BRIAN FLYNN
THE GRIM MAIDEN

BRIAN FLYNN was born in 1885 in Leyton, Essex. He won a scholarship to the City Of London School, and from there went into the civil service. In World War I he served as Special Constable on the Home Front, also teaching "Accountancy, Languages, Maths and Elocution to men, women, boys and girls" in the evenings, and acting in his spare time.

It was a seaside family holiday that inspired Brian Flynn to turn his hand to writing in the mid-twenties. Finding most mystery novels of the time "mediocre in the extreme", he decided to compose his own. Edith, the author's wife, encouraged its completion, and after a protracted period finding a publisher, it was eventually released in 1927 by John Hamilton in the UK and Macrae Smith in the U.S. as *The Billiard-Room Mystery*.

The author died in 1958. In all, he wrote and published 57 mysteries, the vast majority featuring the super-sleuth Antony Bathurst.

BRIAN FLYNN

THE GRIM MAIDEN

With an introduction by
Steve Barge

DEAN STREET PRESS

INTRODUCTION

"I believe that the primary function of the mystery story is to entertain; to stimulate the imagination and even, at times, to supply humour. But it pleases the connoisseur most when it presents – and reveals – genuine mystery. To reach its full height, it has to offer an intellectual problem for the reader to consider, measure and solve."

Brian Flynn, *Crime Book* magazine, 1948

BRIAN Flynn began his writing career with *The Billiard Room Mystery* in 1927, primarily at the prompting of his wife Edith who had grown tired of hearing him say how he could write a better mystery novel than the ones he had been reading. Four more books followed under his original publisher, John Hamilton, before he moved to John Long, who would go on to publish the remaining forty-eight of his Anthony Bathurst mysteries, along with his three Sebastian Stole titles, released under the pseudonym Charles Wogan. Some of the early books were released in the US, and there were also a small number of translations of his mysteries into Swedish and German. In the article from which the above quote is taken from, Brian also claims that there were also French and Danish translations but to date, I have not found a single piece of evidence for their existence. The only translations that I have been able to find evidence of are *War Es Der Zahnarzt?* and *Bathurst Greift Ein* in German – *The Mystery of the Peacock's Eye*, retitled to the less dramatic "Was It The Dentist?", and *The Horn* becoming "Bathurst Takes Action" – and, in Swedish, *De 22 Svarta*, a more direct translation of *The Case of the Black Twenty-Two*. There may well be more work to be done finding these, but tracking down all of his books written in the original English has been challenging enough!

Reprints of Brian's books were rare. Four titles were released as paperbacks as part of John Long's Four Square Thriller range in the late 1930s, four more re-appeared during the war from Cherry Tree Books and Mellifont Press, albeit abridged by at least a third, and two others that I am aware of, *Such Bright Disguises* (1941) and *Reverse the Charges* (1943), received a paperback release as part of John Long's Pocket Edition range in the early 1950s – these were also possibly abridged, but only by about 10%. They were the exceptions, rather than the rule, however, and it was not until 2019, when Dean Street Press released his first ten titles, that his work was generally available again.

The question still persists as to why his work disappeared from the awareness of all but the most ardent collectors. As you may expect, when a title was only released once, back in the early 1930s, finding copies of the original text is not a straightforward matter – not even Brian's estate has a copy of every title. We are particularly grateful to one particular collector for providing *The Edge of Terror*, Brian's first serial killer tale, and another for *The Ebony Stag* and *The Grim Maiden*. With these, the reader can breathe a sigh of relief as a copy of every one of Brian's books has now been located – it only took about five years . . .

One of Brian's strengths was the variety of stories that he was willing to tell. Despite, under his own name at least, never straying from involving Anthony Bathurst in his novels – technically he doesn't appear in the non-series *Tragedy at Trinket*, although he gets a name-check from the sleuth of that tale who happens to be his nephew – it is fair to say that it was rare that two consecutive books ever followed the same structure. Some stories are narrated by a Watson-esque character, although never the same person twice, and others are written by Bathurst's "chronicler". The books sometimes focus on just Bathurst and his investigation but sometimes we get to see the events occurring to the whole cast of characters. On occasion, Bathurst himself will "write" the final chapter, just to make sure his chronicler has got the details correct. The murderer may be an opportunist or they may have a convoluted (and, on occasion, a somewhat over-the-top) plan. They may be working for personal gain or as part of a criminal enterprise or society. Compare for example, *The League of Matthias* and *The Horn* – consecutive releases but were it not for Bathurst's involvement, and a similar sense of humour underlying Brian's writing, you could easily believe that they were from the pen of different writers.

Brian seems to have been determined to keep stretching himself with his writing as he continued Bathurst's adventures, and the ten books starting with *Cold Evil* show him still trying new things. Two of the books are inverted mysteries – where we know who the killer is, and we follow their attempts to commit the crime and/or escape justice and also, in some cases, the detective's attempt to bring them to justice. That description doesn't do justice to either *Black Edged* or *Such Bright Disguises*, as there is more revealed in the finale than the reader might expect . . . There is one particular innovation in *The Grim Maiden*, namely the introduction of a female officer at Scotland Yard.

Helen Repton, an officer from "the woman's side of the Yard" is recruited in that book, as Bathurst's plan require an undercover officer in a cinema. This is her first appearance, despite the text implying that Bathurst has met her before, but it is notable as the narrative spends a little time apart from Bathurst. It follows Helen Repton's investigations based on superb initiative, which generates some leads in the case. At this point in crime fiction, there have been few, if any, serious depictions of a female police detective – the primary example would be Mrs Pym from the pen of Nigel Morland, but she (not just the only female detective at the Yard, but the Assistant Deputy Commissioner no less) would seem to be something of a caricature. Helen would go on to become a semi-regular character in the series, and there are certainly hints of a romantic connection between her and Bathurst.

It is often interesting to see how crime writers tackled the Second World War in their writing. Some brought the ongoing conflict into their writing – John Rhode (and his pseudonym Miles Burton) wrote several titles set in England during the conflict, as did others such as E.C.R. Lorac, Christopher Bush, Gladys Mitchell and many others. Other writers chose not to include the War in their tales – Agatha Christie had ten books published in the war years, yet only *N or M?* uses it as a subject.

Brian only uses the war as a backdrop in one title, *Glittering Prizes*, the story of a possible plan to undermine the Empire. It illustrates the problem of writing when the outcome of the conflict was unknown – it was written presumably in 1941 – where there seems little sign of life in England of the war going on, one character states that he has fought in the conflict, but messages are sent from Nazi conspirators, ending *"Heil Hitler!"*. Brian had good reason for not wanting to write about the conflict in detail, though, as he had immediate family involved in the fighting and it is quite understandable to see writing as a distraction from that.

While Brian had until recently been all but forgotten, there are some mentions for Brian's work in some studies of the genre – Sutherland Scott in *Blood in their Ink* praises *The Mystery of the Peacock's Eye* as containing "one of the ablest pieces of misdirection" before promptly spoiling that misdirection a few pages later, and John Dickson Carr similarly spoils the ending of *The Billiard Room Mystery* in his famous essay "The Grandest Game In The World". One should also include in this list Barzun and Taylor's entry in their *Catalog of Crime* where they attempted to cover Brian by looking at a single title – the somewhat odd *Conspiracy at Angel* (1947) – and summarising it as "Straight tripe and savorless. It is doubtful, on the evidence, if any of his others would be different." Judging an author based on a single title seems desperately unfair – how many people have given up on Agatha Christie after only reading *Postern Of Fate*, for example – but at least that misjudgement is being rectified now.

Contemporary reviews of Brian's work were much more favourable, although as John Long were publishing his work for a library market, not all of his titles garnered attention. At this point in his writing career – 1938 to 1944 – a number of his books won reviews in the national press, most of which were positive. Maurice Richardson in the *Observer* commented that "Brian Flynn balances his ingredients with considerable skill" when reviewing *The Ebony Stag* and praised *Such Bright Disguises* as a "suburban horror melodrama" with an "ingenious final solution". "Suspense is well maintained until the end" in *The Case of the Faithful Heart*, and the protagonist's narration in *Black Edged* in "impressively nightmarish".

It is quite possible that Brian's harshest critic, though, was himself. In the *Crime Book* magazine, he wrote about how, when reading the current output of detective fiction "I delight in the dazzling erudition that has come to grace and decorate the craft of the *'roman policier'*." He then goes on to say "At the same time, however, I feel my own comparative unworthiness for the fire and burden of the competition." Such a feeling may well be the reason why he never made significant inroads into the social side of crime-writing, such as the Detection Club or the Crime Writers Association. Thankfully, he uses this sense of unworthiness as inspiration, concluding "The stars, though, have always been the most desired of all goals, so I allow exultation and determination to take the place of that but temporary dismay."

In Anthony Bathurst, Flynn created a sleuth that shared a number of traits with Holmes but was hardly a carbon-copy. Bathurst is a polymath and gentleman sleuth, a man of contradictions whose background is never made clear to the reader. He clearly has money, as he has his own rooms in London with a pair of servants on call and went to public school (Uppingham) and university (Oxford). He is a follower of all things that fall under the banner of sport, in particular horse racing and cricket, the latter being a sport that he could, allegedly, have represented England at. He is also a bit of a show-off, littering his speech (at times) with classical quotes, the obscurer the better, provided by the copies of the *Oxford Dictionary of Quotations* and *Brewer's Dictionary of Phrase & Fable* that Flynn kept by his writing desk, although Bathurst generally restrains himself to only doing this with people who would appreciate it or to annoy the local constabulary. He is fond of amateur dramatics (as was Flynn, a well-regarded amateur thespian who appeared in at least one self-penned play, *Blue Murder*), having been a member of OUDS, the Oxford University Dramatic Society. General information about his background is light on the ground. His parents were Irish, but he doesn't have an accent – see *The Spiked Lion* (1933) – and his eyes are grey. Despite the fact that he is an incredibly charming and handsome individual, we learn in *The Orange Axe* that he doesn't pursue romantic relationships due to a bad experience in his first romance. We find out more about that relationship and the woman involved in *The Edge of Terror*, and soon thereafter he falls head over heels in love in *Fear and Trembling*, although we never hear of that young lady again. After that, there are eventual hints of an attraction between Helen Repton, but nothing more. That doesn't stop women falling head over heels for Bathurst – as he departs her company in *The Padded Door*, one character muses "What other man could she ever love . . . after this secret idolatry?"

As we reach the halfway point in Anthony's career, his companions have somewhat stablised, with Chief Inspector Andrew MacMorran now his near-constant junior partner in investigation. The friendship with MacMorran is a highlight (despite MacMorran always calling him "Mr. Bathurst") with the sparring between them always a delight to read. MacMorran's junior officers, notably Superintendent Hemingway and Sergeant Chatterton, are frequently recurring characters. The notion of the local constabulary calling in help from Scotland Yard enables cases to be set around the country while still maintaining the same central cast (along with a local bobby or two).

Cold Evil (1938), the twenty-first Bathurst mystery, finally pins down Bathurst's age, and we find that in *The Billiard Room Mystery* (1927), his first outing, he was a fresh-faced Bright Young Thing of twenty-two. How he can survive with his own rooms, at least two servants, and no noticeable source of income remains a mystery. One can also ask at what point in his life he travelled the world, as he has, at least, been to Bangkok at some point. It is, perhaps, best not to analyse Bathurst's past too carefully . . .

"Judging from the correspondence my books have excited it seems I have managed to achieve some measure of success, for my faithful readers comprise a circle in which high dignitaries of the Church rub shoulders with their brothers and sisters of the common touch."

For someone who wrote to entertain, such correspondence would have delighted Brian, and I wish he were around to see how many people have enjoyed the reprints of his work so far. *The Mystery of the Peacock's Eye* (1928) won Cross Examining Crime's Reprint Of The Year award for 2019, with *Tread Softly* garnering second place the following year. His family are delighted with the reactions that people have passed on, and I hope that this set of books will delight just as much.

Steve Barge

CHAPTER I

1

THE YARD HEARS FROM ARBUTHNOT

Anthony Lotherington Bathurst sat in the seat which he favoured. To be precise, he was perched on a corner of the table which graced the room at New Scotland Yard occupied by no less a person than Chief-Inspector Andrew MacMorran. Mr. Bathurst, as was his invariable habit when in this position, swung his legs elegantly but not comfortably. He smiled in the direction of the inspector.

"Andrew," he said enthusiastically, "I'm glad you sent for me. I almost carol with joy. Things have been quiet too long for my liking."

"That's only one way of looking at it. Yours!"

"Very likely. But every man's point of view is important to him. And while we're on the subject, that goes for you, Andrew! You're not excepted from the provisions of the Act. Far from it, in fact."

"And *you're* never satisfied! Peace and quietness don't appeal to you. It's due to your wild, undisciplined nature. Now when I get home to the missus of an evening—*when* I do—"

"Don't tell me you've been working overtime, Andrew—because I shall find the statement most difficult to believe."

MacMorran's eye glinted as he waded into the attack. "When you've done half the work I have—presuming, that is, you live to the late nineties—you'll just be beginning to understand. Mind—I said 'beginning'."

Anthony took a cigarette and handed his case to the inspector. "Don't argue about it, Andrew—spin the yarn. For I'll swear that there *is* a yarn in the offing and that you're dying to get it off your chest. Or did Sir Austin tell you to rope me in? Which is it?"

MacMorran struck a match with a thoughtful expression on his face and lit his cigarette. "Both. In a way—that is. The old man had a letter referred to him on Tuesday—which he passed over to me for attention. He farms out more than ever these days. Nobody who knows him could imagine that to be possible. But it is. He ought to have been a Town Clerk somewhere. Well—I read the letter and then took it back to the 'Guv'nor.' We talked it over. You know how that went—I listened to him. In half an hour he stopped three times in all to get his breath. When he got it finally the upshot of the whole thing was that he suggested I should get in touch with you. I obeyed orders. That's all there is to it at the moment. And that's why you're here. So in the meantime restrain your excitement."

Anthony swung himself from his seat on the corner of the table and put his feet on the floor. "May I see the letter, Andrew? I take it that there is something unusual about it to receive so much attention from two such eminent people. I refer to you and Sir Austin, naturally. Don't misunderstand me. I wouldn't have that happen for worlds."

MacMorran smiled and rummaged amongst his papers. "Here you are, Mr. Bathurst. *The* letter. Read it for yourself."

Anthony found a chair and read the letter which the inspector had handed to him. It was undated and bore no address. It ran as follows. "To the Police Authorities at Scotland Yard. I'm an ordinary man—but I'm frightfully keen on criminology. Have been since I was a small boy. So what—you say? Well—I think that when a man feels in his bones that a crime's going to be committed it's up to him to do all that he can to prevent it. I'm willing to admit that I don't know what the crime in this particular instance is going to be—but that's not my fault. It may turn out to be your job. I propose to call upon you, therefore, and, in a manner of speaking, to follow up this letter at 11.30 a.m. on Thursday morning next, May 22nd. I remain, your obedient servant, Richard M. Arbuthnot."

"H'm," commented Anthony as he gave back the letter to MacMorran, "non-committal certainly. For reasons best known to himself, our Mr. Arbuthnot doesn't intend to put much on paper. He'd rather say it than write it. Well—I don't know that I blame him for that."

"What do you think of it?" asked the inspector.

"Nothing at all. At this stage. How can I? Don't know friend Arbuthnot. He doesn't even tell us where he lives. Therefore, Andrew, why should I theorize? Waste of time. Waste of effort. Compelled to wait till he comes." He glanced at his wrist-watch. "Especially when we consider that Mr. Arbuthnot (if he's punctual) should be with us in about ten minutes' time."

Mr. Bathurst rose from his chair and resumed his former position on the corner of MacMorran's table. "Looked him up in the telephone directory, Andrew? You might get a clue in that way."

The inspector shook his head. "Nothing doing. I looked. He evidently doesn't run to a telephone."

Anthony smiled encouragingly. "Perhaps he's only just moved in. So don't be discouraged. You never know. People do." Anthony persisted. "By the way, Andrew, to whom was that letter addressed?"

"To the Commissioner of Police for the Metropolis. The old man himself."

"Good work by Arbuthnot. Distinguished himself already. I suppose that Hemingway will bring him up when he arrives?"

"He will. The moment he puts his nose inside the doors Hemingway will deal with him. I've given Hemingway the necessary instructions myself."

Like Anthony before him, MacMorran looked at his watch. "Any moment now," he announced, "and we shall be hearing Mr. Arbuthnot's story."

Anthony walked to the other side of the room. He flicked dust with the back of his fingers from the pile of orange-coloured files. His thoughts began to run away with him. If only . . . then he heard the sound of Hemingway's voice and of the door being opened.

"Mr. Arbuthnot, Chief . . ."

"Show Mr. Arbuthnot in, Superintendent."

Anthony wheeled round when he heard the voices. MacMorran, looking eminently business-like, was seated at his square table. A man advanced towards him from the doorway. Anthony saw a young man—about the age of twenty-six. He was all dark. Hair, eyes and skin. A slight moustache tinged and darkened his upper lip. He was of medium height, but all his movements were decisive and quick. Anthony noticed that he was unusually light on his feet and that agility was present in all his actions. Anthony at once classified him as a player of most ball games.

MacMorran spoke. "Good morning, Mr. Arbuthnot. Pleased to see you. This is Mr. Bathurst. In accordance with the terms of your letter we've been expecting you. Sit down."

MacMorran indicated the usual chair. Then he looked a little to his right—that is to say out of the window. The visitor glanced from the inspector to Anthony. He reversed the procedure. MacMorran encouraged him.

"Well, Mr. Arbuthnot—as I stated—we've had your letter. Now what have you come to tell us about?"

2

THE MAN WHO ALWAYS CARRIED THE SAME BOOK

ARBUTHNOT moved a little awkwardly in his chair. When he spoke his voice was light—almost thin in its tone.

"Good morning. I fancy that you must be Inspector MacMorran. I think that was the name I was told when I was brought up."

"Quite right. Supt. Hemingway told you. Cigarette?" MacMorran proffered a packet. Arbuthnot—still looking a little awkward—took a cigarette. He seemed to be feeling more at home than when he had entered, but the process had been very gradual.

MacMorran and Anthony waited for him. They were well used to interviews of this kind, during which, by slowly progressive stages, the diffident become loquacious and the timorous, confident. Arbuthnot however, was not of either of these types. Within a few seconds he had become the Arbuthnot who had penned the letter. A few carefully chosen words and phrases from the lips of Inspector MacMorran started him on his story.

"I'm a bank clerk. London and Home Counties. At the Kingsley Branch. In Surrey. I live at Fosters. That's a little place about three miles from Kingsley. Rather charming. Right in the country. I'm not married. In 'digs' with an old girl named Halsey. She's a widow. Husband was in the Navy. Killed in 1917. I'm pretty ordinary—in most directions. In my spare time I play tennis or go to a flick—sometimes a dance. I'm telling you this so that you can tell better the sort of chap I am. You know—eminently commonplace."

Arbuthnot paused a little shamefacedly. MacMorran nodded encouragingly. Arbuthnot warmed to the nod and proceeded.

"I go to the bank by train every morning. Just a short journey. Three stations. And here comes the interesting part. Now—let's see—what's to-day? May 22nd—isn't it? I'm going to take you back to the end of February. The exact day was the 26th. I'm sure of that. It happens to be pay-day. That's why I remember it. It's always so welcome. I was standing on the platform at Fosters on that particular morning, waiting for my train to come in, when I noticed a chap on the platform near me. I'll describe him as well as I can. Tall and thin. Sallow face. Hair dark brown and worn abnormally long. Large nose. When the train came in he followed me into my compartment. It wasn't by any means overcrowded and he sat opposite to me. He had a book with him. He put it on his lap and I couldn't help seeing the title of it. It was there right in front of me—you see. It was *The Seamark Omnibus of Thrills*. With the mark of the Kingsley Public Libraries service on the cover. He kept the book on his lap until he got out. At Shepherd's Brook. That's the station immediately before Kingsley. Nothing in that you will say. I agree! But listen to the rest of what I'm going to tell you before you dismiss it from your minds. I saw this same man a day or so later. He was seated in the compartment on this second occasion when I entered it. He had the same book with him. On his lap all the time, so that as previously, I was able to see the title. Until he came to Shepherd's Brook again. Still quite ordinary and commonplace, you will say, and I'll still be in complete agreement with you."

Here Arbuthnot stopped again and his keen, alert eyes darted round the room. "But supposing I tell you that on Saturday last, almost three months after the first encounter I had with him, this man was still carrying the same book? This book which, as far as I know, he never opens to read! What would you say then?"

Arbuthnot pulled rather nervously at the knees of his trousers. MacMorran at once exhibited signs of impatience.

"I'm sorry—but I can't for the life of me see what it is you're worrying about. It's obvious what the explanation is. The man takes the book to read in his lunch-hour."

Arbuthnot smiled. "I thought you'd say something of that kind. For three months? The same book? I'm sorry, Inspector, but try as

I will I can't agree with you." Arbuthnot shook his head vigorously in support of his own denial.

MacMorran defended his position. "Even if you can't—what justification have you for anticipating that a crime's going to be committed? As you indicated in your letter to us. I suggest very seriously, Mr. Arbuthnot, that you're allowing your imagination to run away with you."

Arbuthnot glanced towards Anthony almost as though he were beseeching his support. Anthony smiled at him in return, but the smile was benevolently neutral.

"Well, Mr. Arbuthnot," continued the inspector, "you haven't replied to my last question."

Arbuthnot shook his head. "That doesn't mean I'm not going to. Because I haven't told you all, yet. I've kept something up my sleeve. Purposely! In the hope of convincing you. I realized that I had a hard row to furrow, so I deliberately kept one of my best cards back. Listen to this. Last Saturday morning I decided upon a certain course of action. This fellow with his unread book over a period of three months had got on my nerves. I admit all that. Call it a sixth sense, if you like, but I've got it fixed firmly in my mind that there's some dirt coming along in the near future and that he's going to be concerned in it. I've watched him like a hawk for weeks, without him being aware of it. So I resolved to take a chance. As I said— last Saturday morning! I kept in the waiting-room until I spotted him come along the platform complete with book as per invoice. I stopped where I was until the train came in. Then I watched him making for a compartment. At the last moment—so that he should have no chance of seeing me—I came up behind him, right on his heels *literally*, and as he stepped into the train I nudged the book which he was holding under his elbow, and sent it flying. It fell, of course, on the floor of the carriage. I was, however, altogether unprepared for what happened."

Arbuthnot paused and rubbed the tip of his nose. "What did happen?" asked Anthony Bathurst quietly.

"He snatched the book from the floor and turned on me with the most venomous look on his face that I have ever seen on the face of any living person. At the same time—we were both standing, remember—he raised his right hand as though he were about to strike me down without the slightest compunction or hesitation. In the hand I saw the gleaming blade of a curved knife. I don't think I was frightened exactly. It's difficult for me to say when I come to look back on it. I was too surprised. You know—taken off my balance. I apologized for my clumsiness in the best dumb English technique and he muttered something under his breath which I didn't catch and slunk off to a seat in the farthest corner of the compartment. To get out as usual when the train came to Shepherd's Brook. Well— have I made any impression on you now, Inspector?"

Arbuthnot waited for the response. The inspector glanced across at Anthony. The glance was certainly interrogative. Anthony understood and came into the picture.

"When this last incident occurred, Mr. Arbuthnot, were there any other occupants of the compartment?"

Arbuthnot shook his head. "Luckily—no. It was a Saturday morning, as I said. You will realize that considerably less people travel at that particular time on a Saturday than on an ordinary weekday."

"What was the time of the train?"

"8.37. Reaches Kingsley 8.53."

"When does it get to Shepherd's Brook?"

"8.49."

"So that your friend, if he did actually read during his morning journey, would only have a matter of twelve minutes in which to indulge his somewhat peculiar craving for literature?"

"Yes, I know. I've considered all that. But if he read at other times and places surely he'd change his library book more than once in a period of three months? That's common sense—surely?"

Anthony looked at MacMorran with the suspicion of a smile. "I'm inclined to agree with you, Mr. Arbuthnot. So much so that I intend to ask you more questions."

Arbuthnot flushed with pleasure. "I'm gratified. Go ahead at once."

"Why aren't you at the bank to-day?"

"I'm due for a week's leave. That fact influenced me in the chance I took last Saturday. I knew that I would be more or less free during this week and in a position to take certain action, if I considered it had become necessary."

"Good. I've been wondering about that. Now—regarding this unread book. You say it came from the Kingsley Public Libraries and was an omnibus edition of 'Seamark's.' Yes?"

Arbuthnot nodded. "Yes."

Anthony turned to the inspector. "What do you make of that, Inspector? I'm interested."

"Never read it," commented MacMorran curtly, "so that I can't help you."

Anthony continued thoughtfully, "Do you know—I find that description of the book attractive. An omnibus edition! Usually I believe that means at least three volumes bound as one. Most omnibus editions that have come my way have been like that. In other words a largish book, Inspector. Much larger, shall we say, than an average binding. H'm—interesting! There's another point, Inspector, which, bearing in mind your race and lineage, should strongly appeal to you. And that's this: it is the custom of all libraries services to inflict fines on people who keep books beyond a certain time. Money. Coin of the realm—George VI—*inter alia*."

"You can renew a book if you want to," said MacMorran sturdily. "I've done so myself. On several occasions. I remember running all the way once to get to the library before it closed."

"True," said Anthony, "you can. If you remember to. Mr. Arbuthnot—tell me this. Have you ever run across your book-client later on in the day—say on any of your return journeys?"

"Never," returned Arbuthnot emphatically. "I've caught many trains at different times back from Kingsley to Fosters—but I've never yet run across him."

"Ever seen him at other times? Over week-ends for instance? When you've been strolling round the district? It may be assumed that he lives somewhere near you?"

"Never. And I've religiously kept my eyes open for him. Without the slightest success. That morning train has been my one and only point of contact. But that's not been my fault, I assure you."

Arbuthnot closed his jaws with something like a snap. Anthony was impressed by his positiveness. MacMorran scribbled aimlessly on his blotting-pad. It was his habit to do this when troubled. There was an awkward silence. Arbuthnot felt that he was between two vastly different poles of thought.

"At any rate," said Anthony lazily, "one course lies open before us. Its mouth is gaping. Pass me the telephone directory, will you, Inspector—A-K."

MacMorran obliged. Anthony carefully turned the pages at the end of the directory. Eventually he appeared to find the entry he wanted. The two others watched him as he dialled.

"Is that the Kingsley Public Library? Yes? Ask the librarian to speak, will you please? All right, put me through, please." Anthony waited for a little while. Then he began to speak again. "This is an inquiry from New Scotland Yard. Regarding a book which it is thought has been issued from your premises. I'll give you the title. *Seamark's Omnibus of Thrills.* Can you give me the name of the present borrower according to your card index . . . Thank you?"

He winked gracelessly at MacMorran as he waited by the telephone for the information. It came. "Thank you. I'm extremely obliged to you."

They watched him as he replaced the receiver. He turned to them quietly but ominously. "That was the Kingsley librarian, or one of them, gentlemen . . . as you no doubt heard. He was good enough to pass on a piece of highly valuable information. There is no such book as *Seamark's Omnibus of Thrills* in the catalogue of the Kingsley Public Library. And, which may interest you even more, he informs me that there never has been such a book in their catalogue."

MacMorran whistled under his breath. Arbuthnot leant forward with more eagerness than ever and his eyes gleamed with excitement. For some seconds the only sound in the room was the heavy ticking of MacMorran's clock. At last Anthony spoke his thoughts:

"Do you know, gentlemen? I am more than ever inclined to agree with Mr. Arbuthnot. I smell crime round the corner."

Arbuthnot rose. "I'm very gratified to think that my time and my journey haven't been entirely wasted."

3
A DOSE OF MEDICINE

SOME hours after the interview with Arbuthnot, Anthony, back at his own flat was still pondering over the problem of the unread volume, when Emily came upstairs to inform him that a visitor had called who was desirous of an interview with him. Anthony looked at the card which Emily presented to him. The name showed "Doctor Frances Page." Many letters of distinction followed the printed name. But when Anthony saw the address, he was unable to resist a shock of surprise. For the address read "Chandos House, High Road, Kingsley."

"Twice in one day," he murmured to himself. "A coincidence—at least. Show Doctor Page upstairs, will you, Emily," he said to the waiting girl.

Doctor Frances Page, when she arrived, was middle-aged, but undeniably still attractive. Her dark hair was companioned by dark eyes and comprehensively, she was an alert, high-spirited lady who exuded merriment and general good will.

"Mr. Bathurst," she said, as she entered, and her voice was soft and melodious. "I really must start the ball rolling with an apology. But I heard of you and of your extraordinary talent for solving mysteries from Helen Eversley. You remember how you helped her in the Dr. Traquair case. I met her at a party last Christmas. You do remember her, don't you, Mr. Bathurst?"

Anthony nodded and smiled. "Oh—yes. Very well indeed."

"She confided in me some of the inner history of the Traquair case. She told me that she could never thank you enough for the help you gave her." Doctor Page became a little flamboyant.

"I'm afraid that's all intensely flattering. Mrs. Eversley is generous in the extreme." Anthony smiled at his visitor.

"Well—be that as it may—that's why I've come to you. But first of all, I should tell you more. I have not come, Mr. Bathurst, on behalf of myself. I have come on behalf of one of my patients. Does that make any difference?"

"None at all," replied Anthony gallantly.

Frances Page smiled attractively and resumed. "She's a most charming girl. Her father was Irish—her mother English. She lives at Kingsley and her name is Kathleen Regan. She's been under my care for nearly three weeks. She's prostrate almost with worry and anxiety and I'm afraid that unless something can be done for her quickly, she's going to get a great deal worse. In fact I can reasonably anticipate the *worst*. That's where you come in, Mr. Bathurst."

"Tell me," said Anthony. "I'm dying to hear."

Doctor Page flashed her dark eyes at him in gratification. Although he hadn't been at all sure that she hadn't resented his latest remark. Nevertheless she made no comment but carried on with her story.

"Something like a month ago, Mr. Bathurst, Kathleen's only brother disappeared. Their father and mother are both dead and Kathleen and her brother were absolutely devoted to each other. She lives down in Kingsley, near my house, and Terence, her brother, lived somewhere in the Midlands. I can't tell you how long he's been up there as I'm not altogether sure on the point. They each had a little money left them by the parents. I have no idea how much and Terence, I believe, had aspirations to be an artist. At any rate, Kathleen says so. Every week-end, Terence came up to town to see his sister. According to her he never missed doing this. Until about a month ago. Somewhere round about Easter, I think it was. The long and the short of it is, Mr. Bathurst, according to the somewhat hysterical and disjointed story that my patient tells me, that this brother of hers has completely disappeared—vanished from the face of the earth."

"Has Miss Regan been to the police?"

"No." Doctor Frances Page shook her head.

"Why not, Doctor Page—any idea? Surely it would have been—"

She nodded her head emphatically. "I agree. I asked her exactly the same question. In a word—she's frightened. She's a Celt and because of that the word 'police,' to her, means much more I think than it does to us."

Anthony intervened. "It means a great deal to me. I feel that I should point that out. In case we should start with wrong impressions."

Doctor Page smiled rather happily at Anthony's apt rejoinder. Indeed, she almost laughed. "I don't mean what you mean. But I think you know very well what *I* mean."

"Perhaps I do. How old is Miss Regan?"

"Between 25 and 30. I'm not certain—but that's what I should put her age at."

"And the brother?"

"I don't *know*—I've never inquired—but I should *think* that he must be a few years Kathleen's senior."

"Have you told your patient that you intended to consult me?"

"Not quite. I told her that if I possibly could I would try to get you interested in her case."

"Did she agree to the suggestion you made?"

"Agree?" Doctor Frances crinkled a rather attractive nose. "I don't think that it came to a matter of her agreement or even disagreement. If you understand what I mean. I'm her medical adviser and she's my patient and my offer of coming to you upon her behalf was really in the light of professional advice." She smiled. "I do hope I'm making my meaning clear."

Anthony smiled back at her. "I think you are. Would she come here to see me, do you think? Or would she rather I went to her? There are naturally many questions that I should like to put to her. I need not stress to you the value of first-hand information."

"She would come here. I'm sure of that."

"To-morrow?"

"As soon as that? You mean that you will see her, Mr. Bathurst?"

"I do. I shall be delighted. How can I possibly resist the lady's ambassador?"

"Now—now," replied the doctor coquettishly. "I have no illusions. I'll tell Kathleen, then, what I've arranged and what you say. And please accept my most sincere thanks, Mr. Bathurst. Do you happen to know Kingsley at all?"

"But little, Doctor Page. I've been in the town once or twice in my time but no more than that. Usually it's occurred when I've been going up the river somewhere. I've started my journey at Kingsley. Why exactly do you ask?"

"I was going to describe to you where Kathleen Regan lives. In one of the houses quite close to the towpath. Still—she'll tell you herself—if you ever desire to come to see her in the future." Doctor Page held out her gloved hand. "Thank you again. I'll phone you in the morning to confirm the appointment. Or otherwise."

Anthony opened the door for her. As she stood in the doorway, Doctor Page turned and faced him.

"Let me make myself clear. I said I had anticipated the worst. By that I meant self-destruction. I want you to understand. Good-bye, Mr. Bathurst." She waved her hand.

Emily escorted the visitor to the door. Anthony heard the sounds of the Vauxhall as it purred away. He found tobacco and packed it into the bowl of his pipe. As he lit up he murmured his thoughts.

"Now I wonder if Arbuthnot's story fits anywhere into the picture of the vanished Irishman."

He tossed away the burnt match, went to his telephone and rang up Chief-Inspector MacMorran.

4

THE PATIENT OF DOCTOR PAGE

KATHLEEN Regan came to Anthony Bathurst on the following morning. Doctor Page, as she had promised, telephoned him of her patient's visit. Anthony was surprised when he saw Miss Regan for the first time. She was tall and her form was richly developed. She was well-dressed but without the slightest hint of ostentation. Anthony applied the adjective "handsome" as soon as he saw her. Although her tall, full form had quick and alert life in it somewhere, her face was over-pale and her hand and fingers over-thin. "When she is well," thought Anthony, "she would be vivid and challenging with a disdainful almost mocking militant light in her dark eyes." But as he now looked at her her face was grim, hard and set. Anthony waved her to a chair.

"Doctor Page has told me something of your story, Miss Regan. You have lost a brother."

The girl nodded. Her hands were unsteady and her face twitched.

"Tell me," urged Anthony patiently. He waited for the girl to find more composure. Gradually it came. But she spoke tonelessly—almost meaninglessly.

"Terence is my only brother. When my father died, which was a year after my mother, Terence and I were left alone. We have no friends in England. All my mother's relations are dead. I came to live at Kingsley. Because I like to be near the water. We have a fair income. Not a terrific amount—but sufficient for our wants. Terence has always been restless. Anxious to paint pictures. To be a great artist. When I came to Kingsley he went to live at a place called Wroxeter near Stratford-upon-Avon where your Shakespeare lived. We used to write to each other once every week. Nearly every week-end he came to Kingsley and spent it with me. Until the first week-end in April this year. The 5th was the Saturday. Just over six weeks ago. I expected Terence as usual. He never came. He has not come since. I have written, of course. The letter has been returned to me in a post-office envelope. The envelope is marked 'Not known. Gone away'."

The tears showed on Miss Regan's face. "I cannot tell you any more. That is all there is to tell."

Anthony rubbed the ridge of his jaw. "Why did your brother go to Wroxeter to live in the first place? What was the reason?"

"I am not sure. But I think that he answered an advertisement in one of the artistic papers. I do not know which one."

"You do not know for whom he worked or by whom he was employed."

"I knew nothing of that. Terence never told me . . . we never discussed the matter . . . and I was not interested. Only overjoyed to see him each week when he came."

Anthony felt a sense of disappointment. He was getting nowhere, also he was extremely puzzled. By more than one aspect of the matter.

"Have you brought any correspondence with you, Miss Regan? Did you think of it?"

The girl nodded silently and produced two letters. "There is the last letter I had from my brother. Please read it."

Anthony took the sheet of paper from her and read the following: "11, Hampton Rd.—Wroxeter, Warwickshire. Wednesday, April 2nd. My darling Kath, Expect me on Saturday next as usual. Shall be on 5.27 train at Paddington. Arrive Kingsley about half-past seven. Hope you received the heads all right. All news until we meet. With love from Terence."

"There is no doubt, I suppose, that this is your brother's hand-writing?"

"Not the slightest," came the girl's prompt reply. "I should know it anywhere."

"Thank you. It's always as well to be quite sure on matters of that kind. Now—may I see your other letter, please?"

Anthony returned the first letter and the girl passed over the second. "That outside envelope," she explained, "is from the Post office people. The other one is my original to my brother. You see what it says. They opened my letter, I suppose in order to get my address. You can see it for yourself. It can never have reached him. The post-office envelope is addressed to 'Kath,' in accordance with my signature."

Anthony examined the papers. "The enclosed is returned to the sender for the reason stated." Anthony skated over the official phrases. Then he turned his attention to Kathleen Regan's letter to her brother. It was, with regard to the circumstances that it fitted, entirely conventional. Why hadn't he kept his appointment? Was he ill? She was terribly upset not to see him as she had expected. Would he communicate with her as soon as he possibly could and allay her anxiety? Anthony read on. There was nothing in Miss Regan's letter that he found surprising or even interesting. He handed the document back to her.

"Had your brother any personal attachments, Miss Regan?"

"No. Only to his art. Nothing more beyond it. He was passionately devoted to that."

"What did he do? Paint pictures, you say?"

The girl nodded eagerly. "Yes. Yes. Heads. The heads of beautiful girls. He has often shown me examples of his work."

"Do you happen to have kept a copy of any of them?"

"No," she replied round-eyed. "Terence always took them back with him."

"Did he happen to have plenty of money always?"

"Oh, yes . . . but I should explain—we both have some money. My father was comfortably off and what he left came to us. There was no real necessity for my brother to work for his living. So there is nothing in that, you see."

"Did you ever hear him mention any friends he had made in Wroxeter?"

Kathleen Regan wrinkled her brows at the question. "Yes," she returned at length. "I think I did . . . once. I will try to remember the name. It was a common name. I know . . . Brown. My brother referred to a young fellow he had met in Wroxeter named Brown. He was an artist, too. He and Terence had similar tastes. I can recall that."

"When did your brother go to Wroxeter—exactly?"

"In the March of last year. Easter time."

"So that he seems to have stayed there, shall we say, from Easter to Easter—yes?"

"Yes. That would be so."

"How old was your brother, Miss Regan?"

"Twenty-five, Mr. Bathurst."

"Did he have good health always?"

"Oh—yes. Terence was never ill or ailing. Or at least I have never known him to be. You need have no anxiety on that score."

Anthony leant forward to her and spoke seriously. "I feel that there is one question that I must ask you. Why haven't you reported the matter to the police?"

Even the little colour that had remained in Miss Regan's face drained away and her lips twitched with anxiety. Some seconds passed. Anthony repeated his question. At last the girl spoke.

"I didn't like to."

"Why not?"

"I was frightened, I think. My brother has always drummed into me that I should have as little to do with the police as possible. 'Keep away from the police,' he always used to say. 'Shun them like the Devil does holy water'."

"You are sure that you had no other reason?"

"None at all. You can believe me implicitly when I say that." Anthony caressed the line of his jaw. "Tell me, Miss Regan, when you went to live at Kingsley in the first place, who chose the place for you?"

The girl's brows wrinkled. "I told you I liked to be near the river. That was the reason why—"

Anthony interrupted her. "There are many places, not over far from London, that are near a river—or even *the* river. Kingsley is only one of them. What made you select Kingsley?"

"I am not sure. Now that you—"

"Think hard, Miss Regan, did *your brother* suggest it? Did the idea of your coming to Kingsley emanate in the first instance from him. Whip your brain for the right answer."

The girl sat rigid and immovable in her chair. Eventually she found words for her reply. "Yes," she said. "Now that I cast my mind back, I think that Terry did suggest it. But we had no argument about it. I fell in with his suggestion right from the start. I suppose that was what made me forget it."

"I see. Very likely. Now tell me this. Did your brother ever live with you at Kingsley. For a short time, say, before he went to Wroxeter?"

She shook her head. "No, Mr. Bathurst. He never actually lived with me at Kingsley. He went to Wroxeter straight away."

"Did he ever accompany you to Kingsley? When you first thought of moving in, for example?"

"No. I came by myself and made all the necessary arrangements."

"I see. I won't pursue that point any longer, Miss Regan. Where did your brother bank?"

"At the Midland Territorial, Wroxeter."

"Have you written to his bank manager?"

"No, Mr. Bathurst. I thought of it, but I didn't know quite what to say."

"Why was that, Miss Regan?"

She flushed a little at the question. "I'm afraid I'm hopeless at anything to do with business, Mr. Bathurst. It's due to the way I was brought up, I'm afraid."

Anthony drew a slip of paper towards him. "Tell me your address at Kingsley, please."

"I live close to Dr. Page. 'Boscawen,' 311, High Road."

Anthony jotted down the particulars. He extended his hand. "Let me look again at your brother's last letter, will you please, Miss Regan?"

The girl produced the letter for the second time. Anthony read it and frowned over it. "Yes," he said at length, "I thought I had remembered accurately. The word was 'heads.' What is the exact reference here, Miss Regan?"

"My brother sent me a parcel during that week. In it were seven crayon sketches of girls' heads. They were all his own work. I told you that was a speciality of his."

"Was that an ordinary gesture of your brother's? Was it his habit to send you specimens of his work in that way?"

The girl shook her head. "Oh, no, Mr. Bathurst. On the contrary. He had never done such a thing before."

"Now—that's interesting, Miss Regan. Why do you think he did it on this occasion?"

The girl was silent for a few seconds. "Well—I don't know that I thought about it very much. I took it that he wanted to show me how well he was progressing with his artistic studies. What else could I think?"

"Yet your brother mentions them specially in his letter to you."

Kathleen Regan wrinkled her brows. "Specially?" she repeated questioningly—"Do you really think it was specially?"

Anthony nodded. "Yes. I think so, Miss Regan. He betrayed a certain amount of anxiety as to whether you had received them. I think that's true, don't you?"

"I suppose you might look at it like that. But I never did."

"You say these crayon sketches were of girls' heads? Nothing more than that?"

"No, Mr. Bathurst. Just ordinary girls' heads." For the first time during the interview she allowed herself the luxury of a smile. "Pretty girls," she added, "all pretty girls. The other sort never appealed to Terence."

"And nothing else in each sketch beyond the head itself."

She thought over the question. "Only a name under each head in Terence's writing. Or printing rather."

Anthony pondered over the girl's answer. "Can you remember any of the names? You've still got the sketches, I take it?"

"Oh—yes, of course. I wouldn't part with them for anything. I'll try to remember some of the names." She wrinkled her brows again in an effort of remembrance. "I can think of only three," she replied, after a few moments' thinking. "You mustn't forget that it's some little time now since I looked at them closely. But I can remember Edith, Ethel and Edna. The other names were similar. Just ordinary Christian names. Nothing extraordinary about any of them."

"Where have you put these sketches, Miss Regan?"

"On the top shelf of a cupboard in my sitting-room. Would you care to see them at any time, Mr. Bathurst?"

"I rather think I would. But never mind that for the moment. Tell me this. Have you any friends in the Kingsley or Shepherd's Brook or even, say, in the Fosters area? Please think carefully before you answer."

"But I can answer at once. Of course, I have. Several friends. I've lived there long enough to make some friends."

"Forgive my insistence, and please don't mistake my meaning. Any special friends of the other sex?"

A faint colour tinged her cheek. "No special friends, Mr. Bathurst. Or friend—if that's what you really mean. But, as I said, I have various girl friends of my own age."

"What are your hobbies, Miss Regan? Can you tell me that?"

"I like gardening. I cycle a lot. I go to dances and to the 'flicks.' The 'flicks' especially. As a rule, at least twice a week."

"And out of all those associations you haven't developed any specially significant friendship or intimacy."

She shook her head. "No, I can't truthfully say that I have."

There was a silence. Kathleen Regan broke it. "Well, Mr. Bathurst," she said urgently, "do you think that you can help me? To find Terence or to find out what's happened to him?"

Anthony delayed his answer. At his first consideration he thought that the semi-challenge the girl had delivered to him bordered on the unfair. As a result he chose carefully the terms of his reply.

"It would be wrong of me, manifestly wrong, to send you away with false hopes. But I will do all I can. You may rest assured on that, Miss Regan."

He rose from his chair and began to pace the room. "Consider the affair for yourself, Miss Regan. Your brother's last letter to you was posted to you early in April. Now we're approaching the end of May. The scent for me is stone cold. Worse than that, possibly. It may even have been completely eliminated!"

The girl sat with her hands clasped together and resting on her lap. She nodded her head rather pathetically as Anthony made his various points.

"Yes," she agreed eventually. "I see what you mean. And I suppose it's all my fault. Causing the delay, I mean. I ought to have come to you a long time ago. When Terence was first missing."

Anthony turned quickly on his heel and came to a decision. "Look here, Miss Regan, I'll tell you what I'll do. I may, of course, have to make a journey to Wroxeter. That's certainly indicated. But before I go I'll come to your place at Kingsley and have a look round. There are one or two things I'd like to investigate more closely."

She looked at him appealingly, "You won't be too—"

Anthony completed the sentence for her. "Too long? In coming? I assure you, Miss Regan, that if it's convenient to you I propose to visit you to-morrow. How will that do?"

For the first time during the interview Kathleen Regan evinced grateful animation. She stood and faced Anthony and held out her hand to him.

"Mr. Bathurst—I can't possibly thank you enough. You've put new heart and life into me. I shall expect you—at what time?"

Anthony thought. "How about to-morrow morning, Miss Regan? Will that suit you? Say about half-past eleven?"

"I shall be ready for you. And you must stay for lunch. You will?"

"I shall be only too delighted."

Anthony shook hands with her. When Emily had escorted her down the stairs of the flat, Anthony walked to the window and watched her as she walked away. When she had travelled a few yards he saw her stop and signal to a passing taxi.

"Two from Kingsley," he said softly to himself. Then he scratched his cheek. "I wonder! And why did she contradict herself with regard to those heads?"

5

GIRLS' HEADS

THE next morning, as arranged with his visitor of the day before, Anthony travelled to Kingsley. He went from Waterloo, unaccompanied, and arrived at the station of his destination shortly after eleven o'clock. He found the historic red-roofed town good to look upon. There were two main streets with excellent traffic lines, broad footways shaded by stately trees, ancient houses everywhere and at the end of the streets on the western side the gleaming silver of the River Rinn. The shops were good and the sight of the many inns comforted him and warmed his heart with anticipation.

He found "Boscawen" without difficulty and rang the bell more than punctually at twenty-eight minutes past the hour. "Boscawen" proved to be a large, old-fashioned house which had undergone renovations and a certain measure of "modernizing." It had a prim red-and-cream-coloured gate and many clumps of rhododendra in front of its windows. At the back, Anthony had already caught a glimpse of a large and well-laid-out garden. An austere spinster (or so Anthony judged from first impression) opened the door without a smile and raised her eyebrows.

"Miss Regan," murmured Anthony, "I think that I'm expected."

The lady at the door inclined her head in acquiescence and Anthony, following the almost imperceptible movement of her finger, crossed the threshold. He was conducted into a room that his guide described as the "morning-room." At that moment the idea flashed into Anthony's mind that Kathleen Regan lived in what is generally described as "furnished apartments."

"Miss Regan will be with you in a few minutes," said the austere lady.

Anthony accepted the situation as gracefully as he knew how.

"Take a seat, please."

Anthony accepted a seat also and silently prepared to await the coming of Kathleen Regan. His waiting period was of short duration. Kathleen Regan came in to him with hand outstretched. She looked better, he thought, than on the previous day. She had more colour and more mental agility.

"Mr. Bathurst! This is good of you. I was half afraid—"

"Half afraid of what, Miss Regan?" Anthony shook hands with her.

"That you would change your mind and think twice about—coming here. After all—who am I to—"

Anthony raised his hand and stopped her. "Surely, Miss Regan, you don't intend to be uncomplimentary?"

She smiled at him. "I suppose that's really what I am being. But I'm sure you won't misunderstand me. Any old how—you said you'd come, you're here, and that's all that matters."

"Good! Who was the lady who let me in?"

"That's Miss Groves, my landlady. The house belongs to her. She 'lets,' as they say. I have apartments here. She's extraordinarily nice when you know her properly and treats me as well as she would her own daughter. Really—she couldn't treat me better. So don't you dare say a word against her, no matter what else you may do or want to do."

"I shouldn't try, Miss Regan. Believe me."

"That's nice of you. Now you are here, please tell me what you want me to do."

Anthony sat down in an armchair. "Do you mind if I smoke, Miss Regan?"

"Of course not. I'll join you."

Anthony offered her his cigarette-case. Kathleen Regan took a cigarette. Anthony waited for her to settle down before he put his first question. Kathleen Regan made herself comfortable in the armchair opposite to him.

"First of all, Miss Regan, I would like to have a look at the crayon sketches your brother sent you. Can you find them for me without any trouble?"

Miss Regan jumped off her chair. "They're upstairs in a cupboard in my bedroom. Wait down here, Mr. Bathurst, and I'll get them for you."

"Thank you, Miss Regan. I'll wait here as you suggest."

The girl dashed from the room. Everything about her seemed different from the condition of the day before. Anthony found himself wondering as to the real reason behind this. He placed his cigarette-stub into an ashtray and waited for Kathleen Regan's return. She was not away long. Within a few minutes Anthony heard her descending the staircase at a rate very much like a run. She flung open the door minus ceremony and burst into the room with a brown paper parcel under her arm.

"Here you are, Mr. Bathurst. I've found them for you. They were on a shelf in a cupboard in my bedroom."

She placed the parcel on the table and untied the string placed loosely round it. "There they are," she said almost triumphantly, "just as Terence sent them to me. Don't you think they're absolutely wizard, Mr. Bathurst?"

Anthony handled the seven sketches. They were almost exactly as he had anticipated them to be. Anthony was no expert at this particular judgment, but he knew enough of art to realize at once that the work at which he looked was something better than merely good. As Kathleen Regan had told him in his flat, each sketch was of a girl's head. All were dainty, charming, with allure and attraction. There were five blondes and two brunettes. And, again, as the girl had previously stated, each had been given a name by the artist. Anthony searched for the seven names. As he turned the sketches over one by one the names were, "Lois, Edna, Ethel, Miranda, Thelma, Edith and Rosemary." Anthony memorized them. Much more from habit than from deliberate intention. He inspected them carefully and then laid them on the table again. Kathleen Regan stood at his side and watched him. Suddenly his thoughts tangented.

"That letter from your brother that you showed me, Miss Regan, may I look at it again, please?"

"That's in my handbag," she said. "I shall have to leave you again to get that."

"I'm sorry, Miss Regan," Anthony apologized. "Perhaps I ought to have mentioned it to you before. But at that moment it didn't occur to me."

"Never mind," she replied briefly. "I'll go and get it. It won't take me a minute."

Once again Anthony waited for her return. He picked up the brown paper wrapping in which the sketches had been and examined it. The postmark "Wroxeter" was plainly discernible, together with the date-stamp, "April 3rd." Anthony stared at the latter intently. If he were not mistaken—but the return to the room of Kathleen Regan put a temporary stoppage on his musings.

"Here you are," she said, "here's the letter from Terence that you asked for."

Anthony took it from her, checked up on what he desired to investigate and quietly handed it back to her. "I wonder, Miss Regan," he said, "if you would mind refreshing your memory a little. Can do?"

"Of course not. I mean—I don't mind. Only too pleased. What is it you want to know?"

"Go back to the time when you received that letter and this parcel of drawings."

"The first week in April, you mean?"

"That's the idea. Which did you receive first? The letter or the parcel?"

"The letter—no I didn't—I'm wrong! The parcel."

Anthony smiled. "I thought so. Now look at the date the letter was written and after that at the date of the post-mark on the brown paper of the parcel."

Kathleen Regan did as she had been directed. "April 2nd and April 3rd."

"Exactly! And yet, in the letter, written first, mark you, your brother writes, 'hope you received the heads all right.' Which is certainly an indication that he had already sent them to you. Whereas we know now that he hadn't—seeing that the parcel is postmarked a day later than the date the letter was written. Didn't it even strike you in that way?"

She started to nod her head again. "Yes. I'm just a silly little twerp. I remember now. It all comes back to me." Her face held a heightened colour. "The heads *did* come after I received the letter. I thought at the time how funny it was of Terence to do things in that way. I even remember laughing to myself about it. But I've been so worried since that all the details of the business got pushed to the back of my mind. But it doesn't matter in any way, does it?" She looked at him appealingly.

"I don't know, Miss Regan. Yet awhile, that is. But it occurs to me that it *may* matter a lot. It presents me with a situation replete with interesting possibilities. Suppose we have a glance at these ladies again?"

Anthony picked up the drawings. In each instance there was nothing beyond the drawing, the name given to it and the artist's signature in the corner of each sketch, "Terence Regan." He turned them over and looked at the back of each drawing. To his surprise, he saw that they were numbered from one to seven. Anthony arranged the drawings, therefore, in the order of the numbers as assigned by the artist himself. They ran as follows. "Edith—Lois—Miranda—Thelma—Rosemary—Edna—Ethel." Anthony saw the allusion immediately. Taking the initial letters in their precise order as allotted, he had the words "Elm Tree." The point that had occurred to him a few moments previously was abundantly proved. Terence Regan had sent his sister a message. The incident of the dates on the letter and the parcel had caused Anthony to suspect this possibility. He considered the conditions and determined to put some of them to the test at once.

"As I came in, Miss Regan," he said casually, "I caught a glimpse of the garden at the back of the house. Would you be good enough to show me over it before I go? Or even now, if it wouldn't be too inconvenient." Anthony smiled at her. Like many others before her she fell a ready victim.

"I'll take you now, Mr. Bathurst."

Anthony followed the girl through the French doors of the lounge into the garden. He saw at once that his first impressions had been sound and accurate. The garden of "Boscawen" was indeed beautiful. Its lawns were trim and well-kept. The roses bloomed in prodigal profusion even though June was still a few days distant. The kitchen garden at the end was well-stocked and in apple-pie order. But there were no large trees. He saw laburnum acacia, lilac, and a red may but nothing that could even be likened to an elm tree. He turned and spoke to Kathleen Regan.

"It's hot in the sun."

She nodded. "I know. Don't you like it? I adore sunshine."

"So do I. But sometimes—" he broke off and looked round.

"You haven't a tree in the garden to give you any shade. Pity." Kathleen screwed up her eyes to the sunlight. "That's what Miss Groves always says. I've heard her say before now that she wishes she'd noticed it before she bought the house. But there. You see these things when it's too late. That's like life itself." She swung round on him impetuously. "Mr. Bathurst—tell me—why did you ask me to come into the garden? Not surely to discuss sunshine and shade? Won't you tell me—please?"

The suddenness of the verbal attack took Anthony by surprise. He was forced to a quick decision. He decided not to tell her all that he had discovered. He finessed, therefore.

"I thought we could probably talk more freely in the open air than inside the house. And you must admit that it's a glorious morning."

Her eyes held his with a glance of shrewd inquiry. "You're not hiding anything awful from me, are you?" The inquiry in her face gave way to a troubled expression.

Anthony shook his head at her and smiled. "No. I assure you I'm hiding nothing 'awful,' as you call it, from you at all." He grimaced. "See my finger? Wet? Dry? Cross my throat—then. Can't say fairer than that, can I?"

Kathleen Regan caught his mood and half-smiled at it. But she soon reverted to her former condition of anxiety.

"Mr. Bathurst," she caught his arm. "Please tell me! The truth! Do you think there is any chance of your finding my brother. Any chance at all?"

Anthony hesitated a second, perhaps, before replying. "Miss Regan. You ask for frankness. You shall have frankness. And remember I haven't had twenty-four hours on the case yet. But I'll tell you this. I have every hope of finding your brother. Unless—"

"Yes?" She pulled at his arm again. "Unless what?"

Anthony looked at her steadily. "You have asked for frankness, I told you that I should give it to you. I am compelled to make one reservation. Unless your brother is dead."

She put a hand impulsively to her throat. "Dead! Oh—that's what I'm so desperately afraid of. Do you really think that, Mr. Bathurst?"

"No, Miss Regan. And I'm still being perfectly frank with you, I do *not* think so. But—and we must be prepared for any contingency—it's a *possibility* to which we can't altogether shut our eyes. All we can do is to hope for the best."

"If my brother isn't dead why hasn't he communicated with me or anything? That's what I can't understand. When I sit down to think things out I feel that he *must* be dead. It's the only possible explanation of his treating me as he has done."

"Not necessarily."

"I'm sorry, Mr. Bathurst. But what other explanation could there be?"

"Aren't there many that are possible? Let's look at it in the cold clear light of reason. Let's consider the various possibilities: (a) he may be seriously ill; (b) he may have sustained a bad accident; (c) he may be in prison; and (d) he may be in the hands of somebody who is deliberately keeping him a prisoner. As a matter of fact I rather incline to that last-mentioned possibility myself." They had completed the tour of the garden of "Boscawen" and as Anthony let fall his last remark, Kathleen Regan stopped abruptly and faced him.

"What on earth do you mean, Mr. Bathurst? Why should anybody keep Terence a prisoner? We're not living in mediaeval times, are we? And please tell me what makes you think that's the most likely possibility?"

"Three questions, Miss Regan, in quick succession followed by a request. I'll endeavour, to the best of my ability, to answer the three questions and then comply with the terms of the request. Here goes! I mean exactly what I say! I don't know! No! There are your three answers, Miss Regan. The last part is the most difficult for me. To explain to you why I think it's the most likely possibility. Well—I look at it like this. When he wrote to you, your brother was in good health. There's certainly no evidence to the contrary. He intended to visit you at the week-end. If he had had an accident, you should have heard about it. At least, one can reasonably anticipate that happening. I think, therefore, that the balance of probability lies in the direction I have indicated. That he's under some form of enforced restraint. In other words, that he's being kept from communication with you by malice aforethought. If he had been imprisoned by the police authorities for an offence against the law, you can bet your bottom dollar, Miss Regan, that some 'damned good-natured friend' would have let you know all about it. Even though your brother might have wanted the news kept from you. There you are! That's how I view the problem."

Anthony paused and looked at her intently. He saw that her face had become calm and serious again.

"Yes," she said, after a slight pause, "everything that you say sounds logical and feasible. I can't argue against any of it. But what are you going to do? Have you made any plans yet?"

"Oh, yes. What I must do first of all is plain. I must go to Wroxeter. To the house in Hampton Road where your brother lodged. To see if I'm able to pick up any trace of him up there. Who knows? I may strike lucky and get my fingers round a thread. By the way—here's a question I've been going to ask you ever since I arrived. Do you know anybody by the name of Arbuthnot?"

She shook her head. "No. Nobody. But why? Why did you ask me that?"

"No real reason. Put it down as just a bow at a venture."

Kathleen Regan looked at her watch. "I think it's time," she said hopefully, "that you and I went into lunch."

"The resolution," replied Anthony, "has my unqualified support."

CHAPTER II

1

CONFERENCE

ANTHONY sat with Chief-Inspector Andrew MacMorran. "I came to ask you," he said casually, "if you have any developments to report with regard to the gentleman who always reads the same book. As presented by Mr. Arbuthnot. Scene plot by—"

MacMorran cut him short. "None at all. Did you imagine that there would be something?"

"Wasn't sure. Have open mind on the matter. Intend to keep such. But, if you're in the mood for sober confidences, I have something for your receptive ear, Andrew. Is it open for said reception?"

MacMorran grinned. "Ay! Always ready to listen to a Bathurst bed-time story. Spin it, lad."

"Hearken to this, then."

Shortly and concisely, Anthony told him of the visit he had received from Doctor Page and of the events which had transpired subsequently. When Anthony reached the account of the seven girls' heads, MacMorran gave the narrative the closest attention. Anthony came to his conclusion.

"Kingsley twice, Andrew, you'll note—in a matter of a mere twenty-four hours. What say you to our double dose of Kingsley?"

The inspector grunted non-committally.

"What are your immediate reactions?" asked Anthony.

"Not sure. Don't know enough about either of the angles."

"Coincidence?"

"Maybe! After all, Kingsley isn't exactly a village hamlet."

"Too many rude forefathers—eh, Andrew? Well—perhaps you're right. I've done my duty and presented the matter to your notice. Personally, as I said just now, I've an open mind. But, listen, I'm coming forward with a proposal. Just to humour me for the time being, let's treat the cases as *one* with *two* distinct ends. I'll cover one of them. You cover the other. If at any time, we do find them dove-tailing, and, I admit, I've a shrewd suspicion that they will, we can join forces."

MacMorran nodded. "All right. Put as you've put it, it suits me and sounds a good proposition. Which end of it are you tackling?"

"I propose to award myself the treat of a visit to Wroxeter. Armed with a photograph of the missing man which his sister has given me. Seems to me that one of the trails at least, must start from there. I may strike lucky and get on to something fairly quickly. In the meantime, you'll go on keeping your eyes skinned round the

Arbuthnot end in the Kingsley quarter. Whom have you got on it, by the way?"

"Chatterton. I told Hemingway to put Chatterton on it early last week. You couldn't have a better man. Solid and reliable. Not flashy."

"I agree. But I don't envy him his job. Too much akin to the proverbial search for the needle in the hay-stack. Wandering round looking for something that you're not sure you'll recognize when you see it. Chatterton has my sympathy." Anthony grinned. "You can tell him so, Andrew, if you like. It might give him a thrill to know."

MacMorran, however, remained impervious to the raillery. "I don't quite know that Police-Constable Chatterton is the only one."

"How do you mean, Andrew?"

"With a job of the kind you describe. Seems to me we might put Mr. Bathurst himself in much the same category."

Anthony's face cleared when he heard the inspector's explanation. "Oh—you mean when I get up to Wroxeter? Ye-es—in a way perhaps you're right. Still—there's a difference between my job and Chatterton's. That's what you're forgetting, Andrew. I have got a starting-point. A place from which I can jump off. Terence Regan's address. Whereas comrade Chatterton has Sweet F.A. Still—one never knows—perhaps the two lines of inquiry will converge. At any rate, here's hoping, Andrew."

MacMorran looked up from the sheet of paper which had been occupying his attention. "A question for you before you go. Candidly, Mr. Bathurst—what do you think we're up against—*really*? Anything serious? Or something quite trivial?"

Anthony looked grave. "Friend Arbuthnot, to whose intelligence we owe the genesis of the case, is certain that a crime is about to be committed. Frankly, Andrew, I'm inclined to agree with him. That is, of course, if the crime hasn't been committed already."

He spoke the last four words slowly and deliberately. MacMorran was startled. "What are you thinking of, Mr. Bathurst? Terence Regan?"

Anthony nodded gravely in agreement. "You've rung the bell Andrew. I *am* thinking of Terence Regan! God grant that my fears are unfounded."

2

"CHRISTOPHER'S"

ANTHONY had booked rooms in Wroxeter at the "Black Horse" Inn. According to its advertisements, it was recommended by all and sundry. By the time he had been in the place about half an hour, he was reluctantly forced to the conclusion that the recommendations which it flaunted so bravely had been inspired by the twin-spirits of loving-kindness and merciful forgiveness.

His room was small and not over-clean and his first evening meal consisted of the three English inevitables. Tomato soup, roast beef and Yorkshire, apple-pie and custard. On the point of finishing his meal he made certain inquiries of the unattractive waitress who had attended to him.

"What does one do for amusement in Wroxeter?"

The girl pouted her lips and giggled. "There's two cinemas, sir, a dancing-hall and 'Christopher's'. But I'm afraid there isn't much else. Nobody could rightly call Wroxeter a den of infamy, sir. Most of the locals are in bed before ten o'clock."

"I see," commented Anthony. "'Christopher's'? What exactly is 'Christophers'?"

The girl pushed an unruly wisp of dark hair into place. "Well, sir, rightly speaking—it's a bar. You know—drink. Cocktails and such-like at proper fancy prices. The Middleton Hall people get in there a lot. At least—people say they do. Not that I know much about it. Never been in the place myself. I only go by what I'm told."

"I know what you mean," supplemented Anthony—"you mean that anybody who considers that he or she *is* anybody, goes to 'Christopher's' as a habit. Am I right? Yes?"

The girl shrugged her shoulders rather petulantly. "Oh—well, if you like to put it that way, you can, sir."

Anthony smiled. "Tell me where I find it. I promise you that I shan't accuse you of leading me astray."

Somewhat to his surprise, the waitress shed her petulance and smiled back at him. "When you leave here, cross straight over the road and take the turning almost exactly opposite. Then first right and first left. It's in a part of the town called Mardol. But you can't miss 'Christopher's,' sir. It's—er—posh. Got one of those revolving doors outside. Will you be going along there to-night, sir?"

"I might," replied Anthony. "I'll make up my mind later on. And now perhaps you'll be able to help me in another direction. Can you tell me where Hampton Road is?"

"Hampton Road, sir?" The girl picked up the used plates. "Yes. I can. It's not too near here. It's some little way out of the town. On the Dorricot road. Go up past the station and carry straight on till you come to the statue at the cross-roads. It's one of the early Mayors of Wroxeter. Sir Cunnan Foxe. Hampton Road's near there on the left. About five minutes' walk from the statue."

She packed up the plates and walked away. Anthony glanced at his wrist-watch. The time was a quarter past eight. He debated within his mind as to his plan of campaign for the remainder of the evening. He was not long in deciding to visit "Christopher's" as opposed to the idea of finding the house where Terence Regan had lodged during the early months of the year. That could better wait until the next day. It was a lovely summer evening so Anthony walked down to "Christopher's" hatless and outdoor-coatless, in a grey flannel suit and with his hands in his trouser pockets.

He followed the waitress's instructions as to the locality of the bar and was surprised to notice on his journey thereto that there were a good many more people moving about in the streets of Wroxeter than he had anticipated would be in accordance with his assessment of the likely population. Anthony walked at a fair pace and soon came to his destination. Turning a corner, his eye caught the sign showing the words "Christopher's Bar." As he pushed his way round the revolving doors in the front, two or three exceedingly well-dressed women were standing close to him and obviously waiting to come out. Anthony saw that they had a tall and also well-dressed man as escort. A man obviously of a class he wouldn't have expected to meet in a provincial town of the size of Wroxeter.

Inside the establishment the foyer was unusually brightly lighted and from close at hand he could hear the sound of a small orchestra playing. A few paces forward the members of the orchestra became visible to him. There were six performers attired in an evening dress uniform with a colour scheme of red, white and blue. "Coronation relics," he murmured to himself. There were two violinists and they were both distinctly good and well above the average in ability for artists of this class. Coloured lights glittered everywhere and an abundance of alcohol of most types seemed to be in circulation. The majority of the men wore the conventional lounge suit, although about half a dozen were attired in evening dress. Anthony realized at once why his waitress-informant had used the description "posh" and remembered at the same time her allusion to the "people from Middleton Hall."

Anthony wandered up to the bar-counter and ordered a double Scotch and soda. He tendered a ten-shilling note and raised his eyebrows somewhat when he saw the amount of the change that was returned to him. He made no comment, however, but took good stock of the bar-tender who had served him. At a quick judgment Anthony put him down as Portuguese. Whilst he was thinking thus, a man in evening-dress strolled up to the bar-counter next to him, ordered two champagne cocktails and addressed the barman as "Joe."

Anthony glanced at the man who had given the order. He was tall, slim and clean-shaven with a big hawk-like nose. At the same time he gave the appearance of being thoroughly fit in every way and most certainly a man to be reckoned with on most counts. As he accepted his two glasses from the barman he half-turned and gave Anthony a supercilious and disdainful stare. Anthony bore the affront with imperturbability as he allowed the mere suggestion of a smile to play round the corners of his lips. Without looking round too obviously he saw the tall man make his way to a table for two and to a girl there who occupied one of the chairs. She was well-built with heavy dark hair—almost black and her mouth showed as a vividly scarlet gash. The tall man pushed one of the champagne cocktails towards her and then raised his own glass in tribute to her.

Anthony found himself growing inordinately curious as to the reference to Middleton Hall. "Might have done well to have brought MacMorran after all," he commented to himself. "I don't fancy that this country town of Wroxeter is all that it ought to be." As he drank he watched carefully and with interest the various people who came to the bar for drinks and who stood near him. But comparatively few attracted his attention and not one to the degree of the tall, slim man who was now drinking with the black-haired girl. He decided to order a second drink and take it to a table approximate to that where the tall man was sitting with his companion.

He put the decision into almost immediate effect. From where he seated himself he was able to see perfectly the pair who had attracted his interest. The dark girl was talking with animation. Almost with excitement. On the surface the man remained cavalier and arrogant. More than once he shrugged his shoulders at remarks which his companion made to him. A few minutes after Anthony had moved his position, a third person joined the table which he was watching. This was a short, dark, full-necked, florid-faced man, also wearing evening dress. His age, Anthony thought, would be either in the late twenties or the early thirties. The short man took his drink to the table with him and sat down. Anthony noticed that he set his glass on the table and turned the bottom of the glass round three times before he took his fingers away from it.

The tall man spoke. Anthony caught the words. "A great deal of profit can be made on caviare." Anthony thought the remark, in the circumstances, somewhat curious. The short man replied.

"And on *pâté de foie gras*."

Then the thin man came in again. "But there is almost always a loss on *langouste*."

"Yes," came the second reply, "provided you buy in Toulon."

All this, to Anthony's mind, showed a definite development of the unusual. But he was able to bear no more. The short man pulled up his chair more closely to the table and the three people embarked upon what was apparently a serious and important conversation. Anthony lit a cigarette and generally dallied with his drink. He desired to create the impression that he had time to burn. According to what he was able to see of the party near him, the girl now took little part in the proceedings. For the better part of the time she was content to smoke and to listen. Perhaps once or twice she ventured a remark to the tall man, but hardly more than this. Her eyes held a strong suggestion of insolence. The conversation lasted about twenty minutes. The tall man called a waiter to the table and repeated his order of champagne cocktails, which the three quickly drank up and then began to make preparations for departure.

Anthony half-turned in his chair and watched them go. The waiter, who was collecting the glasses, he called to his side.

"Bring me another double Scotch and soda, will you, please?"

"Certainly, sir."

The man was quickly back to him with the drink. Anthony took a quick glance at him and resolved to draw a bow at a venture. He pushed the change along the tray to him. The man pocketed the tip.

"I'm very much obliged, sir."

Anthony drew his bow. "That tall gentleman who was sitting there just now with the dark lady—do you happen to know, waiter, if he's an ex-Army officer? Because if he's not, he's the dead spit of a man I used to know very well indeed. Met him in Durban years ago."

"That's Capt. Trevor, sir. That gentleman. Middleton Hall belongs to him. About two miles from here. Very wealthy man, sir. East India merchant, I believe, sir. Comes here pretty nearly every evening."

"Trevor," said Anthony, simulating reflection. "No—that's not the name I was thinking of. My man's name was Somerville. Extraordinary resemblance, though. Incredible likeness! Anybody who didn't know both of them thoroughly would have a rare job to tell them apart. Middleton Hall—eh?"

"Yes, sir. Capt. Lionel Trevor. The lady with him was a Miss Iris Underwood. Rumour has it, sir, that she's a theatrical lady. On the stage, sir. Capt. Trevor is, I believe," the waiter coughed as an indication of discretion, "rather partial to ladies of that—er—persuasion, sir. At any rate, rumour has it so, sir."

"A rich man, you say."

"Very rich. In the real sense of the word. The hospitality at Middleton Hall, so I am told, sir, if on the lavish scale,"

"H'm. Interesting. Old Clayshire family, I suppose? Came over with the Normans—or something like that?"

The waiter shook his head. "No, sir. Nothing like that. Capt. Trevor came to Middleton Hall about six months ago. It was in the market and he bought it. But he's made things hum a bit in that short time. The week-end parties he gives are the last word in hospitality—or so I am told, sir."

"Really," said Anthony, "you surprise me. East India merchant—eh? Ah, well—that's very interesting."

He then deliberately side-tracked the inquiry. He wanted to stifle any idea in the waiter's mind that he was exhibiting inordinate curiosity in the subject. He rose, therefore, as though about to leave.

"Are you always as crowded as this?" he asked casually.

"About average to-night, sir, for the middle of the week. Week-ends it's much thicker. It's a bit of a tussle then to get across the floor. Like bees round a honey-jar."

It was on the tip of Anthony's tongue to inquire with regard to Terence Regan, and the possibility of his having visited "Christopher's," but he was wary and checked the inclination. He felt, on consideration, that the better plan would be for him to work under cover. Certainly for a time, at least. So he bade the communicative waiter a brisk "good evening" and returned to the tender mercies of the "Black Horse." On the whole, he considered, he had not fared too badly. "Christopher's" looked like providing many interesting possibilities and Wroxeter itself appeared, on first and early acquaintance, to hold many points and features dissimilar to the majority of towns of its own type. Anthony therefore went to bed and slept soundly.

3

THE TREE IN THE GARDEN

THE "Black Horse" breakfast was of considerably better quality than the "Black Horse" dinner. Anthony, indeed, was agreeably surprised. He was in good spirits, therefore, when he set out for the house in Hampton Road where Terence Regan had lodged up to a date in early April. Guided by the information his waitress had given him with regard to locality, he had no difficulty in finding the statue of that mayor whom the burgesses of Wroxeter had decided to honour, and, passing it, in coming upon Hampton Road comparatively quickly.

The house he sought was the sixth house on the left-hand side as he turned into the road. Anthony took a good look at it and he saw at once that it was unoccupied and that there was no condition present that even by the generous interpretation of a rate collector could be justifiably termed beneficial occupation. It was a house of the villa type, small and probably inconvenient to live in, but semi-detached. Similar in type to many he could see in the road. Its market value he assessed in the region of six hundred pounds.

He walked down one side of the road and then up the other before coming to a decision. He meant to enter number eleven, if it were at all possible for him to do so. The gate at the front was held back by a brick placed beneath it. Anthony went through and saw at once that he could get to the garden at the back by walking past the side of the house. There was no barrier of any kind to prevent his taking this course. And, bearing in mind that he was more interested, perhaps, in the garden than in the house itself, this discovery brought him a considerable amount of pleasure. He walked straight through, therefore, to the back garden. Naturally, considering that there was no occupation of the house, the garden was neglected and overrun with weeds. But there were certain signs extant that there had been some attempts, at least, towards cultivation of moderately recent origin. Certain designs of flower-beds were still to be observed and Anthony could see the remains of a fair-sized rockery at the far end of the garden.

But Anthony's primary angle of interest, on this particular morning, was the discovery of an elm tree or elm trees. And he saw them at once! At the bottom of the row of gardens there ran a line of elms. They were of great age, Anthony thought, and the particular tree which was still to be found at the end of the garden of Terence Regan's house of stay looked as though the end of its days was well in sight. Its branches had been thoroughly lopped, but it had been a fine tree in its hey-day, and Anthony walked towards it full of interest and well-foundationed curiosity.

It might well be, of course, that the idea with which he was toying would prove to be unsound. The allusion he was considering might be other than he was anticipating, but on the whole he was feeling well pleased as he advanced towards the tree and fortified also by a strong belief that he was on the right track.

The tree stood at the back of the garden and almost exactly in the middle. Anthony had to cross what had evidently been a bed for *Brassica*, to reach it. A few decaying months-old Brussels sprouts were still protruding from the ground. Directly he got the tree in full and complete view Anthony began to rub his hands. For he saw a fair-sized cavity at the bottom of the trunk on the right-hand side of it—that is to say on the opposite side to that by which he had approached. Anthony saw at once that this hole might well have been used as a hiding-place and his heart began to beat a little faster at the prospect of what he might find within it.

He scanned the various doors and windows at the rear of the neighbouring houses to see whether he was being observed. But he could see nothing of that nature to cause him any disquiet. His entry to the garden of the empty house had not been noticed. Or at any rate he held strong hopes that this was so. So he squatted on his haunches before the trunk of the lopped elm and thrust his hand into the cavity. To his surprise, his fingers grasped a large object which felt at first acquaintance like a slab of wood. Anthony pulled it out. For a moment, when he looked at it, he was uncertain as to what he held. But realization came to him quickly and he saw that the object which he held in his hands was a discoloured brass plate such as is used by professional and business men outside their places of operation to publicize their trades or professions. Anthony rubbed the front of it with his handkerchief in an endeavour to decipher what was on the brass plate. He had no difficulty. The brass brightened up quickly under the attentions of the hand-kerchief and Anthony was enabled to read the following, "Doctor Cranmer, M.D., and Doctor Sellers, M.B., 22 Hathaway Street, Stratford-upon-Avon. Hours of Consultation, 10 a.m.-4 p.m. daily except Thursdays. Sundays, 6-8 p.m."

Anthony pushed one hand through his hair. An extraordinary object, he thought, to find secreted in the trunk of an old tree. And originally from Stratford-upon-Avon. Anthony remained squatting on his haunches for a minute or so and then put the brass plate on one side and thrust his hand again into the cavity. His next find was a small book. He withdrew it and saw that he held a pocket-diary. This promised better things. He glanced at the opening pages. Yes! The name and address had been inscribed on the fly-leaf. "Terence Regan, 11, Hampton Road, Wroxeter." He promptly transferred the diary to his coat pocket with the intention of examining it thoroughly at his leisure. Anthony then made a third hand-incursion into the hole in the tree-trunk. A largish envelope rewarded him on this occasion and from the first feel he had of it, it seemed that the contents were bulky. An elastic band had been placed round it to hold these contents in position. Anthony took off the band and extracted the contents. To his amazement he found a packet of currency notes—each in the value of one pound. Without counting them he placed these on top of the brass name-plate and made further investigations. He pushed his fingers in all directions, but nothing more was in the hole.

Anthony stood up to think matters out. (a) A brass plate of two doctors who practised, or who had practised, in Stratford-upon-Avon, (b) a diary and (c) a packet of currency notes. In truth—a miscellaneous collection of effects. He took some time in deliberating as to what his next step should be. His mind eventually made up, he returned to the front of the house with his various finds and knocked on the door of the house next adjoining. A thin, elderly woman answered his knock whose elbows were cupped in her hands. Anthony apologized for troubling her. But could she give him any information concerning a Mr. Regan, a young gentleman who had resided next door up to the early days of April?

The thin woman shook her head. She had not seen him for some weeks now. And Mrs. Kirk, her neighbour and Mr. Regan's landlady, had vacated the premises about the middle of May. She was a widow and had gone to live with her married daughter in the North of England somewhere. Anthony explained that Mr. Regan's relatives had received no news of him. Did the lady think that Mrs. Kirk had had any?

The thin woman doubted it strongly. If Mrs. Kirk had received any before she went away she had never mentioned the fact to her neighbour. There was the possibility, however, that the neighbour on the other side might know. She was, perhaps, more friendly with Mrs. Kirk than she herself was. She herself had always been one to keep herself to herself!

Anthony made it clear that he understood her point of view perfectly. But she wouldn't mind, he took it, if he had a word with the lady on the other side? The thin woman stated that she would have no objection at all, so he wished her a gallant good-day and repaired to the house numbered nine in Hampton Road.

His knock here was greeted by a woman who was the almost complete antithesis of the lady to whom he had just spoken. This second personality was short, fat and with a good-natured florid face. Anthony used the same opening gambit that he had used before. Concerning any information that there might be had in relation to young Mr. Terence Regan. But he met with no greater measure of real success than had rewarded him previously. All the short woman could do was to tell him what Mrs. Kirk had told her. Which, summed up, amounted to this. That young Mr. Regan "had gone away." She *believed* that he had returned to a place somewhere near London. And to the best of her recollection, Mrs. Kirk had informed her that young Mr. Regan had telephoned her to this effect.

But his belongings—what about them?—inquired Anthony. The stout woman nodded sapiently in agreement with the justice and the force which lay behind the gentleman's questions, but she fancied that the young fellow had come in one afternoon when Mrs. Kirk was at the pictures, packed his bag and left the money that was owing for the rent on Mrs. Kirk's kitchen-table—he was always the gentleman, she could say that for him!

This seemed pretty conclusive, so Anthony shifted the point of his attack. Could the lady tell him anything more about Mr. Regan? Had he made any friends in the neighbourhood as far as she knew? Had he any hobbies? What were his general habits? What inclination or direction did they take? But Anthony drew blank on each and every count. All that she knew with regard to Regan was that he had lodged next door and had departed thence almost as suddenly as he had arrived.

Anthony realized after a time that little or no good purpose would be served by his persisting in the inquiry. He therefore bade the lady as equally a gallant good morning as he had extended to her predecessor, closed her garden gate behind him and slowly walked back to the "Black Horse." Nevertheless he had made progress. There was no gainsaying that. And there was also another string to his bow waiting to be loosed. In his pocket there lay the diary of Terence Regan. To say nothing of a certain number of currency notes.

4

THE DIARY OF TERENCE REGAN

ANTHONY went straight to his bedroom at the "Black Horse" and deposited therein the three finds he had made that morning in the tree trunk at the back of the house in Hampton Road. He placed the brass name-plate on the floor by the side of the dressing-table but the wad of currency notes and Regan's diary he put on the small table which stood at the side of the bed. He then pulled a chair up to the table and proceeded to count the notes. There were fifty.

For a time Anthony sat quiet. Here was a problem indeed! Why should Regan hide the notes and then go away and leave them in their hiding place? Unless he intended to return! Yes—it must be conceded that there was a distinct possibility in that angle. With an almost violent movement, Anthony snapped the elastic band round the notes again and tossed the bundle on the bed. He would turn his attention to the diary. It was a small diary of pocket size. Dark blue in colour. Of the type that can be purchased at a moderate price at most stationers and the like at the season of Christmas and the New Year. Opening it he saw that there had been no serious attempt to "keep" it, employing the verb in its usual and relevant sense. All that Anthony could discover on any of its pages were stray written observations which obviously had no relation whatever to the dates under which they had been inscribed.

Anthony found them in this order. There were eleven of them. 1. Hon. Michael Polhill-Scott; 2. The Skipper—circular; 3. ? The menu; 4. Doctor Sellers—? address; 5. ? did Lovegrove know all; 6. At Christopher's; 7. Odd-coloured eyes; 8. Silver patch; 9. Note—call at the gardener's house—? distance; 10. Mrs. Ardsley Spuyten; 11. Sir Curtis Littlehales—Eureka! Anthony could find no other entry between the beginning of the year and the third of April. From that date to the end of the year the pages were blank. Regan had not made a note on any one of them. But right at the end of the book on the back page Anthony found a few more words scrawled. They ran thus: "See April 25 for all." He thereupon referred to that date in the main body of the diary. The whole page, however, on which this date occurred was entirely innocent of writing!

Anthony puzzled over this. To no avail. Eventually he returned to the consideration of the eleven entries he had found in the early pages of the diary. He placed them in categories as follows: Names (3); Queries (3); Definite statements (4); Definite statement with query attached (1). Of the names of the three people mentioned, all, he thought, bore unmistakable indications of upper class and well-to-do people. Two, presumably, British and one, also presumably, American. The "Eureka" after the last-mentioned name might well be significant. Of the queries, one related to a menu, one to an address and the last to the possible knowledge of a certain person described as Lovegrove. The definite statements were mixed. The first required explanation. The second he understood, having already visited the place in question, but the third and fourth were obviously physical references to a man or men or to a woman or women. The last allusion—that of the definite statement with query attached—had evidently been specially noted by Regan as a reminder to himself. But who was the gardener and how great was the distance? And in addition to this what was the point in the date of April 25th?

Anthony rose from his chair and began to pace the room. As he did so he cursed the conditions of delay which had made his problem all the more difficult of solution. Footprints obliterated, scent cold, memories dimmed and faint. If people in trouble would only act or seek advice quickly! As far as he could see he had several procedures open to him. He explored several of them mentally as he walked up and down the room. As a result of these mental excursions he decided on one course which he would take at once. He put the currency notes into a small parcel and with them he put the following short note which he addressed to MacMorran at Scotland Yard.

"My dear Andrew. Run your eye over the enclosed. I can't possibly overlook the natural appeal they will make to a man with a name like yours. I *think* they were left behind by young Regan when he cleared away from here. That is to say 'cleared away' or '*was* cleared away.' I have told nobody of this discovery. Don't trouble to reply as I hope to be with you as soon as any letter you sent would be with me. But I have made one or two interesting discoveries and I am interviewing the local police this afternoon. In the meantime what's the price of 'Arbuthnot Deferreds.'? I shall expect to hear something in that direction when we meet. Till then, A.L.B."

He took the packet to the post-office himself and registered it. That effected, he returned to the "Black Horse" for lunch. Before cudgelling his brains over the various fragments which he had unearthed from the diary, he intended to apply an entirely practical test. To that test, he considered that the local police authorities were the most likely agency to supply the correct answer. If they failed to do that, he must cast his line in another direction but he hoped that this alternative would not be necessary. That there was crime close at hand, he now harboured no doubt. Perhaps inexplicable and unpredictable crime, radiating from this centre of Wroxeter. He knew from the avenues of his own experience that there were men abroad in the land who were both desperate and degenerate and who would stick at nothing if sufficient profit came to them as a result of activities which were hideous and evil. With these thoughts dominating his mind, Mr. Bathurst turned his attention to the inevitable tomato soup. On this particular occasion it was, if anything, a little worse than usual!

5

THE POLICE AT WROXETER REMEMBER

ANTHONY entered the police station at Wroxeter at almost exactly three o'clock. It was a glorious afternoon. With haze everywhere. The sun rode high in the heavens, and everybody who could, took life as easily as possible. Dogs lay quiescent and cats basked in the sunshine. Even the insects, with all sorts of summer industry on hand, seemed to have reached a basis of agreement that the afternoon's work could very well wait for a later date. Anthony, who had presented his card to the station-officer, was passed to a Sergeant Singleton. The last-'named received him cordially and requested him to take a seat and make himself comfortable. Anthony did so.

"I'll tell you what I want, Sergeant," he said. "I want to trace a missing man. A man who was in Wroxeter up to somewhere about the first week in April. His name was Terence Regan. By profession he was an artist and he lodged with a Mrs. Kirk at 11, Hampton Road."

Singleton pulled a file towards him and turned over papers. Anthony let him. "April, you said," remarked the sergeant.

"The first week in April."

After a time Singleton shook his head. "Nothing reported to us here concerning a missing man named Regan."

Anthony nodded. "I'm aware of that, Sergeant. In fact I knew that was so. He had no relatives in the district and I understand that he told his landlady he was on the move. But I am not sure that I altogether accept that position."

Singleton looked fixedly at him. "Why not? Why do you say that? What are your reasons?"

"His sister, who lives at Kingsley, which as you know is in Surrey, has heard nothing whatever from him since the early days of April. Previously they corresponded regularly and she was to have met him within a few days of receiving his last letter. Frankly, Sergeant, I'm worried about the man."

"You mean you suspect foul play—or something like it?"

"Frankly—I do." Anthony's hand went to his pocket. "There's a photograph of Terence Regan, Sergeant. I brought it along with me. It will give you some idea of what the man was like."

Singleton took the photograph and regarded it critically. It struck Anthony that he was exercising a definite line of thought. "Recognize him?" he inquired of Singleton.

"No. Not exactly," came the drawled response—"but all the same I'll admit that you've started the grey matter working. I'm not sure but I may be—"

He got up from his chair and walked to the door leaving Anthony wondering. "Is Beaumont there?" he called out. Anthony couldn't hear the reply but after a second or so's wait he heard Singleton say, "Well, then, find Beaumont and tell him I want him in here pronto."

The sergeant returned to his place opposite Anthony. He grinned as he did so. "Maybe I'm barking up the wrong tree—but on the other hand—maybe not. You never know. Anyway Roger Beaumont'll tell us."

Anthony was inquisitive. "On to something?"

"You wait," returned Singleton—"I never like jumping at anything. Not my form at all."

Anthony grinned back and waited in patience for the arrival of the (to him) unknown Roger Beaumont. Some minutes passed. Singleton tapped on his desk with the points of his fingers. Every now and then he looked straight over Anthony's right shoulder out of the window and into Wroxeter's main street.

"Sorry to keep you waiting so long," he ventured eventually, "but I expect Beaumont's engaged somewhere." He tilted back his chair and began to talk again. "You see, Mr. Bathurst, I'm not quite sure as to where I am. That's why I want Beaumont in on it."

"I understand. And I am content to wait."

Suddenly the door opened softly and a uniformed constable came in. He looked at Sergeant Singleton and smiled affably.

"I was in the mortuary, Sergeant, when your message came over. They took a woman from the Wroxe this afternoon. Suicide case, I fancy."

Beaumont was tall, fair-haired and blue-eyed. Anthony liked his looks on the spot.

"That's O.K., Beaumont. This gentleman here is Mr. Anthony Bathurst. You've probably heard of him. He's come for any information he can get concerning a missing man who resided here in Wroxeter. There's the missing man." Singleton passed the photograph to Beaumont.

Anthony watched intently for reactions. But Beaumont took everything with the utmost sang-froid. He put the photograph on Singleton's desk face upwards.

"I think I know what's in your mind, Sergeant. And if you're looking to me for confirmation it's yours for the asking."

"I was right then, was I," said Singleton quickly, "in that case, Constable Beaumont, let this gentleman here have the whole story. It will come from you better than from me."

Beaumont squared his shoulders. "Well, Mr. Bathurst, you hear what the sergeant says. My story's this. Early in April—I'll check up on the exact date for you later on—this fellow here," he indicated the photograph of Regan, "or his twin brother, was picked up dead on the road to Stratford-upon-Avon. A motor-cyclist spotted him late one night and phoned to us here at the station. I was on duty and took the call. I sent an ambulance out for him and it brought him back here to the mortuary. I took him in. This is the guy all right. Not the flicker of a doubt."

"I thought you'd say so," contributed Singleton in an undertone.

"How was he killed?" asked Anthony curtly.

"Run over by a fast and heavy car, in all probability. His ribs and one of his arms were smashed. Crushed like matchwood. Death must have been pretty well instantaneous. The divisional surgeon gave him the once-over—said he'd been dead probably for some hours when the cyclist spotted him under the hedge."

"I see. Now tell me this, Constable. Why wasn't any—"

"I know what you're going to say," interrupted Beaumont good-humouredly. "And the explanation's this. There was absolutely nothing whatever on him or in his clothes that identified him. Not a sausage!"

Anthony nodded slowly. "I see."

Beaumont went on again. "We had it all broadcast. No car driver came forward. No friends or relations made any inquiries whatsoever. So the poor stiff was buried, after the coroner had had a look at him, in what some of the old-fashioned novelists used to call a nameless grave. To be precise—in Wroxeter Parish Churchyard. And the long-suffering ratepayers footed the bill. Not for the first *or* the last time."

"There you are, Mr. Bathurst," intervened Sergeant Singleton, "Constable Beaumont has told you just what I expected him to. But he knew the man's face better than I did, better than any of us did, in fact, so I thought I'd get him to confirm my own pretty shrewd suspicions."

Anthony debated within himself as to the particular line he should take with them. He decided that he would raise no awkward questions at the moment and accept the information that had been given to him with little comment.

"That's very sad," he announced, "and it means that I have nothing but bad news to take back to his sister. That's the lady for whom I'm acting. As far as I know, she's the only living relation the man had. The one thing about it that's satisfactory is that it clears the job up. He's dead, I can report how he came by his death, and she must realize that no power on earth can bring him back to her."

"That's about all you can do," replied Singleton, "and although it's sad, it's the only sensible way you can look at it. I wish everybody that comes in here with a bundle of trouble would look at matters in the same way."

"There's one thing before I go," said Anthony, coming round to Constable Beaumont again, "if you could tell me the exact date of Regan's death, I'd be obliged. You promised to check up on it for me, if you remember. If it's not putting you to too much trouble."

"No trouble at all, sir," responded Beaumont, "just give me a couple of minutes and I'll be back with the dope."

"Smart man that," commented Singleton, "you were lucky to find him on duty. There's very little that comes his way that he forgets. With any break he'll make a name for himself in the 'Force.' Marvellous memory. We often refer to him as 'Datas'."

"I suppose," said Anthony meditatively, "going back to the Regan affair, that the motor-cyclist who spotted his body was above suspicion all right?"

"Oh—quite. That end of the case was tested very thoroughly. Nothing could be pinned on him. He wasn't within a hundred miles when Regan had been killed—according to our Divisional-Surgeon's time. I remember that I—"

The door opened to admit Constable Beaumont. "Here you are, Mr. Bathurst—here's the data you inquired after. The body was picked up by the police ambulance at twelve minutes past eleven on the evening of April 8th. It was found on the Stratford-upon-Avon road about two miles out of Wroxeter. The name of the cyclist who found him was Arthur Allchin. His address was 17, Ledbury Cottages, Swindon. We checked up on that—it wasn't the Swindon in Wiltshire but the village near Dudley. There was nothing for us on Allchin—I can assure you of that."

Beaumont looked up from the file which he had been reading. "There you are, sir. That's about the full extent of what I can do for you. Sorry I can't make it any more."

Anthony rose and thanked the two uniformed men for the assistance they had given him. He walked back to the "Black Horse" with his mind full of conflicting ideas. But that Regan had met with foul play he hadn't the slightest doubt.

6

CONFERENCE WITH MACMORRAN

ANTHONY left the comfort of the "Black Horse" early that evening on the understanding that he would be back within a period of twenty-four hours. Before eleven o'clock he was in consultation with Chief Inspector MacMorran in the latter's room at New Scotland Yard. Anthony assumed his customary seat on the corner of the table.

"I take it you got my wire, Andrew?"

"I did that. And I formed the conclusion that you'd got your hooks in something. Am I right?"

"You most certainly are, Andrew. But tell me before I start my yarn—has there been any Arbuthnot development?"

MacMorran shook his head. "Nothing at all. Do you still persist in connecting the two ends? Because if you say you do, I'll tell you candidly I can now see no grounds for your so doing."

Anthony smiled. Almost to himself. "Well, I do, Andrew. I've got a hunch. But we'll leave the argument out of it for the time being. Let me get back to the Regan end." He lit a cigarette. "Regan was murdered. You can take that for gospel. Ah-h—I thought you'd be sitting up and taking nourishment when you heard that piece of news. I'll pitch you the whole yarn, though, and you can form your own judgment. Listen to this."

Anthony told MacMorran the whole story. Right from the crayoned heads of Terence Regan down to the interview he had had that day with Singleton and Beaumont in the police station at Wroxeter. MacMorran listened without comment. Occasionally he nodded his head. When Anthony had finished, he put a question.

"Why was Regan murdered?"

Anthony shrugged his shoulders.

"Either he knew too much or he found out something which he shouldn't have known."

"It's easy to say that. But what about?"

Anthony grinned. "Can't answer that at the moment, Andrew. You're asking too much. See me this time next week and I'll see what I can do for you."

The inspector ignored the levity. "You went to the police. What about the bank manager—I think you said it was the Midland Territorial where Regan banked?"

"I haven't been there yet. It can wait till later and I had to move quickly. As a matter of fact I kept away on purpose." MacMorran grunted. "Have you told the girl?"

"No. Not yet. Candidly, I don't fancy the job."

MacMorran's mind went back to its more normal business. "These local police. At Wroxeter. They don't show up as over-bright, do they? The way they handled it. A dead body in the road with nothing on it whatever to identify it. Positively screams for an investigation. Don't you think so?"

"I do. But, as most people do in similar circumstances, they took the line of least resistance. It was 'easy'—the way they acted. The divisional-surgeon probably had a date, or wanted to play golf. So he accepted everything at its face value. That's the probable explanation, Andrew—you can stake your life on it."

"H'm. Sounds plausible the way you put it."

Anthony came to closer grips. "Those currency notes I sent on to you, Andrew. Any news for me?"

"Not yet. They've been passed to an expert for investigation and report. It may come in later on to-day."

Anthony rubbed the ridge of his jaw. "It's difficult to know where to attack. At Kingsley we have Miss Regan and the Arbuthnot incident. The one, I admit, may have nothing whatever to do with the other. I'll say that to please you. Although I can think what I like myself. That's beside the point. At Wroxeter we have the dead Regan. In addition to several other highly interesting possibilities. According to the dead man's sister, Regan was friendly at Wroxeter with a man named Brown. Observe the patronymic, Andrew!

Of all names—Brown! Had it been Smith or Jones, now, we might be feeling—"

"Obviously chosen for the purpose," growled MacMorran. "You can't expect too much jam put on your plate."

"I don't," grinned Anthony in return. "My friends always accuse me of pessimism rather than its opposite number. But to get back. Try as I will I can't avoid coming to this conclusion. Regan fell foul of somebody and—what is more—*knew* that this condition existed. In a way he endeavoured to warn his sister. He paid for his knowledge. Whoever it was he was up against silenced him."

The inspector nodded.

"I agree with you that it's difficult. We've so precious little to go upon. But there's one thing at least I think you ought to do. And that's have a few words with the divisional-surgeon at Wroxeter. Seems to me that something might be picked up from him. He saw the body when it came in on the ambulance."

"Yes. I think you're right, Andrew. I'd better get back to the Midlands. But I must see Regan's sister first and break the bad news to her."

"Yes," replied the inspector. "I suppose you must."

7

ANTHONY IS REMINDED OF ARBUTHNOT

ANTHONY went to Kingsley on the following morning and was ringing the bell at "Boscawen" soon after half-past ten. Miss Groves informed him that Miss Regan was in. Anthony waited for her. She came towards him impetuously with her hand stretched out towards him.

"Take me out into the garden, Miss Regan—where you took me before."

"You have news of Terence! I am positive you have news of my brother. It's true, isn't it?"

"Yes, Miss Regan. It's true. But come and sit down over here." Anthony took her over to a wooden seat right in the heart of the garden which held many roses. Kathleen Regan caught him by the arm as he seated himself next to her.

"Tell me your news, Mr. Bathurst," she said with a quiet simplicity.

"That's why I have come, Miss Regan." He looked steadily into her eyes. "You must be brave."

She paled. "Is it bad news that you have brought me? Is it? Is Terence dead?"

Anthony nodded his head. The tears came to her. Anthony knew that they would bring her some relief and that it was good that they should fall. He said nothing to her while she cried. When the first flood was finished, she said, "Tell me, please, how did he die? Was he ill? If he were, why couldn't he have sent for me?"

"I can't give you all the details," Anthony answered her, "yet awhile. I expect we shall have to wait some time before we can piece everything together. But it is believed that your brother was run over and killed by a motor-car. His body, badly injured, was found on the road between Wroxeter and Stratford-upon-Avon."

She looked at him with a frightened look in her eyes. "When did this happen, Mr. Bathurst?"

"According to my information, on the evening of April the 8th. His body was found by a motor-cyclist, who reported the matter to the Wroxeter police."

"But I don't understand," she cried. "Why was it all hushed up? Why wasn't I—"

"I know what you're going to ask. I asked similar questions. There was no clue on him as to his identity when his body was picked up. And no news of any kind came in with regard to him. An inquest was held and he was buried at Wroxeter. The police had no information at all to work on—you see."

He watched her face grow hard and grim. She turned to him impulsively. "Something you said! You said 'it is believed' my brother was killed by a car. You had a reason for putting it like that. You had—hadn't you?"

Anthony had feared that these questions would come. He replied non-committally. "Perhaps."

"But you had!" Her declaration now was fierce and insistent. "It's no use your trying to stall me off. You mustn't hide anything from me. I implore you not to. You must tell me the truth." She almost shook his arm in her anxiety and impatience.

"Very well, Miss Regan. I will be as frank with you as you wish me to be. I am *not* satisfied. And I'm very much afraid that your brother was the victim of foul play."

"But why, Mr. Bathurst? There *must* be a sane reason for an awful thing like that to happen. And I can't think there is. My brother hadn't an enemy in the world."

Anthony shook his head. "You're running on too fast, Miss Regan. Murders aren't always committed by reason of enmity, hatred or malice. They are sometimes occasioned by other motives. Fear, for example, can be cited as one of them."

"Fear!" she exclaimed incredulously. "Who would be afraid of Terence? Who in Wroxeter, especially?"

Anthony shook his head again. "It might not have been fear of your brother in exact terms. But there might have been fear of, shall we say, *what he knew*. Knowledge often may mean power. Power may cause sour resentment in the subjugated. Resentment such as that has been known to resolve itself into murder. There you have the normal chain."

She was silent. Anthony went on. "You can help me. Why did your brother go to Wroxeter? Tell me again. Think hard. I need details."

"He had work offered him there. Work that was congenial to him. He went to a man named Brown. Brown was an artist like my brother was."

Anthony's brow furrowed in thought. "Didn't you tell me before that your brother answered an advertisement? In one of the papers?"

"I think that is what he told me. But I am not definitely sure."

"And you can't remember your brother ever coming to Kingsley before he took the job at Wroxeter?"

"No, Mr. Bathurst."

"But you agree that he suggested you should reside in Kingsley in the first place?"

"Yes. I agree that he did."

"Thanks. If I'm able to get all these details right it's going to help me considerably."

"Where is Terence buried?" she asked in a flat, toneless voice.

"According to the police, in Wroxeter Parish Churchyard."

"I must go and see his grave. As soon as ever possible."

"I shall be returning to Wroxeter. I've brought one or two matters away with me that need investigation. I'll make arrangements for you to come down there and—"

She put her fingers on his arm again. "Tell me, Mr. Bathurst. And please don't think me a stupid, foolish girl for asking you—but I'm frightened."

Anthony's eyes searched her face. "Why, Miss Regan? Why should you be frightened?"

She shook her head. "I don't know. But I am."

"That's not giving me any reason."

"No. I know it isn't." She fell to silence again. Anthony left her alone. Suddenly she looked up and started to speak again. "Perhaps I've a sixth sense at work somewhere inside me. Perhaps even I'm what is sometimes called 'fey.' But I'm sick with fear and foreboding. For myself—and none other. I'm afraid that the terrible evil which caught and killed Terry is reaching out to pluck hold of me—and that, whatever I do, I shan't be able to contend with it."

Anthony shook his head. "You're giving way to an obsession. You mustn't allow yourself to. You must fight against it with all the natural forces at your command. For, as I see things, there is no danger that threatens you."

"You are trying to reassure me. I appreciate that. But the feeling of disaster that I described to you has got me in its grip. I just can't shake it off."

"You've had a shock, Miss Regan, and a pretty substantial one at that. And what you're feeling is but a natural reaction to that shock. Now come into the house again. As I told you just now I intend to return to Wroxeter almost immediately. Certainly not later than the day after to-morrow. My address will be the 'Black Horse.' In the High Street. When I'm back there I'll communicate with you again."

Anthony got up from where he had been sitting. The girl followed suit. Silently they returned to the house. As he was preparing to depart, Kathleen Regan spoke to him again.

"I've been thinking things over, Mr. Bathurst. I realize more than ever now that I must place myself absolutely in your hands.

Which means that I shall do nothing until I hear from you again after you've gone to Wroxeter."

"That's very sensible of you, Miss Regan. I agree entirely."

Anthony took his leave of her. As he left "Boscawen" he noticed a man lounging about near the gate of the front garden. Anthony took good stock of him. The man's attitude and demeanour struck him as curious and a little suspicious. The man was tall and spare. His hair was worn long. He wore a dark suit and a cap and his nose was unduly prominent. Also, to Anthony's keener interest, he carried a book under his arm. Anthony remembered the description which Arbuthnot had given to MacMorran of the man who travelled on the train from Fosters to Shepherd's Brook.

As Anthony watched him the man seemed suddenly to become aware that he was an object of interest. He turned on his heel and walked away. Anthony decided to follow him at a respectable distance. After a journey of about a quarter of a mile Anthony, at a distance of fifty yards, saw the man turn into a shop. Anthony quickened his pace. When he came abreast of the establishment where the man had disappeared Anthony saw to his annoyance and disappointment that it was the Kingsley branch of "Woolworth's." He lost no time in entering. But he was too late. The place was crowded. Quick movement was impeded everywhere. He could see no sign of the man whom he had followed. But he noticed, to his chagrin, that there was an exit door at the rear through which, there was little doubt, his quarry had had ample time to make his escape. Anthony realized that he had been outwitted.

All the same though, he told himself on his journey back to town, he had information for MacMorran re the Arbuthnot end of the tangle. On the whole, he felt some greater degree of satisfaction. For he was certain that the man he had seen *was* the man who had troubled Arbuthnot and that they were at last getting to grips with a tangible reality and not pursuing a mere figment of an exaggerated imagination. Which was all to the good, considered Mr. Bathurst!

CHAPTER III

1

MR. BATHURST REVISITS WROXETER

Anthony passed on his news concerning the man at Kingsley. MacMorran received it with avid interest. He promised to take further steps in that particular district. On the next morning Anthony caught an early train to the Midlands and booked up again at the "Black Horse."

Within the next three hours he had contrived two personal interviews—the first with the manager of the Wroxeter branch of the Midland Territorial Bank and the second with the divisional-surgeon to the Wroxeter police authorities.

The bank manager's name was Poulton and Anthony found him both courteous and obliging. Anthony explained the purpose of his visit and produced his credentials. Poulton comprehended the position at once.

"Yes—I remember young Regan very well. Very decent chap. I interviewed him when he came in here on the first occasion to open his account. I'll find out for you how it stands." He picked up a telephone and spoke into it. "Mr. Palmer! Bring in Mr. Terence Regan's account, will you, please? 11, Hampton Road the address. No—ordinary current account. Thank you. We'll soon see how it stands," he said with a smile.

The clerk instructed brought the account into the manager's room. "Thank you," returned Poulton, "I'll let you know if I should want you again."

"Thank you, sir."

The manager turned over the pages briskly. "Regan—Terence. Here it is. 11, Hampton Road. Balance in his favour to date—seventy-one pounds fifteen shillings and elevenpence. No transactions—either debit or credit—since April the fourth. H'm—time ago."

Anthony nodded. "The reason being that it is feared Regan is dead. I don't think there could possibly be a better reason." Poulton stared at him. "But if that's the case, Mr.—er—Bathurst, it's a rather strange—"

"I think that I can explain that to your entire satisfaction, Mr. Poulton." Anthony proceeded to inform the bank manager of the details of Regan's death as given him by the police.

"It's rather incredible," said Poulton when Anthony had finished. "Of course, it's nothing to do with me from that particular point of view, but it almost suggests that everything may not have been all above board. Don't you agree with me, Mr. Bathurst?"

"I do indeed—hence these inquiries. I called here to-day to confirm the position as indicated by the deceased's account. You have confirmed it and I thank you."

"Only too pleased—and if there's anything more that I can do in the same direction please don't hesitate to ask me."

The two men shook hands on it and Anthony made his way, for the second time, to Wroxeter police station.

"I got your phone message," said Sergeant Singleton when he greeted him. "This is Inspector Foster and this gentleman is Doctor Sandford, the divisional-surgeon, the gentleman you want to see. Now I'll leave it to the inspector."

Anthony thanked him and sat down. Foster took up from where the sergeant had left off.

"I've had a word with the 'Yard.' I spoke to Chief-Inspector MacMorran as you suggested." He smiled. "He tells me that everything is all right and that I'm to oblige him by giving you all the information possible."

Anthony nodded. "Thank you, Inspector."

Foster smiled again, showing a mouth filled with fine white teeth. "I told him I'd be pleased to. Never know when you'll want to be on the right side of the 'Yard.' Must keep one's bread buttered. So here we are, including Doctor Sandford, our divisional-surgeon. You'll want to ask him some questions. Go ahead, Mr. Bathurst." The inspector sat back in his chair.

"You're very encouraging to me, Inspector. I shall be pleased to." Anthony turned to the divisional-surgeon. "You've been told no doubt, Doctor Sandford, of the case concerning which I'm seeking information. A young man named Terence Regan. The name, I understand, was unfamiliar to you until a few days ago."

Sandford's shrewd eyes lit up as Anthony made this statement. "It was," he remarked, "entirely unfamiliar. But I remember the case very well. Just you let me refer to my diary for a second. I remember that I made a note of it at the time. Hang on for half a second, will you?"

Sandford fished a book from his pocket. "Yes—here you are," he said eventually, "I've a note against the evening of April the 8th. The body was that of a young man aged about thirty. Perhaps a little younger. It was healthy and well-nourished. There were severe injuries. The ribs were crushed and the left forearm was broken. These injuries, allied with shock, were the cause of death."

"As the body was found in the roadway you were satisfied that the deceased had been knocked down by a car, and the injuries caused in that way?"

"Well, yes—I suppose I was. What else would you have? Aren't the odds a thousand to one on a car?"

Anthony grinned. "So they may be, Doctor, but the long-priced outsider comes home sometimes, you know, Doctor. I do—and to my occasional cost. Wouldn't be any fun if it didn't. And in this instance I don't think Regan *was* killed by a car."

"That's all very well," returned Sandford. "How was he killed then?"

"I don't know. It's no use my pretending I do. But do you mind if I ask you a question or two?"

"Not a bit. And I'll do my best to answer them. Shoot!"

"Do you remember the state of Regan's body—at all clearly?"

Sandford shut his eyes. "Let me think a minute. Yes . . . I can remember it. I examined it at the time and I think I can revive most of my impressions."

"That's excellent, Doctor. What I was hoping for. Can you recollect if there were any unusual bruises on it?"

Sandford denied the suggestion without a second's hesitation. "Oh—no. No bruises. Certainly no bruises. The body was in splendid condition in every way."

"Were there any peculiar marks on the body?"

"Marks? You don't mean such a thing as a birthmark, do you?"

"No. Let me put it like this. Were there any tell-tale marks?"

Sandford repeated the adjective Anthony had used. "Tell-tale?"

"Yes. I chose the word deliberately."

"I don't know that I quite understand what you mean. What's the tale they're supposed to tell?"

"Any tale that wouldn't be—shall we say—normal?"

Sandford rubbed his forehead. "You're asking me something, you know. And it's over a couple of months ago, don't forget. Can't you be more—specific?"

"I didn't want to be. I didn't desire to lead or guide you in any way. But needs must, I suppose, when the—er—doctor drives." Anthony grinned at him. "Here goes then. Were there any marks on the wrists, for example?"

Sandford shut his eyes and passed his hand across his forehead again. "I'm trying to visualize the body as I had it on the P.M. table."

There was a silence. Anthony watched Sandford and neither Foster nor Singleton spoke. After a time of meditation, the divisional-surgeon opened his eyes.

"Yes," he answered quietly, "you've rung the bell. I do remember that there were slight rednesses round the two wrists. But they weren't bruises, they weren't injuries—so I paid but scant attention to them. That's not an 'apologia'—that's a solemn statement of fact. But tell me, Bathurst, what's your actual point? What are you attempting to establish?"

"I'm coquetting with a theory—that's all, Doctor Sandford. And you're fanning the flames of the flirtation. Coming back, though, to a practical interpretation of your question, might those rednesses you mentioned just now have been caused through the tying of Regan's wrists? Would that be a reasonable proposition, Doctor Sandford? I've no wish to force an agreeable answer. If I'm wrong, please tell me so unmistakably."

"That's all right, Bathurst. No need to sound the warning note. You're barking up the right tree this time. The red marks I noticed most certainly *might* have been caused through the man's wrists having been tied up in some way."

Inspector Foster leant forward to the company, his arms planted firmly on the table. "Here, you two! What's all this talk of yours leading up to? It seems to me this is where I come in. Or, if I don't,

I ought to." He shifted a little in his chair and addressed himself directly to Anthony. "What are you after, Mr. Bathurst?" he asked with an ominous quietness. "Is it—murder?"

Anthony was equally direct in his reply. "I'm very much afraid so, Inspector. And I hope you'll request the 'Yard' to co-operate—seeing that we've brought the cat out of the bag, as it were, and placed it on your own doorstep."

Foster made a rueful grimace at Anthony's statement. "I'm afraid we shall have to—seeing how far it's already gone. But what do you know?"

"Nothing, Inspector Foster. Or as good as nothing. But I *suspect* a hell of a lot. I'll tell you."

Anthony recounted the story of Doctor Page and her patient and of how he himself had come to Wroxeter to encounter Constable Beaumont's information. He made no mention of the brass name-plate, of Regan's diary or of the pile of currency notes which he had found in the cavity of the elm tree. Nor did he refer to the consignment of the seven crayoned heads. He desired to consult with MacMorran before he played these cards. Foster and Singleton listened to him attentively. When he had finished, the former came in with an immediate reply, and a warning shake of the head.

"I think your story's thin, Mr. Bathurst. Thin as can be. And that's telling you candidly."

"I want you to be candid. And I'll be equally candid with you. Why do you regard it as thin? To use your own word."

"No evidence! Not a shred! To say nothing of an entire absence of motive."

"As far as I know!"

"Well—have a heart—I can't go further than that, can I?"

"Perhaps not."

"Well—there you are then. And as I said—with regard to evidence—"

Anthony interrupted him. "I hope to be in a position to supply certain evidence before many days have passed. Till then I must ask you to possess your soul in patience."

"We may expect to hear from you again then, Mr. Bathurst?" asked Inspector Foster.

"You may—and you most certainly will," replied Anthony.

"And in the meantime we do nothing—eh? Just sit tight? Is that O.K. by you?"

"Entirely," said Anthony. "I won't ask you to make any move until you hear from me again. Which won't be over long, I assure you."

The three Wroxeter police officials rose and Anthony shook hands with them. He returned to the "Black Horse" feeling more positive than ever that he was on the track of something big. It might even be, he thought, that more than one cat would emerge from the bag!

2

THE OFFENCE IS RANK

ANTHONY heard from MacMorran early on the following morning. To be precise, the post was brought in to him as he sat at breakfast. The chief-inspector's note was brief and to the point.

Dear Mr. Bathurst,

Just a line to let you know that both Carrington and Denman (the two experts) have made a thorough examination of the currency notes you sent from Wroxeter. They are 'dud.' But extremely well done at that. Carrington says that in all his thirty years' experience he has never set eyes on better 'phoney' stuff. This gives us something to work on and I have already started the ball rolling in more than one direction. Developments, therefore, may be expected. All the best and with kind regards.

Yours, etc.,

Andrew MacMorran.

Anthony read the letter carefully twice and then tucked it away in his wallet. This was decidedly interesting news. And as MacMorran had written, certainly gave them a clearly-defined starting-point. Anthony thought that he was beginning to see the shape of things much more clearly. To a point, that is! He proceeded, therefore, to eat his breakfast with some degree of satisfaction. Just as he was finishing he had another surprise. The waitress who usually attended him brought him the buff-coloured envelope of a telegram. He frowned at it before he opened it. Probably MacMorran again with some white-hot news. He was wrong, however, and it was with added surprise that he read the following:

"Thanks for message. Arriving at 11.15 this morning. Kathleen Regan."

Anthony was shocked to read this, as well as surprised. After a couple of minutes' intensive thought he pushed back his plate and made a straight way to the receptionist's office.

"I want Kingsley 5995," he said, "will you try to get me connected at once. It's an urgent call."

"I'll let you know, sir," replied the girl, "as soon as I get the number."

"Thank you. I shall be in the lounge. You won't forget it's urgent, will you?"

"No, sir. I'll do my best. You can rely on me."

Anthony walked back to the smoking-room and waited for the call to be put through. The receptionist was as good as her word and he had his Kingsley number in under a quarter of an hour. He explained who he was and asked if he might speak to Miss Regan. As he thought, when he had first heard her voice at the other end of the line, the speaker was Miss Groves, the landlady at "Boscawen."

"You're too late, Mr. Bathurst," said the lady. "Miss Regan has already left for Wroxeter. Actually she went away from here this morning within half an hour of receiving your message."

Anthony was thunderstruck. "My message, Miss Groves? When was that, if you please?"

"Why—shortly after seven o'clock this morning. When you telephoned through before."

Anthony decided to dispense with explanations. To do so would save time and words. "No, Miss Groves," he said quietly, "there's been either a mistake or a misunderstanding, I'm afraid. I have not telephoned before this. Still, the mischief's done now—I'll make arrangements to meet Miss Regan's train when it comes in here. Thank you very much for all your trouble and my apologies for disturbing you."

He hung up thoughtfully and returned to the lounge. This last business had put an entirely different complexion on matters. He felt decidedly uneasy. After a time he resolved to consult an *A.B.C.*, but immediately discarded the resolve and substituted for it a journey to Wroxeter railway station. Arrived there, an examination of the time-table told him that after leaving Paddington the train stopped at three stations before reaching Wroxeter. At Reading, Stratford-upon-Avon and Bridge Ferry—the last-named place being, according to his reckoning, about five miles distant from Wroxeter. This fact brought him an acute problem. One, indeed, of many. Further inspection of the time-table showed him the train which was bringing Miss Regan was due at Stratford-upon-Avon at 10.44. The time was now ten minutes past ten. And there was no train that would get him there in time. But he had seen that he *could* get as far as Bridge Ferry. There was a train which left Wroxeter at 10.46 arriving at Bridge Ferry at 10.58. The London train, carrying Miss Regan, was scheduled to arrive at Bridge Ferry at 11.3. This would give him a matter of five minutes to spare.

He went to the booking-office and bought a return to Bridge Ferry. He knew that he was taking a chance. With the odds, if anything, just a trifle against him. It was obvious, he thought, that if an attempt were being made to waylay Kathleen Regan it would have to be executed somewhere between Paddington and Wroxeter. The three adjacent stopping-places of the train, Stratford-upon-Avon, Bridge Ferry and Wroxeter, did not, in his opinion, present equal chances. As he considered matters the odds were heavily in favour of Bridge Ferry. It was a quiet, out-of-the-way place, so he imagined, which fact in itself would give much greater opportunity for an attempt of the kind he was envisaging. His only worry at the moment as he stood on the platform waiting for the train was his mere margin of those five precious minutes.

As his train arrived, he glanced anxiously at his watch. The time was 10.48—two minutes late. The train went through a small halt-station without stopping—Courthope, he fancied the name was from the glance he got of it—travelled another half-mile or so, slowed down and then stopped! Anthony sat in his compartment and fumed at the delay. His precious margin of time was suffering rapid erosion. He consulted his watch again. Unless the train started moving again almost immediately—then his spirits brightened appreciably. There was always the hope that the London train would be as late or even more so. But his train stayed put. Impatiently he looked out of the carriage-window. No hope from that direction. The signal was still against. Anthony chafed still further at the annoyance. When at long last the train did start on its journey again, the time was two minutes past eleven—a bare minute before the London train was due to arrive at Bridge Ferry. He still remained optimistic, however, and watched the line all the way, as his train chugged along with a maximum of engine-effort and a minimum of speed. Then, to cap his aggravation, just as his train was a hundred yards or so from the station at Bridge Ferry he saw what was obviously the London train pass by in the direction of Wroxeter. Even now with a modicum of good fortune he might still be able to—he jumped from the train before it came to a standstill and ran up the flight of steps to cross the line to the other platform. To his dismay, not a soul was in evidence. But eventually he found an ancient ticket-collector-cum-porter-cum-general station-attendant leaning on a wicket-gate which gave access to the King's highway.

"Ticket, sir," announced this worthy in a sepulchral voice.

Anthony surrendered the appropriate half of his ticket and attacked immediately.

"I wonder if you could help me," he said hopefully.

"What about, sir?" came the response.

"Well—it's like this. I had hoped to meet the London train here but my connection from Wroxeter, as you know, arrived late."

"It often do," replied the museum, "more's the pity. Company ought to do somethin' about it. Very upsettin' to passengers."

Anthony smiled in benison of the suggestion. "Good idea," he agreed, "but unfortunately too late for me. My trouble's here at the moment."

"If you're wantin' another train, sir, the picture ain't too bright for you."

"God forbid," said Anthony, "that my desire should be so avid. No—what I wanted was to meet some people who were supposed to be on the London train. Did you happen to notice if a young lady was amongst those who got out here?"

"I did that, sir. I had to, seein' as how I had to take their tickets. It were a young lady and a gentleman with her. They were the only passengers. And another young gentleman met them here with a car." He paused and then continued again with even more of the sepulchre in his voice. "They drove away a few moments before you came up in that direction over there." He stabbed with his forefinger in a direction which, to say the least of it, was mildly uncertain.

It was at this moment that Anthony felt the full flow of his annoyance. "It's a crying shame," he declared, "that your company can't run trains to time. And when I say 'time,' I mean moderately reasonable time."

"I've often thought the same way, sir. But there you are!" He shrugged his antique shoulders in a gesture of martyred resignation. "May be some day, sir, someone important will take the matter up and complain about it. Till then, sir, I'm afraid it's a case of what can't be cured must be endured. That was my old grandfather's favourite saying, sir."

"I'll take your esteemed word for that," responded Anthony, "and please don't bother to tell me what your grandmother's was. The only information I want now is this, what were the men like who accompanied the lady and what was the car they drove away in. Can you help me there?"

"The men were tall. Both of 'em. I couldn't say any more than that. My eye was fixed on their tickets. That was my job—and every man to his trade, say I. It don't do to let your mind wander off your job. That's how mistakes come to be made."

Anthony groaned inwardly. "What about the car?" he asked in a still small voice.

"The car? Well—I don't know that I'm much of a hand at describin' cars. Don't hold with the contraptions too much if I tell the honest truth. Spoil the countryside, if you ask me—with their noise and smoke. But I did notice the one to-day as it happens."

"Good," said Anthony, a faint hope surging in his breast. "What was it?"

"A blue one, sir. A dark blue one."

"Excellent. With the usual number of wheels presumably?"

"Quite so, sir."

Anthony gravely handed him a shilling. "It would be impossible for me," he said, "to say how much I value your information."

"Only too pleased, sir," came the inevitable rejoinder. "I like to keep my eyes open."

Anthony walked away—pondering as to his next step. Several possibilities presented themselves to him and he considered them all carefully and from every conceivable angle. Eventually he decided to get into touch again with Inspector Foster at Wroxeter. There was a train back within three-quarters of an hour's time and Anthony travelled on it.

Back in Wroxeter he phoned the "Black Horse" and then he went straight to the police station and was quickly in consultation with Inspector Foster. Foster was inclined to be sceptical of Anthony's forebodings.

"What can I do?" he asked almost plaintively. "What have I to go on? You can't even be certain that it was Miss Regan who left the train at Bridge Ferry."

"If she didn't," replied Anthony doggedly, "she would be at either Wroxeter station waiting for me or at the 'Black Horse'. She's at neither of those places. I've just come from the station and I've telephoned to the hotel. 'No can do' in each instance."

But Foster remained unmoved. "You don't even know for certain that she caught the train she intended to catch. She may have missed it."

Anthony stuck to his guns doggedly. "She got out at Bridge Ferry—with escort."

"That again—with the greatest possible respect—you don't know. You conjecture. It's all mere surmise."

"I'm convinced that Miss Regan is under forcible restraint somewhere in this district. As her brother was before her. Her brother who was murdered."

"All right. Supposing I grant you all that? Where?"

Anthony shrugged his shoulders. "I agree it's pretty hopeless. Still—do this for me, will you? Try to trace a phone call from round here somewhere to Kingsley 5995, before seven o'clock this morning. The earliness of the time will narrow it down considerably."

"All right. I'll do that. We shall find it was put through from a public call-box without the shadow of a doubt."

"Maybe. It's worth trying, anyway. Here's another line of inquiry I'd like you to take up. Will you try to trace a young artist named Brown who may have lived in this district up to fairly recently?"

Inspector Foster grimaced. "Brown—eh? You do pick 'em out, don't you? If you'd said Jones now, or even Smith—all right, you win—I'll have a go. Come in early this evening and I may be able to let you know *re* the telephone call. Mind you—I only said 'may'." He grinned at Anthony.

"I'll be generous," said the latter, "I'll give you until to-morrow morning. Expect me at ten o'clock sharp."

"That's O.K. And I'll do my best for you. I can't say fairer than that, can I?"

Greatly troubled in mind and spirit, Anthony walked back slowly to the "Black Horse." Almost all his previous optimism had evaporated.

3

DEATH REPEATED

ANTHONY stood at the entrance to the "Black Horse" which bore the superscription "Hotel." It opened on to a cobbled-stoned courtyard of respectable antiquity. He had just finished dinner and was enjoying the customary post-prandial cigarette. The evening was glorious, soft and full of summer. He debated in his mind as to how he should spend the remainder of the evening. It was just on nine o'clock. Should he have another look at "Christopher's" or should he put in an exercise of concentrated and intensive thought on the late Terence Regan's diary? On the whole, he was the more attracted by the first-mentioned possibility. He felt drawn towards "Christopher's" with an almost irresistible urge.

He finished his cigarette and decided to stroll down there exactly as he had done on the previous occasion. But he wanted one or two things from his own room before he started out. He went upstairs, obtained what he wanted and came down again. As he reached the bottom stair, he almost collided with the hurrying receptionist.

"Oh, Mr. Bathurst," she said breathlessly. "I've been looking everywhere for you. You're wanted on the 'phone in my office. The caller's hanging on."

"Thank you," said Anthony, "I'll come along at once."

The caller was Inspector Foster. "Is that you, Mr. Bathurst? I'm sorry to worry you at this time of the evening, but if you could come along to the station at once. I'd be very much obliged to you."

It occurred to Anthony that Foster was talking under the stress of emotion. "All right," he replied quietly, "I'll be with you in a few minutes."

He hung up the receiver, thanked the girl and walked straight out of the hotel. Foster had evidently discovered something unusually important to call him like this. There would be no visiting "Christopher's" for him that evening. He walked briskly to the police-station and the officer on duty, acting doubtless under special instructions, showed him straight in to Inspector Foster.

"Here I am, Inspector," he announced himself, "utterly and entirely at your service. What's blown up? Got your teeth into something? Because I don't suppose you've sent for me on account of my personal charm."

To his surprise, Foster shook his head. Instead he reached for his hat and put it on. "Come with me," he replied curtly. "I've got something to show you."

Anthony raised his eyebrows and followed him out. They crossed a small rectangular yard at the rear of the police-station proper and Anthony waited patiently while the inspector felt in his pockets and then fumbled with a bunch of keys.

Anthony realized what the destination was going to be. He found the right key and opened the door. Anthony saw at once that his guess had been correct and that they were standing in the police mortuary. That an ambulance was drawn up in the yard outside, was a second observation he made as he crossed the threshold.

"Over here," said Foster as curtly as he had spoken before.

He walked forward and, as before, Anthony followed him. It was a matter of but a few seconds for Anthony to know the worst. The body at which he looked was the body of Kathleen Regan.

4

BROTHER AND SISTER

A HOT wave of resentment surged through Anthony as he looked at the dead girl. The girl who had come to him for help, and by reason of that action had gone to her death! Unjustly perhaps, he felt embittered towards the inspector at his side. But for Foster's scepticism—He heard the inspector speaking.

"Well—pretty ghastly, isn't it?"

"When did it happen?" asked Anthony in a low voice.

"We had a call at the station about a quarter to nine. Just as happened in the other instance. Dead body in the road—evidently the victim of a car injury. When I got it, I tell you frankly it worried me. Worried me like hell. I couldn't forget those two interviews I'd had with you, you see, and your views generally on the matter. They were on my mind and on my nerves as well." Foster paused. "The ambulance went up and brought her back."

"Where was she?" asked Anthony tonelessly.

"Not in the main road on this occasion. Down a side road."

"Suitable for a car to travel along?"

"Yes. I'm told so. Just about."

"You know why the body was found in a side road, don't you?"

Foster shook his head. "Don't know that I've thought about it yet. Never mind! Tell me! Why?"

"It was comparatively light. Different time of the year. To drop a body on the main road between Wroxeter and Stratford-upon-Avon would have been much too dangerous. A side road was easier and presented much less risk of disaster. But we're running on too fast. How did she die?"

"I'm waiting for Sandford now. He should be along any minute."

Anthony went and looked down at the body again. "Inspector," he said at length, "I don't quite know yet what we're up against. I'm not going to pretend that I do. But it's *big*'—whatever it is. It's brutal and merciless. Anybody who stands up to it, or even in its way, is murdered. There are no half-measures. The offenders are removed. And it will give me exquisite pleasure, Inspector," his voice grew excessively quiet, "to send the beasts who murdered this poor girl to their own place—the gallows and hell."

Foster looked at him. This was a Bathurst the inspector hadn't seen before. He was on the point of saying something when a footstep sounded outside and there came a rapping on the door.

"The doctor," said Foster with a turn of the head, "do you mind, Mr. Bathurst? Oh—and by the way—the call you were anxious about was put through from a call-box."

Anthony nodded and went across to the door and opened it to admit the divisional surgeon.

"I don't know a curse, Foster, which would be sufficiently appropriate. Why in the name of all that's sacred do you have to drag me—"

The inspector silenced him with a quick movement of the hand. Sandford understood at once and his face changed simultaneously with the understanding. He went over to the body.

"Dear, dear," he said almost to himself, but his words were summarily checked by the realization of what he saw in front of him. Then he began to mutter words only audible to himself. Anthony strained his ears in an effort to hear, but could catch nothing. After a time the divisional surgeon began to busy himself on the body with his hands and fingers. Eventually he came back to Anthony and Foster.

"The seven 'true' ribs are broken. Crushed to a jelly." He lapsed into technicalities dealing, as far as Anthony could make out, with costal cartilages, intercostal arteries, tubercules and transverse processes. Anthony allowed him to proceed with the description for some little time. When Sandford showed signs of subsiding he intervened with a question.

"Anything similar here to the multiple injuries you found on the body of Terence Regan?"

Sandford stared at him before a wave of appreciation seemed to break over the doctor's features. He whistled softly under his breath. Then he slowly nodded his head.

"By Jove—I see what you're getting at. You caught me on one leg for the moment. Something I hadn't been considering." He rubbed his cheek.

"Let me put my question in a different form," continued Anthony. "Are these injuries on this dead girl consistent with having been knocked down and killed by a car?"

Sandford glanced quickly in the direction of Inspector Foster. Anthony went on. "Because that's what my first question to you was really intended to convey."

The doctor began to speak slowly. "The injuries *are* like those on Regan's body—but only to an extent. It's difficult to explain. They are different in—er—scope. For one thing, they are much more extensive. Much more severe. And candidly, I don't think that they have been caused by a car. Regan's, though, might have been. You see what I mean."

"Might," replied Anthony deliberately.

"I said 'might.' I've got to be careful, you know! You're putting me on the spot rather. If I may put it like this, Regan's body seemed to have put up, shall we say, more *resistance* to whatever caused the impact than this girl has done."

"I see," replied Anthony slowly. "I'll try again, Doctor Sandford. Might these injuries on this girl this evening have been caused by the same weapon or agency as caused those on the body of Terence Regan? Please let me have your fully considered opinion."

"Why—I remember a point you put to me when you were asking me about Regan. You asked me if I found any marks on his wrists— or near his wrists. I told you that I had. Well—I've just been over to look at the girl again. There are no red marks on her wrists. No marks of any kind near the wrists. Perhaps I've anticipated a question and answered it?"

Anthony shook his head. "No."

"No?"

"No. I had already looked myself. As a matter of fact, Doctor, I didn't expect to find anything of that nature in this case. But I looked merely to make sure."

Sandford raised his eyebrows. "Why did you say you looked then?"

"To make sure. Wasn't I clear in the first instance."

Sandford looked a little annoyed. Foster noticed it. "I'll tell you what it is, Doctor," he said, "I'll be frank and admit it. Mr. Bathurst here has a damned good opportunity of saying to me, 'I told you so.' And so far he's refrained from saying it. It's a temptation which few people are able to resist."

The divisional surgeon looked doubtfully from one to the other of them. "I'm afraid you'll have to do a bit more explaining, Inspector."

"I've been expecting that. Well—here goes. The dead girl over there, according to Mr. Bathurst here, and I've no reason to disbelieve him, is Kathleen Regan, sister of the dead Terence Regan. That's what's eating Mr. Bathurst."

Sandford took the news quietly. His eyes were fixed on Foster, as though he were prepared for the inspector to make further revelations. Foster sensed this. He shook his head.

"Sorry, Doctor, and all that, but you know almost as much as I know, now that I've told you that."

Anthony sat with his shoulders hunched. His *amour-propre* had just sustained a shattering blow. The death of this girl, in the circumstances as he knew them, had shaken him profoundly. After all, she had come to him for help! His help had brought her disaster. Worse than disaster—death!

"I'm as sorry, Doctor, as the inspector. Every bit. All I can do is to suspect. But I'm fumbling and groping in the dark. I know nothing that I can reasonably demand you to translate into action. That's how it is with me. But somebody has seen fit to murder a brother and sister. Until I know why—I can't hasten along the way."

Sandford stood there uncomfortably. Foster drummed with his fingers on a table. Anthony looked up.

"Something I haven't asked you yet, Inspector. I meant to but it slipped me. Miss Regan's body was found, so you said, down a side turning off the main road."

"Yes. Down a lane. To be precise, Sharnbrook Lane."

"How far from the spot where her brother's body was found?"

"Come into my room again and I'll tell you almost exactly. I've got a large-scale map in there and you'll be able to see for yourself."

Anthony accepted the invitation and he, with Doctor Sandford, followed the inspector back into his own room. As they went out, Foster was careful to produce his keys and lock the door of the mortuary building. Inside his room, he pointed to a map hanging on one of the side walls.

"Here," he said, indicating a point with his forefinger, "is the place on the Stratford-upon-Avon road where Terence Regan's body was found. And here is approximately the spot where the girl was picked up." His finger traced one of the side turnings from the same main road. "Distance?" he said questioningly—"Well, what shall we put it at? It's certainly not very great. Let's see—on this scale—between a mile and a half and two miles."

"Not a lot," observed Anthony.

"Not a lot, as you say, Mr. Bathurst," confirmed the inspector.

"When you sent for me this evening," said Anthony casually, "I had just made up my mind to stroll along to 'Christopher's.' I had found myself at something of a loose end and 'Christopher's' was going to be my way of tightening it. Then your telephone call came and remodelled my plans for the evening."

"'Christopher's' is all right once in a way," declared the divisional surgeon, "if you don't particularly mind being stung for your liquor. That guy who runs the place certainly knows how to charge."

"I suppose he does, to tell the truth. But I've only been there once so I'm far from being an authority on the place."

Foster had made no reference to the matter. Anthony, therefore, put a direct question to him. "What do you think of it yourself, Inspector Foster? Is it as bad as Doctor Sandford makes out."

Foster frowned as though Anthony's question had awakened within him a collection of disagreeable memories. "'Christopher's'? I can't say that I'm struck on the place myself. I've been there two or three times—naturally. They seem to behave themselves and they certainly don't give us any trouble which I suppose is one of the main considerations from a policeman's point of view. In other words, Mr. Bathurst, no complaints."

"Well—that's very gratifying to know, Inspector. I shall have no qualms whatever now with regard to going there. Meanwhile—" he paused meaningly.

"Meanwhile—" repeated Foster after him—"what's your point exactly, Mr. Bathurst?"

Anthony smiled. "Meanwhile—what steps do you propose to take? *Re* the Regans? That was what I meant."

Foster fidgeted uneasily in his chair. "H'm. That's a pretty big question. I don't know that I'd made up my mind yet."

"Are you prepared to take a suggestion from me?"

"What's that, Mr. Bathurst?"

"Call in the 'Yard.' After all—Miss Regan came from Kingsley. There'll be nothing *infra dig.* about it."

"I wasn't thinking along those lines so much. I shall have to submit it to the Chief Constable. Till that's been done, I'm afraid I can't promise anything."

"I understand that," replied Anthony, "and I make no comment on it whatsoever. I shall return to London early to-morrow and I'll explain the whole position to Inspector MacMorran at the 'Yard.' Till we hear from you at this end, we shall have to be content to possess our souls in patience. Good-night, Inspector Foster. Good-night, Doctor Sandford." The three men shook hands and Anthony, heavy at heart, returned to the comparative comfort of the "Black Horse."

5

LEGACY FROM TERENCE REGAN

Two hours after Anthony arrived back in London he had conference with MacMorran. He gave the latter the full facts as he knew them, with regard to the death of Kathleen Regan. The inspector sat up and took notice. His eyes were hard and unyielding by the time that Anthony had finished his narrative. Anthony then undid, in full view of MacMorran, an oblong-shaped brown paper parcel.

"That brass name-plate," he said, "came from the hollow of the tree in Regan's garden in Hampton Road, Wroxeter. I can tell you nothing more about it than that and up to the moment of going to press, I've made no inquiries. Events crowded upon me so thick and fast that I had to push the matter of that professional plate well into the background."

MacMorran nodded. "I agree it can wait."

"Good for you, Andrew. Then there's this." Anthony produced the Regan diary. MacMorran picked it up and turned it over.

"In the tree, too?"

"A-ha! And little doubt, either, that Regan himself put it there. I'm not equally sure of that in the case of the name-plate."

"Anything of value in it?" asked MacMorran.

"Don't know yet, Andrew. Not sure. Think there may be."

"In what way?"

"There's a list of names that may mean something and there are also two or three rather indirect allusions. It's difficult to say at this stage what these may mean. I shall have to put in a spot of work on them before I can say either way."

"I suppose it's murder all right," commented MacMorran.

"You've said it," returned Anthony, "and unless I'm an extremely bad judge it's going to start with '*l'affaire* Arbuthnot.' I don't know how and I don't know why. But I'll bank on it."

"It's a pretty far cry from Kingsley to Wroxeter. And I can't see what on earth the connection is."

"It may be. But the Regans bridged it."

"So they may have," retorted MacMorran with a spice of triumph. "That doesn't mean a thing as far as Arbuthnot's concerned."

"You've had no luck, I take it, regarding our friend with the book?"

"None," replied MacMorran gloomily. "Since you were down there and he gave you the slip, I've given the district no rest. But I've toiled several days and nights and caught nothing."

"I was hoping to hear something more encouraging than that. Still—can't be helped—I'm going back to Wroxeter. There's a vital clue down there somewhere and it's up to us to pick it up. Maybe I shall get a break and be fortunate. My plan will be to hang around and watch points." Anthony paused.

"You don't seem over-hopeful, if I may say so, Mr. Bathurst." Anthony replaced Regan's diary in his pocket. "I don't know that I altogether agree with you, Andrew. I've got this, you know." He patted his pocket. "It may yield me something when I get right down to it. I'm certainly cherishing hopes in that direction. And once I've made a start who knows where I may be guided?"

MacMorran nodded. "I agree. You've had less data in the past more than once, and arrived somewhere eventually. Let's hope you'll be equally successful over this journey."

"I shall want help from you, Andrew. In more than one direction."

"Let's have it, then I shall know where we stand."

"I want you to keep me posted as to any developments that may come from the Arbuthnot end, and also with regard to the 'dud' notes issue."

MacMorran nodded again. "I've a further investigation in progress with regard to that and there should be a second report within the next day or two. Will you be staying at the same place?"

"Yes. Care of the 'Black Horse,' Wroxeter, will find me. In the meantime, too, you may be hearing from Foster or the Chief Constable. I'm rather anticipating that they'll take the advice I threw at them and rope you in."

"In that case I'll come down there myself, Mr. Bathurst."

"As you know only too well, Andrew, there's nothing that would suit me better."

MacMorran found his pipe and leisurely filled it. He fumbled in his pocket for matches. "I don't know that in all my career I've ever found a case which looked so vague or so . . . er . . . unpromising. At each end all we have is vagueness and indefiniteness. A man with a book. And two people found dead at different times, in the roadway. It *might*—now mind you, I only say 'might'—be nothing more than a coincidence." He eyed Anthony shrewdly to see how he took the suggestion attack.

Mr. Bathurst shook his head emphatically. "I can't have that, Andrew. All my reason and all my intelligence are in red revolt against it. The two Regans, Andrew! A boy and a girl, brother and sister, from the same family. I can't stomach your coincidence theory when I remember that. The odds are far too fantastic. No! The Regans knew something about somebody. Terence got on to it first and either Kathleen followed up, or the aggressors feared that she knew that her brother knew and *would* follow up. She therefore travelled the same dark and dreadful road as her brother had before her. That's how I see it, Andrew!" He stopped—to resume in a graver and quieter voice. "I intend to get the people that killed that girl if it's the last thing in this life that I ever do. She came to me for help, Andrew, and I failed her. I failed her living, but I promise to God I won't fail her dead!"

And MacMorran knew of old, that when Anthony Bathurst spoke like that, he meant business.

CHAPTER IV

1
ANTHONY QUESTING

Anthony Lotherington Bathurst sat in his room at the "Black Horse," Wroxeter. He had finished dinner and had set himself a task. In front of him, on a small table, lay the pocket diary of Terence Regan. He meant, if it were humanly possible, in the time at his disposal, to wrest the secret of the diary from its pages before he went to bed that evening. Even though that intention might delay his rest until the early hours of the morning. First of all he collected the names that were mentioned therein and listed them. He would get MacMorran to make inquiries about the people and report back to him. As far as he could see, he could do nothing beyond this for the moment. Not a single one of the names conveyed anything to him.

The inclusion of the Greek verb part "Eureka" by Regan obviously meant that he had discovered something. And Anthony thought that the use of the term denoted a condition something akin to enthusiasm or even triumph. That he had, at last as it were, happened or hit on something which for some time, probably, had been baffling him. This particular Greek verb part, Anthony thought, was nearly always employed to meet circumstances of that kind. Well—this was all to the good. For it coincided comfortably with Anthony's own theory. Namely—that Regan had in some way become possessed of highly dangerous knowledge. Dangerous in a double sense. To Regan himself and also to a third party whom Anthony designated to himself for the time being as Monsieur X. This brought him to the personal touches. To the presumably individual characteristics. "Odd-coloured eyes" and "silver patch." Personal peculiarities, no doubt, which Regan had applied to a person or persons whom he had encountered during his stay at Wroxeter. It would be necessary for him to put himself in the dead Regan's place and keep his eyes skinned for anybody possessing either or both of these rather unusual physical idiosyncrasies. Again, this was no more than he reasonably could do, situated as he was.

Then came the entry "See April 25th for all." The essential meaning of this seemed impenetrable. For it might, conceivably, mean *anything*! "For all"! For all what? People? Actions? Explanations? There was no clue of any kind as to what the word "all" might refer. The remainder of the diary carried no further hint or indication. The date—April 25th? Anthony decided to concentrate on the date. Had it any particular significance? Anthony rose, went to his suitcase and took out his copy of *Brewer* which he had purposely packed in connection with the investigation he was now undertaking. A reference to April therein yielded him nothing. He racked the recesses of his memory. Was there any special matter or incident dedicated to April 25th? Then he had a brainwave. Might it be a Saint's Day? Anthony ran through his saints—the better known ones, of course. His memory failed to associate one with April 25th. He decided to check up, therefore, on the dates of the less popular ecclesiastical figures and he commenced with the more unknown of the twelve apostles. This exercise took him just on an hour and yielded him nothing. Then a tiny something began to titillate his brain. A half-remembered fragment of a line of poetry which seemed to give him, out of the hinterland, an excursion into the month of April.

He strove hard for adequate remembrance and at last it came to him. It was a fragment of Keats that he had been striving to recall. Gradually, Anthony brought the full verse back to him. Yes—it came from *Cap and Bells*. Anthony repeated the lines to himself. "Look in the Almanack—Moore never lies—April the twenty-fourth—this coming day, Now breathing its new bloom upon the skies, Will end in St. Mark's Eve. You must away, For on that eve alone can you the maid convey." There it was! For if April the twenty-fourth were St. Mark's Eve, then April the twenty-fifth must be the day dedicated in the calendar to the evangelist, St. Mark. St. Mark, in the opinion of some historians "the young man who went away sorrowing" after Christ had answered his question concerning the inheritance of eternal Life.

Anthony thereupon fitted St. Mark into the appropriate part of the Regan sentence. "See St. Mark for all." What did that really signify? The Gospel according to St. Mark? If so, what particular portion of it? He repeated the words to himself again. "See St. Mark"—and the truth came suddenly out of the blackness and hit him. "See Mark," or in a slightly different form "Seamark," and, of course, "for all" was literally construed as "omnibus!" The *Seamark Omnibus*. There it was—just as he had hoped to prove it would be. The point he had desired to establish was on firm foundation at last. Regan had definitely linked up for him the Kingsley end with the Wroxeter end. And it meant this: Regan must have made contact with somebody during his stay in Wroxeter who had been connected with the *Seamark Omnibus* in some manner. And in such a manner as to impress upon Terence Regan the necessity of recording it in a form, no doubt, which he considered would be secret and understood only by him.

Anthony sat back in his chair and rubbed his hands. He had now taken a definite step on the long road that had started with the bank-clerk, Arbuthnot. This would be news for Andrew MacMorran! That Regan had adopted his crude form of cryptogram to record what he had discovered. Yet it was consistent with what he himself already knew of Regan. He had used a somewhat similar method of conveying information to his sister. Regan had run true to form. Which, from an investigator's point of view, was all to the good. Anthony lit a cigarette. One thing was beginning to disturb him and an additional question raised itself in his brain. What had Kathleen Regan known? Had she known *anything*? Or were the aggressors merely frightened at what she might have known? This alternative, to his mind, was a distinct possibility, and, on the whole, he rather inclined to its acceptance. The problem now was what should he do next? What was the next step that he should take, which was likely to be the most profitable?

Anthony thought over this, long and hard. Eventually he came to a decision. He would write to Andrew MacMorran that same evening. One of his most favoured axioms had always been "that there was no time like the now time." In this belief, you will see that he shared a taste with the man and poet Francis Villon. He procured writing-paper, therefore, and wrote to MacMorran as follows: "My dear Andrew, I am confident that you will be interested to hear that I have established *beyond a doubt* (in my own mind) that '*l'affaire* Arbuthnot' has one leg in Wroxeter and that the man who travels by train and neglects to read his library book, is connected somehow with the murders of the two Regans. I was able to determine this highly important factor in our case after an intensive study of the various items in the Regan diary. I am unable to go beyond that *at the moment*. But to-morrow is also a day and who amongst us knows what any morrow may bring forth? Be assured, that while I stay up here, both my eyes and ears will be excessively receptive. I have already decided upon one or two lines which I shall speedily cast and at least one bow which I shall draw. And I'm not admitting that it will be necessarily drawn at a venture. But of those things more anon. I am still awaiting your further report as promised *re* the 'phoney' currency notes and any possible centre concerned with their circulation activity and in the meantime—despite all that—behold me pressing you for even more information. Please let me know as soon as you possibly can full details of the following personalities. You will remember, from what you saw of it, that they have been culled from Regan's diary once again. Here then are the names in question in appropriate batting order: 1. Lovegrove; 2. Hon. Michael Polhill-Scott; 3. Mrs. Ardsley Spuyten; and 4. Sir Curtis Littlehales. With regard to these people, glean, or get gleaned, relevant data all and sundry. For I am moderately certain that the late Terence Regan did not take the trouble to list these names in his diary simply for the purpose of sending them Christmas cards or obtaining their telephone numbers. In the meantime I have seen Foster again—that's the local inspector in case your memory's faulty—and I must say, to be fair all round, that he has been extremely helpful in all directions. But he is still hanging on for the 'all right' from his Chief Constable *re* co-operation with your good self and your colleagues at H.Q. Until that signal comes, you will, of course, be destined to remain on the fringe of the affair as far as this particular end is concerned. Which may not be too healthy or pleasant from your point of view but which may, Andrew, bring strategical benefits which might not be ours were our full hand to be displayed to the enemy right at the very outset of the campaign. For campaign it is going to be, I feel absolutely certain. The affair is *odd*. That condition, however, will give an added kick to my investigations. At its present stage it's in a very hell of a muddle. The muddle is mainly due, I'm willing to concede, to this condition of 'oddness.' As a rule when I begin to sleuth in on a case, I set myself the primary task of deliberately *looking for* the 'oddnesses.' Because they invariably mean so much. I haven't known one case yet wherein they didn't. And, nearly always, sooner or later as the Deity wills, one of them rears its ugly head and—hey presto—there it is in front of you, all ripe and ready for the plucking. This little problem, though, of unread books and crayoned heads and brass plates and 'snide' and strange deaths of crushed bodies lying on the King's highway (or near thereto) bristles with so many of these damnable oddities that they grimace at you from all the points of the ruddy compass. My job will be to separate them—those that count from those that don't. By the time you come barging in, I hope to have that particular piece of work completed both to your satisfaction and my own. So you will arrive, my dear Andrew, accepting my successes (if I have any) as a mere tribute to your own powers of discrimination, and justly rebuking the incidences of my failures (note the plural) and ultimately dismissing them as still further evidences of those projections of mine which you always find such relish in describing as mere 'theories, Mr. Bathurst, and if I may say so, rather fantastic theories at that.'

"It is possible, of course, that I shall hear from you before you receive this. But I certainly think that something ought to be picked up from the *Seamark Omnibus* clue lying right at the Arbuthnot end (or beginning, if you like) of our little problem. That book *must* have been bound somewhere, and that somewhere may have been Kingsley. Or at least, a Kingsley environment. Inquiries at the various bookbinding establishments in that district might well prove profitable, Andrew, and I've been hoping, for some days now, that I shall be hearing from you that you are on to something. Perhaps that hope of mine will be realized just round the corner. This is all for to-night. Except that I am going to put in an hour or so in the saloon-bar. Not only for the sake of liquid refreshment! Yours till the next time (hullo—I'm stealing signatures or at any rate 'hall-marks'). Anthony L. Bathurst."

Anthony read his letter carefully and then placed it in an envelope. Half an hour later he walked out of the hotel and found a pillar-box. An examination of the time-plate told him that he was in ample time for the last post. The fact pleased him. It meant that Andrew MacMorran would have the letter in his hands by midday on the morrow.

2

MORE LIGHT

As ANTHONY had anticipated might be the case, the letter he had written on the previous evening, crossed the one which MacMorran had sent to him. This latter letter was in the letter-rack in the breakfast-room when he came down to breakfast in the morning. This is what MacMorran had written.

"Dear Mr. Bathurst, Pleased to say that I have some news for you at last. You will find it interesting. A vast amount of 'dud' paper has recently been circulated in the provinces generally. This applies to both the Midlands and the North Country. Birmingham, Wolverhampton, Sheffield, Leeds, Halifax, Bradford, Manchester, Liverpool, Bolton, Blackburn, Wigan and Preston are amongst the many towns from which this state of affairs has been reported as 'rife' for some little time now. Other smaller places similarly cited include Stratford-upon-Avon, Alcester, Banbury, Shrewsbury, Ludlow, Dudley, Newark, Shifnal, Wombourne, Kidderminster, Worcester and Grantham. The range, you see, is pretty extensive. It is quite probable, too, that the headquarters of the organization which is directing the job may be somewhere pretty near to where you are at present. You will observe that it is, perhaps, a little significant, from the point of view of the connection under notice, that the name of Wroxeter does *not* appear in the list I have furnished of the smaller places which have been affected by the 'dud' circulation.

The merits or demerits underlying this omission, however, I leave to you and your judgment. There may be something in it. On the other hand, there may not! As I said, I leave it to your judgment. Nothing has as yet come through to us here from Wroxeter, with regard to the matter of the 'Yard' consultation. Perhaps the local police get off the mark slowly as a matter of general habit! Shall be pleased to hear from you as often as you care to communicate. Especially if the report is 'progress.' The Commissioner joins me in the sending of kind regards. Yours sincerely, Andrew MacMorran."

Anthony digested this over his coffee and bacon. And again, he found a measure of satisfaction. The information which the inspector had forwarded fitted into the general pattern of the problem. It was not one of the "oddnesses" to which he had referred in his own overnight letter to MacMorran. What more likely than that the H.Q. of the organization at whose existence MacMorran had hinted, was based in Wroxeter itself or in the adjoining district? Certainly, there were far more unlikely contingencies.

Anthony thought matters over very carefully. How should he proceed to inaugurate his campaign? He felt that he must have a definite plan of action fully developed in his mind before he embarked upon anything. Any other form of activity would inevitably end in disaster. Anthony sat late over his breakfast. All the other people who had breakfasted in the room with him, had long since made their respective departures when he himself rose to go. By the time he reached his bedroom he had determined upon his first step. He would take an external look at the house known to him as Middleton Hall. Discreet inquiries of his waitress made in the recent past had given him a rough idea as to its locality and he imagined that he would experience but little difficulty in finding it.

Following the waitress's instructions, Anthony took the Dorricot Road—the same direction, let it be said, as he had taken to reach the Regan house in Hampton Road—and walked until he came to where the road forked towards Templeton Magna. Anthony followed this fork to the left and traversed it for close on a mile and a half and then in the distance he had his first sight of Middleton Hall. It stood on an eminence which he guessed to be the well-known Templeton Hill. The village of Templeton Magna lay farther along the road and consisted, according to a local guide-book which he had consulted, of an ancient inn, a row of almshouses, a few comparatively modern dwellings, three shops (including a general store), a post-office, a telephone exchange, a church and a vicarage. From the road where he stood, Anthony took a good look at the house on the hill. He saw the thickly wooded country behind it. In shape, and bearing in mind the distance he was away from it, the house reminded him of a large windmill. For the reason that two curious wings rose on each side of it.

Anthony began to move towards the house. From now on, the walking was of the roughest description. The lane down which he had been compelled to turn was full of loose stones. Anthony began to ascend. On both sides of him he could see soft marshy hollows and green moss. Gradually and by dint of careful walking, Anthony approached nearer to Middleton Hall, an uphill journey for him all the way. The nearer he came to it, the more he saw of it. He saw a pair of iron gates, a lodge, and what, at that distance, looked like a shrubbery at the end of the house and a terrace overlooking a small stream. As far as Anthony was able to judge, a distance of close on half a mile separated the gates from the house itself. Also, there were many rose gardens with blooms rioting in prodigal profusion.

Then his eyes caught sight of something else. From the terrace there was a flight of stone steps which led to a small bridge thrown across a sunken fence to meadows which lay beside the same stream which Anthony had previously observed. Everything about the house spoke of wealth and opulence. Anthony determined to get as close to it as he could. So he ascended the hill all the way until he came to the iron gates. From where he now stood, he could see a flagged pathway that led past the many terraces of a rock garden. Near by was a tall pergola covered in the scarlet splendour and crimson beauty of dense clusters of rambler. Certainly no expense had been spared to increase and enhance the natural attractiveness of Middleton Hall. As he stood there he heard the sound of an approaching car. This car was coming up the hill towards the house. But his ear told him that it was still some distance away and he hoped against hope that he had not been seen by the people in it. He considered it would be better, for the time being at least, if he kept himself well out of the Middleton Hall picture and perspective.

Turning quickly he saw a clump of three or four small bushes away to his right. He made rapidly for them and the hiding-place they offered. When he had gained the comfort of their shadow, there was still no sign of the car as far as his eyes were concerned. But he could hear it away in the distance, coming nearer and nearer. Anthony reckoned that his luck had held and that he had not been seen. He crouched down in the bushes, therefore, and waited for the oncoming car's appearance. He had to wait but a matter of seconds. A big blue car flashed by and ran to the iron gates where he had been standing a few moments previously. As it flashed by him he thought of the porter's words on the platform at Bridge Ferry when the abduction of Kathleen Regan had been discussed. Once again—the pattern fitted!

Then Anthony, craning his neck, caught a glimpse of something else. A short, squat man, who was evidently the lodge-keeper, came out from the lodge and unlocked the gates for four people who stood outside them. There were three men and a woman but Anthony's position made it impossible for him to see any more than this. But he found an inordinately acute curiosity mounting in his mind concerning Middleton Hall, its functions and its occupants, and at the same time he began to question his prudence in entering upon a contest, to all intents and purposes, single-handed. He heard the car drive in through the entrance and the noise of the iron gates coming together again. He was in a quandary now as to the best course for him to pursue. Should he wait a little while in the seclusion of the clump of bushes or should he make his way back again? He chose the latter course, scrambled out of the bushes and started to descend the road by which he had come. To his relief nothing in the way of traffic passed him and he was able to return to the "Black Horse" without incident or mishap.

What he had seen of the externals of Middleton Hall had given him furiously to think. There was definitely something sinister about the house and he was conscious that the exhalations from it were evil. Anthony realized more acutely perhaps than he had before, that he must gang warily and watch his step. Any false move that he might be lured into making, would, he felt certain, exact from him an inevitable and far-reaching penalty. The case would demand the most careful handling even though that care carried with it an admixture of audacity and he decided that he would feel better about it when he knew what the local police intentions were with regard to Scotland Yard. Till he had that knowledge, he must possess his soul in patience. Perhaps he would receive more news by the evening post. MacMorran might have picked up something additional.

3
ANTHONY MOVES

NEITHER the afternoon nor the evening post brought Anthony any further news from MacMorran, and at half-past eight, having had dinner, Anthony's impatience and inaction chafed him so successfully that he determined upon a bold step. He would take the war into what he had a shrewd idea was very much akin to the enemies' camp.

Shortly before nine o'clock he strolled down Mardol for the second time and into "Christopher's Bar." Once through the revolving glass doors, his mind became much clearer as to what he intended to do from the point of view of a plan of action. The orchestra was playing as usual—the same six in personnel that had been here on the occasion of his previous visit. By this time Anthony's idea had taken shape in his mind and he resolved to put it into action at the first favourable opportunity. The coloured lights were all ablaze, the waiters were bustling to and fro, doing much good work with their trays, and there seemed an even larger company present than on the evening he had been there before.

As he had done formerly, Anthony strolled to the bar and ordered a "Gin and Ginger beer." He was thirsty. The evening air of Wroxeter invariably had this effect on him. The man who looked Portuguese served him. Anthony thought of him as "Joe." The drink came up and Anthony burnt his boats. He deliberately crossed the Rubicon. He put the glass on the counter and turned the bottom round three times before releasing his finger from it. Not altogether sure that Joe had seen the action, Anthony repeated it after the lapse of a few seconds. There was no doubt that Joe had seen it on this second occasion. He looked up under his eyebrows and spoke in an undertone.

"The Skipper's not here yet, sir. He'll be a bit late this evening. I don't expect him for another half hour or so. But I'll pass the word along to him directly he comes in. That suit you, sir, or are you in a tearing hurry?"

"No," replied Anthony coolly—"it's all the same to me. Half an hour's not a matter that I shall ever quarrel over with anybody. In addition to which, it's understood by everybody that all the best things in life have to be waited for patiently. I'll be over at one of the tables when I'm wanted."

"Very good, sir. I'll tell the 'Skipper' directly I can get a word in his ear."

"Thank you, chum," said Anthony, "that's very nice of you." Taking his drink with him, he made his way to one of the tables, near, as far as he could judge, to the place where Trevor had sat on the occasion of Anthony's previous visit. The minutes passed. The noise of the band grew louder but they played well. To-night there were a piano, two violins, a banjo, a drum and a saxophone. At odd moments ladies retired through curtained archways. Twice Anthony beckoned a waiter to his table and ordered more drinks. The general atmosphere of merriment developed rapidly. Then, suddenly, Anthony saw one of the men for whom he had been look-ing. The short, dark, full-necked, florid-faced man whom he had seen talking to Trevor. Anthony took a good look at his eyes. They were certainly not "odd" coloured. Each was of a reddish-brown tint. The short man walked up to the bar-counter and conferred with Joe. For some few minutes their two heads were very close together. Anthony saw Joe gesture in the direction of the table at which he was sitting. He felt certain that he himself was the subject of discussion. Then somewhat to his surprise the short florid man left the bar-counter and sauntered over to the table where he sat, carrying his drink with him.

"Is this seat taken?" he asked Anthony.

Anthony shook his head. "Not to my knowledge."

"Mind if I park here?"

"Not at all. It has been rumoured that we live in a free country. And you know what rumours are."

The man looked him up and down. "New in these parts, aren't you?"

"No-o," replied Anthony—"this is not my first visit. But I am sometimes compelled by reason of my business to pass an evening in Wroxeter—and, well, candidly, this place makes as much appeal as any other. It can scarcely be argued that Wroxeter hits the high spots in the way of entertainment."

"Too true," said the short man, with a shake of the head, "you've said what I've often said myself."

Almost absent-mindedly he turned his glass round three times as it stood on the table. Anthony affected to disregard the incident. He was rewarded by seeing a puzzled look come into the short man's eyes, as though their owner was feeling his way and was definitely uncertain of himself. Anthony waited for his companion to make the next move. He hadn't to wait long.

"The Skipper's on the late side this evening. He's nearly always here by this time. Must be detained somewhere, I suppose."

"Couldn't tell you," said Anthony, still on the cool side.

"He's pretty busy these days, you know, and I expect he finds that it makes a difference. Rare lot of new stuff coming in."

"You're probably right."

The short man appeared to show surprise. "I hope I haven't made a bloomer! You're acquainted with the 'Skipper,' of course?"

"By sight only. I hope to improve that acquaintance as soon as possible."

The man appeared again to heave a sigh of relief. "That's all right, then. D'ye know, for the moment, you had me guessing a bit. I was just a wee bit dubious. Doesn't do to make mistakes, you know, in any direction where the 'Skipper's' concerned. He'll tear you off a strip as soon as look at you. But I expect you've heard that from others as well as from me." He seemed to invite an answer to his statement.

"No," replied Anthony, "all I've heard about him has been favourable. That is to say, 'favourable,' bearing in mind all the circumstances."

The short man nodded. "I think I understand what you mean."

"I'm glad of that," declared Anthony—"it makes me feel easier in my mind, too."

The man stared at him with an undisguised hint of admiration. "You're a cool card, bless my soul if you're not! If I'm any judge the Skipper'll take to you like a duck takes to water. Birds of a feather—if you ask me! Early impressions mean a lot with him I can tell you."

"I find it a comparatively easy matter to be cool in this country. The opportunities that one gets in the opposite direction seem to me to be very strictly limited."

The man grinned and showed his teeth. "You know what I mean. You're stalling now! Putting me in my place and all that. But you've got me all wrong. There's no need to take offence—I give you my word."

"Don't then," replied Anthony—"I assure you that I shan't. My primary considerations were for you."

"Look here," said the other man, "let's have a drink, then we shall know where we are with each other. There's nothing like good liquor for mutual understanding and agreement."

"I don't mind having a drink," responded Anthony, "but I know where *I* am, even without that pleasure. As for your remark with regard to an *entente cordiale* existing between us—well—let it pass." His companion nodded and gestured to a waiter who was hovering in their vicinity. The man came up to the table.

"What will you have?" asked the self-appointed host.

"Make it a pint," accepted Anthony, "in a tankard for preference."

The short man raised his eyebrows. "Sure you wouldn't care for something else?"

"No. A pint of beer will do me very nicely, thank you."

"That's quite all right. Every man to his taste. Although I didn't think you were drinking beer when I blew in on you. I'm for a short myself." He gave the order.

"I wasn't," said Anthony, "but does that matter? I'm a tremendous believer in the benefits which arise from change and—er—variation. It's nature's characteristic expression, surely."

His companion's eyes narrowed noticeably. "I don't know that I get that. How do you mean exactly?"

"Would you like me to explain?" asked Anthony.

"Perhaps I would." By now there had just come a slight suspicion of truculence in the short man's tone.

"Let me give you," said Anthony, "a practical illustration of the argument that I was just advancing. The charm of nature is in her changing moods, surely? The pageant that each year brings to us. Spring, summer, autumn and winter. Each day with its dawn, its light, its twilight and then its darkness. See what I mean? And then the English climate itself. Changing all the time. Heavy rain, light rain, ordinary rain, drizzle, fog, sleet and snow. All a matter of variety—you see."

The short man seemed to be regarding him with some measure of suspicion. Anthony, however, affected not to see it. He continued in his vein with a disarming smile attached.

"I'm sure you are following me. This desire for change is inherent in every one of us. Many men, indeed, and not a few women have died in its cause."

"Died?" queried his listener.

"Yes," said Anthony innocently, "'by the route of the nine o'clock walk. You know what I mean!" He made an expressive gesture with his fingers to his throat and neck. "I could recite the names of quite a number. Mabon, Rouse, Mrs. Bryant, the late lamented Dr. Crippen, everybody who knew him by the way describes him as a charming little chap, Mrs. Thompson, Bywaters—"

His companion interrupted him. 'Yes, I get you. I suppose you're right. And if it's any information to you, the Skipper's just barged in. He's talking to Joe. Take a dekko yourself."

Anthony turned his head and looked towards the bar-counter. As be expected, there stood the man whose name had been given to him as Capt. Lionel Trevor. He seemed to be questioning Joe rather sharply. The barman didn't appear to be too comfortable under the barrage. More than once he spread out his hands deprecatingly and shrugged bis shoulders. Something very much akin to anger showed on Trevor's face and smouldered in his eyes. Anthony turned his attention to the man who sat with him. He wanted to see how he was reacting to the little scene which was thus being played so relatively near to them. Anthony thought that the short man was not entirely devoid of a certain amount of uneasiness. No doubt, too, on his own behalf. Suddenly he lightened up and generally pulled himself together, as it were.

"The Skipper's coming over to us," he announced quietly. "I hope that you'll—"

Anthony was not destined to hear what this hope was. Trevor had come abreast of their table.

"Evening, Skipper," said the short man. Anthony couldn't miss the sycophancy in the voice.

"Evening, Stanhope," replied Trevor. He frowned—and the frown was all-embracing. Stanhope moved uncomfortably under it.

Trevor sat down in the chair that Stanhope had vacated. Anthony took a cigarette from his case and lit it. He carelessly tossed the burnt match-stub into an ash-tray and waited for the inevitable, A moment or two passed. Anthony looked with steady composure at the man seated opposite to him. As before, he was in evening-dress attire. Anthony took in the steely-blue eyes, the rather heavy eyebrows and the predatory nose. Yet the man would be accounted handsome by some tastes and by nearly all women. His hands, Anthony saw, were large and fleshy and the veins showed prominently on the back of them. Suddenly Trevor, as though aware that Anthony was taking stock of him, drank from his glass, placed his two arms on the table and leant forward.

"I understand," he said in a hard voice, "from Joe—that's the barman—that you have an idea of doing business with me. Am I right?"

Anthony smiled easily. "I think that might be one way of putting it, Capt. Trevor. In fact, I'm certain of it."

Trevor raised his eyes. "You know my name, then?"

"I made it my business to before I decided to come here."

"Really! May I hope for a similar condition with regard to yours?"

"Certainly, Capt. Trevor. My name is Lotherington."

"Who introduced you?"

Anthony had his story all ready. He had prepared for an overture of this kind. "A man named Brown."

"Brown? Not a very strong identification. What were the man's initials?" Trevor's tone was the reverse of cordial.

"I couldn't tell you. I met him in Wroxeter somewhere about a couple of months ago, I should think, perhaps a little more. I can check up on that. It was round about Easter time. If it would help you at all to remember him—he was by way of being an artist of sorts."

"I'm not too sure that I recall the man. And that being the case—"

Anthony waved a nonchalant hand. "That's all right. I understand your difficulty. You're taking no risks. I don't blame you. If you're in doubt—forget all about me. I daresay I can manage to get fixed up elsewhere."

He picked up his tankard and drank from it. His attitude, however, had the exact effect that he had desired. Trevor was loth for the matter to drop as summarily as all that. As Anthony had judged, his curiosity had been whetted. He was guessing. He came again.

"Just a moment, Mr. Lotherington," he said, with a slight mollification of manner, "I don't know that that follows. As you put it Brown may be quite sound. But I've had dealings with more than one Brown and it isn't exactly an easy matter to sort them all out properly at a minute's notice. That isn't to say, though, that I can't try. What was the nature of the business that you thought we might find mutually an attractive proposition?"

The blue eyes glinted dangerously, Anthony's grey eyes met them unwaveringly. He was on the point of taking a big risk—and he knew it. If Trevor called his bluff—! Anthony burnt his boats. *Toujours l'audace!*

"Shall we say on the matter of restaurant profits?" He could feel that the beat of his own heart had quickened as the words left his lips. The glint went from Trevor's eyes and they became wary. Anthony thought that he was endeavouring to make a quick assessment of the merits and implications of the situation. As though he knew that he too must make up his mind rapidly. Trevor cleared his throat and spoke.

"Restaurant profits—eh? So that's the line in which you're interested. Well—I must say that it suits me. I've no quarrel with any profits that accrue to me from keeping a restaurant, you under-stand, *of the right sort*. I always insist on that." He paused.

"Naturally," said Anthony, playing for time.

Trevor nodded—evidently communing with himself. "I'm glad that you agree with me."

"I should hate to do otherwise," replied Anthony with a show of but little concern.

"As long as," continued Trevor, "one remembers this. One fact that must never be allowed to be relegated to the background. The background of finance. A great deal of profit can be made on caviare."

Trevor ended his sentence summarily and leant back in his chair. Anthony still appeared to be unconcerned.

"Again I agree with you." Like Trevor a moment or so ago, he paused. He felt that his companion was watching and waiting for him with suppressed excitement. Anthony dallied, therefore, with deliberation. He handed his cigarette-case to Trevor, and then took a cigarette for himself. He lit it, waited for it to burn properly, shook the flame of the match out and tossed away the charred end. Trevor was now leaning forward, waiting for him. Almost like a huge cat about to pounce.

"And on *pâté de foie gras*," declared Anthony.

Trevor's mouth twisted into a crooked smile. "But," he said, "on the other hand, there is almost always a loss on *langouste*."

Anthony nodded. "Yes."

Trevor's mouth straightened. His old mood of dubious expect-ancy returned to him. The glint came back to his eyes. Anthony sighed. "Provided you buy in Toulon," he added. Trevor pulled his chair forward and put his arms on the table. Most of the suspicion had vanished from his eyes. "Brown, I think you said the name was?"

"That's right—Brown!"

"Funny! As I said, can't call that particular merchant to mind. Still—that's neither here nor there now. A rose by any other name—"

He laughed rather boisterously. Anthony decided to sit tight for the moment. He was a little uncertain as to what the next move was to be so he resolved to let Trevor make it. Trevor was speaking again.

"You prefer—er—restaurant profits to . . . er . . . my more ordin-ary and orthodox accounts?"

"I think so," returned Anthony, "bearing in mind all the circumstances."

"I . . . er . . . angle . . . in many different waters. As a result, of course, I catch more than one kind of fish. You understand me, Mr. Lotherington?"

Anthony inclined his head. "All doubtless of excellent and satisfying flavour."

"Yes. I can accept that statement. Otherwise the exercise would scarcely pay me. And as a business man—" Trevor shrugged his shoulders ostentatiously.

"Of course," corroborated Anthony—"it would be impossible for you to put it more plainly, situated as we are."

"I'm glad that you see my point. We must have a drink on the strength of this understanding."

Trevor turned round in his chair and made signs to a distant waiter. The man came up with alacrity and Trevor spoke to him in a low voice. The waiter nodded and disappeared.

"I've ordered a bottle of 'bubbly'," said Trevor in explanation. "I haven't the slightest doubt that you're a devotee and I consider that the occasion calls for it. So I'm not anxious on that score. They keep some very decent stuff here. Besides the other kind. But, of course, they have to know you before they dish it out to you. I'm by way of being *persona grata* and get the real McCoy."

Anthony smiled his appreciation. The waiter came up with the wine.

"You try that," said Trevor a minute later, "it's a comparatively young wine but it has an undoubted distinction. You could go a long way and fare worse. Try it for yourself."

Anthony sampled his champagne. The evening so far had gone a little beyond his anticipation. Trevor drank appreciatively.

"Very nice tonic. Personally, I like it morning and evening. Does me good at my time of life. Puts pep into me."

"How long," asked Anthony, "have you been connected with the restaurant trade?"

Trevor's expression changed. His face grew hard. "Why do you ask that? I'll tell you, my dear Lotherington, here and now, that I have a rooted antipathy to answering personal questions." Anthony affected to miss the antagonism. "It's of no consequence. After all, I must take you on trust just as you must do the same with me."

Trevor put down the glass that he had raised to his lips. "I'll say this for you, Lotherington, you're not lost for it."

"As your possible . . . er . . . associate . . . surely that's just as well? From your point of view, I mean."

Anthony knew that he was playing high. Trevor seemed somewhat taken aback. "I suppose it is. When I come to think of it. You're a cool card, I must say."

"You are not alone, Capt. Trevor, in thinking that. Well . . . do we get to business or is the deal off? My time is not without value to me."

Anthony was forcing the pace deliberately, now. In his judgment, this was the safest course to pursue.

"I think that we shall be able to do business. In fact I'm sure we shall. But not to-night. I'm not in the mood. To-night I'm more in the mood for what dear old Charlie Hawtrey as 'Ambrose Applejack' used to describe as 'dalliance'." He glared round the room. The drink, evidently, was beginning to have its effect on him. After a little while, he jerked himself back to the matter in hand. "I'll tell you what, Lotherington, you must come up to my place to see me and have a chat. Then we can get down to brass tacks. I'll give you my address."

He fumbled in his pocket until he was able to produce a visiting card. He flicked it over to Anthony. "Capt. Lionel Trevor, Middleton Hall, near Wroxeter, Warwickshire."

Anthony frowned as though the address was puzzling him.

"Middleton Hall," he questioned. "I don't think that I—"

"That's right. Middleton Hall. That's the name of my little outfit. It's no distance from here. About a couple of miles. The road's a bit rough but not too bad on the whole. Now let's see! When shall I expect you? According to my idea, the sooner we get down to real business, so much the better. You can't negotiate matters of that kind in a joint like this." He grinned. "I've always been a stickler for the proprieties. Well, Lotherington, does my suggestion suit you?"

"Yes. I think so. I've certainly no objection to it."

"Good. That's settled then. Now when shall I expect you?"

Anthony considered the question. He had no wish to make too long a delay in the acceptance of Trevor's invitation, in case the latter's suspicions were aroused. "I should have liked to have made it to-morrow but I'm afraid that's out of the question at such comparatively short notice. Let's say the day after. On Friday. That suit you?"

"Suits me all right," replied Trevor lazily—"what time?"

"Morning or evening?"

"Oh—I don't know. Evening I think. Yes—make it evening. After dinner. I'm generally at my brilliant best then. We'll meet at my place instead of gravitating here. Won't do me any harm to give this place a miss for once in a while."

"Nine o'clock?"

"Right-o. Nine o'clock. I'll book the appointment now."

He produced a small book and made an entry in it. Anthony watched him curiously. Trevor replaced the book in his pocket.

"Now there's one more thing I want to say to you, Lotherington. If it suits you you can regard it as a warning. No! We won't call it that. That's a bit too steep. Call it a piece of reasonable and seasonable advice. When you start on your activities, if we agree to a business proposition between us, you may run up against trouble. If you do—you'll have to get out of it yourself. It won't be any good running to me, or squealing for me to come to your assistance. I always make a point in my operations of remaining in the background. And when I say the background—I mean the background. If you join, you join on your own and you paddle your own damned canoe. I hope you understand that much, Lotherington."

Anthony stuck out his jaw. He knew that it was necessary for him to impress Trevor and that any other line would be sheer futility.

"My dear Trevor," he said, "you've spoken straight to me. I don't mind that at all. I prefer straight talk to any other kind. But sauce for the goose is sauce for the gander. So I'll talk straight to you in my turn. I shouldn't come to you as I have, if I were in the habit of sheltering behind other people's skirts. My own line of action has always been good enough for me and I hope it always will be. When it isn't any longer, I'll throw my hand in. So you can set your uneasy mind at rest on that point." He leant back and looked Trevor straight in the eyes.

"I see," remarked Trevor dryly. "So that's how you feel about things, is it?"

"It is. And we'd better know where we stand, from the moment the tapes go up."

"All right," said Trevor, with a sudden change of voice. "That's O.K. with me. See you on Friday, then." He rose and lounged off.

Anthony stayed at his table for a few moments longer before he, too, took his departure. Trevor, standing by Joe at the bar, watched him leave the premises. As Anthony passed through the door, Trevor grinned and chuckled.

"Joe," he said in a tone that implied the passing of a confidence, "there goes a guy who, if I'm any judge, thinks he's going to play me for a 'sucker.' What, my excellent Joseph, do you think will become of him? You can answer that question as well, if not better, than the next man." By the time he had finished speaking there was a nasty edge on Trevor's voice. The barman heard it and recognized it. It was by no means new to him.

"I guess, Captain, that that guy will wish he'd never had a mother."

As he spoke, Joe shivered. Trevor looked him up and down with critical insistence.

"For once, Joseph, I find myself in complete agreement with you." He tossed off another drink and then began to whistle softly between his teeth.

4

PROTECTIVE ACTION

ANTHONY read MacMorran's letter. The chief inspector had supplied information with regard to the list of names which Anthony had sent him. This was the information:

No. 1. Hon. Michael Polhill-Scott. Aged 33. Third son of Lord Clamness. Educated Eton and Christchurch. Married Julia Schuyler, only daughter of Felix Schuyler, iron magnate of Pittsburgh, Pa. One child. Suzanne, aged 5. London address 11 Bryanston Square.

Clubs, Diadem and Royal Cygnet. Note (this had been added in MacMorran's own handwriting)—inherited over a million sterling from his aunt, the Countess of Lefroy, who died a few years ago without issue.

No. 2. Lovegrove. Very little information to pass on to you here. Especially in the absence of any initials. There is no *well-known* Lovegrove. But a Walter Lovegrove, a native of Stoke Newington, disappeared some months ago from his home and nothing whatever has been heard of him. It is just possible that this is the man.

No. 3. Mrs. Ardsley Spuyten. Aged 37. Widow of Chester Spuyten, millionaire, ex-Chicago pork trade. Chester Spuyten died as a result of motorcar accident at Pillerton Priors not far from Droitwich in 1937 whilst touring in this country. Mrs. A.S. has one child. Aged 4. Dudley Lee Van Houten Spuyten. Address, Little Clancy St., Mayfair.

No. 4. Sir Curtis Littlehales. Aged 43. Son of the late George Littlehales, silk manufacturer. Educated Felstead and Clare College, Cambridge. Married Ada Butler-Baring, second daughter of Thomas Bartholomew Butler-Baring of Kynaston, Warwickshire, and niece of Lady Colkett-Hardy. One child, Imogen, aged 3. Address, Ingots Court, Margretham, Essex. Note (this again had been supplied by Andrew MacMorran himself)—Sir C.L. is reported to be one of the six richest men in England. There is big money on both sides of the family.

Anthony pushed the letter to one side and concentrated on the information it contained. In problems of this nature, he always looked for the common factor and also for the intruder. That is to say for the two extremes, as it were, of the progression. He quickly saw and recognized more than one common factor, ignoring the presence of Lovegrove in the list.

Each one of the three people was extremely rich as far as the things of this world were concerned. Each one could justifiably be placed in the (to use the common expression) millionaire class. Polhill-Scott had inherited a huge sum from the Countess of Lefroy, Mrs. Ardsley Spuyten was the widow of a modern Croesus, and Sir Curtis Littlehales was actually reputed to be one of the six richest men in England. Here then was common factor Number

One. Common Factor Number Two was to be found, and equally quickly. Each one of the three people had one child. Polhill-Scott a daughter, Mrs. Spuyten a son and Sir Curtis Littlehales a daughter. Mrs. Spuyten was the intruder from one point of view—she was a widow—the marriage partners in the other two cases were alive—and from another angle, Sir Curtis Littlehales intruded—there was no mention in his case of any American connection. Anthony then looked at the respective ages. Polhill-Scott was 33, Mrs. Ardsley Spuyten was 37 and Sir Curtis Littlehales, 43. The children were 5, 4, and 3 respectively. Only children according to MacMorran's records in each instance. Here, considered Anthony, was delectable food for thought.

Then he tangented. Who was Lovegrove? From where did Terence Regan pick this name up? A Lovegrove had disappeared, thereby, according to Anthony's present line of reasoning, placing himself in the same category as Terence Regan himself and his sister, Kathleen Regan. Lovegrove, too, was a Londoner, assuming that MacMorran's Lovegrove equalled Regan's Lovegrove. A Londoner from Stoke Newington. What part had he played in the Trevor *ménage*? MacMorran had not mentioned the missing Lovegrove's trade or profession. Pity that! The information would have been valuable. It might be, thought Anthony, that the man was an artist, similar to Terence Regan. Then another thought occurred to Anthony. Perhaps "Brown" may well have been Walter Lovegrove, again assuming that MacMorran's man was the authentic one. Certainly the entire problem presented many interesting features and possessed tremendous possibilities. Possibilities which grew the deeper he delved into the case.

Anthony then thought over the circumstances of his encounter with Trevor, of the previous evening. He had definitely elected to walk straight into the enemy's camp—he knew that—but he had made the choice deliberately and with his eyes open. It was risky. More than that—it was perilous. The slightest mistake might well mean the end of him. The people against whom he was pitting his intelligence were ruthless and, as he knew perfectly well, would stick at nothing to achieve their desire. With two—and perhaps three—murders in their ledger, they would not be deterred by the contemplation and execution of a fourth. But Anthony had always believed in the efficacy of bold action and he was determined to make no exception in the case under review.

He turned to MacMorran's letter again, almost idly, and saw that there was a P.T.O. direction which he had previously missed. More than ordinarily interested, he turned the page. Andrew MacMorran had scrawled a message across it. "Just heard from Chief Constable—he is calling in 'Yard.' Coming down myself. Meet me at Wroxeter station, 11.40."

Anthony rubbed his hands when he heard this. He was overjoyed, for, coming at this moment, he couldn't possibly have had better or more comforting news. An effort on his own was an entirely different proposition from an effort assisted by MacMorran with all the vast resources of Scotland Yard behind him. The inspector's assistance would give him also greater assets of strength, a second line of defence, and—which was at least equally important—a stronger bargaining power, were he ever to force a bargain.

Anthony looked at his watch. MacMorran would be with him in little more than an hour. Things were definitely moving!

CHAPTER V

1

COMBINED OPERATIONS

ANDREW MacMorran stepped from the train to the platform at Wroxeter with the spring of a two-year-old. Anthony met him and the inspector grinned broadly in recognition.

"This is Inspector Foster," said Anthony. "Chief-Inspector MacMorran."

The two professionals shook hands cordially. "I've a car waiting," said Foster, "we can drive straight back to the station. Unless, of course, you'd rather—"

MacMorran shook his head. "Your original idea, Inspector Foster," he said waggishly, "will suit me very well. And we'll cut the 'shop' talk until we get to the station."

Foster nodded. "That's all right, sir. I shan't offend—you can rely on that. I didn't start in the Force yesterday."

When the car reached the station, Anthony gave MacMorran a surprise. "I'm going to leave you two experts for a short time," he said, "you'll be able to get on very well without me. But at 1 p.m. precisely, Andrew, I shall expect you to lunch with me at the 'Black Horse.' I can't promise you anything in the nature of a banquet—but it will be passably adequate. At one o'clock sharp, Andrew—don't forget."

Before Andrew could either refuse or accept, Anthony had alighted from the car on the roadside, turned on his heel and walked away. Foster watched his retreating figure.

"What's he after?" he asked, almost to himself.

"Don't know," replied MacMorran, "but whatever it is, I'll lay even money he'll catch up with it."

Foster raised his eyebrows. "Like that, is it?"

"Every time," declared MacMorran, "and then some, as our American cousins would say."

Anthony returned to the inn, wrote three letters, posted them in the nearest pillar-box and waited for one o'clock and Inspector MacMorran. The latter was five minutes late in arriving, but bustled in eventually and announced himself as more than ready for his lunch that was to follow. Anthony took him to a table and got him settled in front of the soup before he said anything beyond the conventional. After a time, MacMorran began to open out.

"Had a long chat with Foster. Seems to me they've got the case all round their necks. As I expected! These local people are always the same. Always start moving when it's too late."

Anthony smiled at him. "You mustn't be over-critical, Andrew. Don't forget one thing. They haven't the organization of the 'Yard' or anything like, and in that respect they're handicapped."

MacMorran grumbled. "They can always call us in, if they're in the dirt. But they don't. Unless it's to carry the can back."

"Human nature being what it is, can you blame them? But I want some information out of you, Andrew. Did you tell Foster of the 'phoney' notes?"

"I did that. And also the news that I gave you *re* the supposed centre at Stratford-upon-Avon."

"Did you mention the details that were found in Regan's diary?"

"No. They may not be relevant to the case. I've left that to you, to work on at your own sweet will. But you can bring Foster in on it whenever you feel you want to. I shan't object or complain."

"Right. That's understood then. Now I want a few words with you regarding myself. From now on, I'm not going to be seen in public with you. Even now, I feel that I'm taking an unnecessary risk in lunching with you here."

MacMorran looked up at him from his plate. "What are you talking about? What's biting you?"

Anthony crumbled bread on the table-cloth. "Listen to me, Andrew. I want you to go to 'Christopher's' to-night. It's a bar. Otherwise a haunt where they serve alcoholic drinks at exorbitant prices. I shan't be there. I'm going to keep away on purpose. You'll see why in a moment. I want you to get a line on two or three people. By name, Trevor, Stanhope, and the bar-tender, Joe. I'll describe the first two to you now."

Anthony gave MacMorran word-pictures of Trevor and the man Stanhope. MacMorran let the data soak into his mind.

"Got that, Andrew? Good. Now my idea is this. There's a racket of some kind being run from Trevor's country house. That's about a couple of miles from here. The name of the place is Middleton Hall."

Anthony stopped abruptly with a far-away look in his eyes. MacMorran noticed it.

"What's the trouble now? Thought of something else?"

"Ye-es," replied Anthony slowly. "Regan's notes are becoming more clear to me every day. I'll tell you of the particular point I've just thought of, in a moment or so. I think there's something in this case beyond 'snide.' We shall see. Regan's diary put me on to it and since I've been to 'Christopher's,' I've made a certain amount of progress. But listen. What do you make of this?"

Anthony told the inspector of the sign of the circular movement of the drinking-glass and of the conversational answers and statements concerning possible profits made by restaurants.

"Put those sentences down somewhere, Andrew—word for word. It's on the cards they may be useful to you some day."

MacMorran did as instructed. Anthony saw him frowning as he entered the words in his note-book. "Bit unusual, isn't it? Never met anything before quite like it. Still—the yarn's interesting. Get on with it."

Anthony went on and described his encounters with the man called Stanhope and with Trevor himself. From time to time, MacMorran nodded. Eventually he spoke.

"So you're due there to-morrow evening—eh? Bit venturesome, don't you think?"

Anthony grinned at him. "I did, I'll agree with you, until I got your news that you were coming down here. That caused me to take a different view. I consider that strengthens my hand a lot. I've always got you in the background. I can bring you up as my reserves, as you might put it, when, and if, I'm in sore need. Do you get the idea?"

MacMorran peppered his potatoes in profusion. "That's all very well as far as it goes. I might happen to arrive too late."

Anthony grinned again. "Must risk that, Andrew. Damn it all, man—we've taken risks before, you and I—in this game. And history goes on repeating itself."

"I guessed you'd say that. But tell me more of your plans, so that I may fix mine in with them."

"I've had one look at this place, Middleton Hall, from outside. It's well looked after, believe me, Andrew. But Regan had got on to it in some way. I'll tell you how I know that. That was the reference I made just now. In Regan's notes was this sentence: 'Note—call at the gardener's house—query distance?'" Anthony paused. "Well, Andrew, have you arrived?"

The inspector shook his head, knife and fork poised over his plate. "To be truthful, can't say that I have. Seems a pretty ordinary statement to me. Commonplace! What's your special interpretation of it?"

"I think this. 'Gardener's House' equals 'Middleton Hall.' Don't forget your B.B.C. programmes, Andrew! Regan desired a quick synonym and that was the first his brain thought of. It was topical."

"It's an idea, certainly. I'll admit, though, that it didn't occur to me. Go ahead, Mr. Bathurst."

"I'm going along there to-morrow evening as I've already informed you. I shall be able to have a look-see at the inside of the place and I hope to get an insight also into the essentials of Trevor's operation. He *may*—I stress the 'may'—confide in me—*to an extent*. If I'm to be included in the racket—whatever it is—he's almost bound to give more away to me than he has up to the present. That's one of the reasons why you and I have got to part company—temporarily and ostensibly. Any other condition would be far too risky. Agree on that?"

"Ay! That's sound enough. On the surface. But have you considered the possibility, my boy, of Trevor *suspecting you* from the moment you sat down with him—or he sat down with you—to be precise—and of him playing his cards accordingly? Seems to me there's a distinct chance of that." MacMorran shook his head.

For some seconds Anthony made no reply. "Even then, Andrew," he replied at length, "I must take my chance. I feel strongly about it. Let me try to explain. I've a hunch that this business at Middleton Hall is more evil than mere ordinary crime. I can't give you logical reasons for thinking thus. I just do think it. Whatever the racket is, there are black-hearted men behind it and it's up to you and me, Andrew, to lay them by the heels. If I get inside—and I'm due to get inside to-morrow, don't forget—the vital clue may come to me. That particular clue in every case which makes all the difference. If Trevor is playing spider to my fly, which you say you consider is a distinct possibility, and the worst come to the worst, you must come in and get me. We must make definite arrangements before we part now with regard to that. But you'll at least know where I am."

MacMorran shook his head doubtfully. "As I said before, Mr. Bathurst, it may be too late. My arrival, I mean. All I may know is not where you are but where you *were*. And knowing that won't help you much, if you're in danger or up against it. I'm a Scot and I'm a wee bit cautious."

MacMorran finished his lunch and pushed away his plate. Anthony thought it the better policy, as things were, to agree with him.

"Yes. I know how you feel, Andrew. And in the event of our respective positions being reversed, I expect I should feel as you do. But we'll have a definite cut and dried plan for emergency before we part company this afternoon. I'll meet you here the day after to-morrow at the same time as we met to-day. But in a private room. Not in this public luncheon room. They may have got 'tabs' on you by then. I don't think they've had time to do so to-day. I had to risk that. If I don't meet you, you'll know that the fat's in the fire and that I'm close to the fat. Which means that you'll have to don your best thinking-cap and come in and get me."

"Dead or alive, I suppose?"

Anthony grinned at him again. "The latter preferably, of course."

MacMorran was gloomy. "I don't like it. And it's no use my saying I do. And it's all—as you map it out—much sooner said than done. Much too risky altogether for my liking."

"You'll have to use your ingenuity, of course. That goes without saying."

"All the ingenuity in the world won't bring you back if you're a stiff. That's the part of it that worries me."

"Don't be so damned pessimistic. You're yammering like an old midwife. I shall be all right, I tell you. If I'm not, it's my funeral."

"Exactly, Mr. Bathurst. And that's just what I'm afraid of."

Anthony was forced to laugh at this. "Good for you, Andrew. You got home that time. The wheel went full circle. Nevertheless, I'm determined to do what I say and carry out my plan. And if I'm any judge, we'll have lunch here, as I said, the day after to-morrow. If I'm not here—it's up to you. Is that a bargain?"

MacMorran grumbled. "I suppose it will have to be. I notice that when you want your own way—which is always—you invariably get it."

"Right, Andrew. Then that's a bet. And we'll finish up today's proceedings with a couple of Kümmels."

Anthony suited his words by beckoning to the waitress. The inspector waited in pleasant anticipation.

2

INSIDE THE ENEMY'S LINES

ANTHONY Bathurst looked at his watch. For the second time within a week, he was travelling the not-so-good road which led to Middleton

Hall. The time showed at twelve minutes to nine. He felt reassured. He always liked to be on time for all opportunities. He had come prepared—torch, a whistle, a length of rope round his middle, and a revolver in his pocket. Judging by the distance he still had to cover, he would be at the iron gates of Middleton Hall with at least a couple of minutes to spare. A touch of exhilarated elation came to him. He smiled to himself as he remembered an old belief, that the soul, on the point of the body's death, finds cause for rejoicing and jubilation.

"Pretty grim that," he muttered to himself.

He arrived at the gates and pressed the bell. Soon after, he heard the sound of approaching footsteps. A man had emerged from the lodge and was coming towards the gates. This man, silent and almost preoccupied, opened the gates and gave Anthony a somewhat curt invitation to pass through. Anthony nodded to him conventionally and did so. The gates closed again. Surprisingly or so it seemed, the man spoke. It was the man Anthony had seen before.

"You have come to see Capt. Trevor, I believe?"

"That is so," replied Anthony.

"Then follow me, if you please. You have some little distance to travel yet before you come to the house. Come this way."

Anthony could have replied that he was aware of that, but he judged it prudent to keep the knowledge to himself. So he contented himself with following his guide to the house known as Middleton Hall. As he passed them, one by one, Anthony recalled the landmarks that he had noticed when he had taken his first and clandestine look at the exterior of the house and he attempted to memorize, in addition, new features which had, on the first occasion, eluded him. They came to a turning which lost itself in a beautifully-kept gravel drive and the man who was with him stopped dead in his tracks.

"There is no need for me to come any further with you. You can find your way easily. If you walk straight ahead you will come to the main entrance."

Anthony took a good look at him, thanked him for his services, and walked on as he had been directed. A matter of a hundred yards or so brought him to the main entrance as his guide had stated. Before he could reach the door it opened and a figure stood in the porch. Anthony saw that it was Trevor himself. Trevor advanced to meet him.

"Evening, Lotherington. You're on time, I'm pleased to say. I'm glad of that. I simply detest waiting about for people who simply can't keep appointments. Makes me see red. And I practise what I preach! I'm never late for an appointment or an assignation. Come inside, will you?"

Anthony, thus invited, entered Middleton Hall. Trevor led him to an arched door, through which they passed into a room which suggested a museum much more than anything else. Coats of armour, old weapons, and stuffed specimens of all types of animal and fish predominated.

"This, Lotherington," said Trevor, with an expansive wave of the hand, "is my chief interest in life—next to making money. I'll admit that with candour and without fear or favour."

There was a desk in the far corner of the room and a man was seated there. On a raised platform by the side of the desk was a large box with a small padlock attached to it.

"Brodhurst," called out Trevor, "this is Lotherington whom I mentioned to you yesterday. I told you he was coming along this evening. Come and be introduced."

Brodhurst slid out of his chair and came forward to meet Anthony. As he met the fellow face to face, Anthony became acutely conscious of two unusual physical features. He had odd-coloured eyes and a small triangular patch of silver on one side of his head which showed conspicuously in his black hair. Anthony knew once again, without the shadow of a doubt, that he was talking where Regan had talked and walking where Regan had walked. Brodhurst had a long thin face but was a man of some weight. His expression, Anthony thought, was "foxy" and as he looked at you there came a stabbing bluish-grey glint from his most unusual pair of eyes. His gait was almost shambling and his hands were restless and the fingers unsteady.

"This is Lotherington," said Trevor again. "Ralph Brodhurst. My chief technical assistant."

Brodhurst thrust out a hand which Anthony took. "Pleased to meet you," said Brodhurst in a tone which belied the meaning of the words. His entire expression was the reverse of cordial.

"Thank you," said Anthony.

"Come into the lounge, both of you," said Trevor, "and we'll have some drinks brought in. May as well start as we mean to finish."

Anthony followed Trevor and Brodhurst into the room which Trevor had designated as the lounge. It was tastefully furnished, with a low-lying open hearth and fire-place. Trevor rang for Scotch and soda and waved Anthony to a seat.

"Sit down, Lotherington, and make yourself thoroughly comfortable. Regard yourself as being in your own house. That's my idea of hospitality."

"Thank you," said Anthony again. His eyes were watchful and he was ready, he hoped, for any contingency or emergency. Trevor handled the siphon with an adroit skill which betokened long practice.

"Say 'when', Lotherington." Anthony said it. Trevor handed him his glass. "I asked you here," he went on, "because I felt that we could be useful to each other. To say nothing of the fact that you had been properly introduced. I wasn't overlooking that, of course. It wouldn't pay me to."

He turned and spoke directly to Brodhurst. "Lotherington comes to us from Brown. The artist, Brown. Remember him?"

"Can't say that I do. But that doesn't mean much. Our artists have been ten a penny in recent years. I took an extremely poor view of nearly all of them. What line does Lotherington want to take up?"

"He claims to be interested in restaurants." Trevor spoke slowly.

Brodhurst raised his eyebrows. "Really? That's most interesting. In that case, then, Trevor, we could start him off on the preliminary work at once."

Trevor nodded. "So I thought myself. What shall we give him? K, X or Z?"

"What do you think yourself? You're more in touch at the moment than I am."

Trevor found pencil and paper and from what Anthony could see began to make calculations. After a time he looked on his task. "Z, I fancy, Brodhurst," he declared. "Z certainly needs a considerable amount of attention. It's been neglected for far too long. The receipts recently are most unsatisfactory."

"That's only too true. All right, then. I agree to Lotherington being put in charge of the Z group."

"That's settled, then." Trevor came back from Brodhurst and spoke to Anthony. "You heard that conversation. Brodhurst is ready to fall into line with my idea. You shall take over the Z's. I refer, of course, to our own special branch of restaurants, treated by us in the manner that we have made entirely our own and over which we exercise entire control. Now look here—banishing all ideas except those to do with strict business—here's the list you will be expected to handle. I've no doubt you're thinking it's all a bit on the cryptic side."

Trevor rose and walked to a small side table. He pulled open a drawer and took out a file of papers. The top one, Anthony saw, was a cardboard stiffener. On this outside sheet, he saw a large capital Z done in bright green ink. The ink, to his eye, looked new. Trevor began to flick the papers over one by one.

"The first," he said, "is Zancomi's, High Street, Stratford-upon-Avon. Followed by Zappelli, Woodstock Road, Dudley. Then comes Zaruni's, Hurcott Avenue, Kidderminster. After Zaruni's, we have Zerusti's of Bulwer Road, Banbury. But I need not detail the entire list." He flicked over the pages with careless indifference. "I'll hand it over to you, Lotherington, for executive action. That's my first step."

Anthony still kept silent. He was determined to let Trevor carry on. Trevor obliged him. "I said 'executive action,' Lotherington. You are wondering no doubt what I meant by that. Your wonderment is natural. I want you to call at each one of the places that has inclusion in this list." He handed over the list. "You must exercise extreme care in your initial approaches. It is necessary that you are warned with regard to that. You will never refer to me by name. You will invariably allude to me as 'The Skipper.' Never anything other than that."

"The Skipper," repeated Anthony after him. "I see. Always the 'Skipper.' I must remember that."

But inwardly the news pleased him for the reason that it took him back to Terence Regan again and he knew, without a doubt, that he was on the track of something pretty big. Trevor nodded.

"That's the idea. I will continue with my explanation to you. After you have introduced yourself as my . . . er . . . emissary—agent is the better word in the circumstances, perhaps—you will make the announcement that you already know." Trevor smiled. "Concerning what you yourself were pleased to describe to me as 'restaurant profits.' You are equally aware of the response that your announcement should evoke and of the subsequent verbal exchanges *which are vital to a complete understanding*. If you are satisfied—and the responsibility will be held to be entirely yours, my dear Lotherington—you will collect certain moneys. You will find that the respective amounts are shown on the appropriate pages of that file I've just handed to you. You will, on no pretext whatever, accept a cheque of any kind. You will then give—in my name, never any other—just 'The Skipper'—a receipt for the money you take. Our clients will almost certainly insist on this procedure. Is that clear so far?"

Anthony nodded his understanding. "Quite—thank you. I sign the receipt in the sobriquet of 'The Skipper.' Everything is perfectly clear to me as far as you've gone."

"Good. You hear that, Brodhurst? We've a recruit here after our own hearts. Now where was I? Oh—I know—after you have given the receipt for the cash you've taken, you will say 'July—Either the 8th or the 22nd—which do you prefer?' That will be the date of your next call—whichever date the particular client chooses. The selection is entirely up to him. You'll jot down the answers, naturally, on the file there."

"Yes," returned Anthony laconically. "Or else commit them to memory."

Trevor gave him a look of searching inquiry. "Er—yes," he replied, "provided you don't slip up on any of them. We don't tolerate mistakes in this outfit, do we, Brodhurst? You may as well know that at the very beginning. If an agent of ours does happen to make a mistake, we are compelled to take action. We have no other possible course. To protect ourselves, my dear Lotherington, if for no other object. Can you blame us? In fact we usually transfer him to our Nuremberg office. That's the form the punishment takes. Where conditions of employment aren't anything like as comfortable as they are here."

He broke off and chuckled but Anthony heard and shrank from the cold-bloodedness in the chuckle. Brodhurst laughed openly.

"Nuremberg," he repeated—"that's the idea—certainly."

Anthony judged it prudent, at this juncture, to ask a question. "And what is my procedure in the event of the proper replies not forthcoming?"

"Ah," said Trevor, "I've been waiting for you to ask me that question. Good for you! In that event, you will make one remark, and one remark only. You will say 'Good morning'—if it happens to be morning of course—and then this, 'There are many virtuous maidens in Nuremberg.' Having said that, you will not say another word but leave the restaurant immediately. Believe me, the person to whom that remark may be addressed will understand your meaning perfectly."

"I see," returned Anthony. "And how many of this Z class have I to visit?"

"I really couldn't say without reference to that book. But you have the file there in your hands. You can easily tell. Count them now and see for yourself."

Anthony turned over the foolscap leaves of the file. As he turned them he counted. "Thirty-two," he announced eventually. "There are 32 Z contacts."

"Good," said Trevor, with a nod of the head. "32—eh? That's rather more than I should have said if I'd been asked. They're probably pretty well scattered over the Midlands so I'll give you a week to make the total cover. Say a week from to-day. Are you in agreement with that, Brodhurst?"

"A week? For thirty-two cases? Cutting it pretty fine, aren't you? Oh—yes, judging from previous experience that should be just about right." Brodhurst's reply had been given immediately.

"Good. I'm glad you agree with me. Both of us shouldn't be wrong. Right-o, then, Lotherington. Report back here a week from to-day. We shall be in a position to tell then, what sort of an agent you're likely to make. You ought to bring back a tidy sum from those thirty-two cases. Provided you handle them in the right way. There's a good deal in that, you know. Probably more than you're inclined to think. The novice always thinks it's easier than it is. Before he gets the necessary experience. Afterwards, when he's been blooded as it were, he finds it a vastly different proposition. Personality and initiative weigh a great deal. Experience counts everywhere."

Rather surprisingly, Brodhurst added his tribute. "That's very true. There's no argument about it. Capt. Trevor never spoke sounder words. We see the truth of that many times over in the course of every year. And you'll find it so, Lotherington, directly you start in on the job."

Anthony rose. "I think I'm clear."

Trevor put up his hand. "Just a minute, my dear b-boy, before you make your personal observations and also your farewell oration. You observe the extent to which we are trusting you. You will have and hold in your possession a considerable sum of money belonging to me. On that collection—whatever it is, there's absolutely no limit—I am willing to pay you five per cent. That will be anything between £150 and £200, if my opinion's worth anything. Not bad for less than a week's work, Lotherington? What do you say yourself? If, on the other hand, you double-cross me and decamp with my money—an alluring prospect which may appeal to you—I promise you that I shall have you followed, I shall run you to earth, and life, shortly after your discovery, will, I assure you, cease to interest you."

Anthony started to speak but again Trevor stopped him with uplifted hand. "Let me finish, if you please. I don't think any of that need be seriously feared. I trust you because I am satisfied that you have been sent to me from an approved source. My agents invariably satisfy themselves as to a candidate's credentials. They know perfectly well that I am prepared to employ the very best—and only the very best. That's all. I have nothing more to say. You can talk."

"Thank you. As I said, I think I'm clear. I take five per cent of all I collect, provided I hand it over to you in a week's time. I shall remember the details of your various instructions. But there's one point on which I should like a little more light thrown. What happens after I return a week from to-day?"

Trevor smiled and turned to Brodhurst. "What do you think of him, Ralph? In a ruddy hurry, isn't he? Wants to run before he can walk—eh? Ah well—it's not a bad quality when all's said and done." He came back to Anthony. "My dear Lotherington, please understand this. There are other letters in the alphabet for which I need representation. And the general process continues—it doesn't summarily cease to function. Does that information satisfy you?"

"Thank you. I accept the underlying suggestion. That's all I wanted to know." He looked round the room with studied deliberation. "Unusual place you have here, Trevor."

"You think so?"

"I most certainly do. Don't know that I've ever been in a show quite like it."

"Don't suppose you have," said Trevor, with a wealth of meaning in his voice. "Bit of an optimist, aren't you? Do you expect Middleton Halls to grow on every bough? Because if you do—you can take it from me that they don't. Have another drink. Brodhurst—fill up Lotherington's glass. Not our form—neglecting our guests. Not done, Brodhurst. Definitely not done!"

Brodhurst gave Anthony another Scotch. Anthony, however, still hoped against hope that Trevor would respond to his cast and show him over Middleton Hall. But he was destined to disappointment. To his inward annoyance, Trevor deliberately changed the subject.

"To-day week, then, Lotherington. That's an arrangement between us. Till then, the best of luck."

"Thank you," returned Anthony quietly. He realized that he would have to accept the rebuff. To come again, in the same vein, with no appreciable interval of time, would be to court disaster, and that, he, certainly at this stage, must *not* risk! Five minutes later he said "good night" to both Trevor and Brodhurst and commenced making his way back to the "Black Horse" and comparative tranquillity.

3

THE LAST LETTER OF THE ALPHABET

ANTHONY welcomed Andrew MacMorran into his private room of the "Black Horse". MacMorran's face, hitherto clouded, cleared when he saw Anthony waiting for him. Anthony grinned at him as they shook hands.

"No deception, Andrew. It's the man himself. Same gentleman going the other way. Unharmed and free from the scars of conflict. But sit down. I've prevailed on the management to serve a couple of lunches in here for us. As I indicated when we were last together. While we're disposing of the grub, I'll talk to you. Tales of far Kashmir, old man. I'll give 'em a ring."

Anthony rang the bell and his lunches were duly brought, the table laid and the meal started. The inspector stated that he had not yet been as far as 'Christopher's'—he had not had the time. Anthony told the story of his visit to Trevor at Middleton Hall and of the arrangements Trevor had made with him. MacMorran listened attentively until Anthony had finished the account.

"Well, there you are, Andrew," said the latter. "What do you make of it? That the answer's a lemon?"

MacMorran grunted. "The whole affair seems crazy to me. Let's have a look at that file of papers Trevor gave you. It's on the cards that I may be able to make something of them."

Anthony handed him the file. The inspector turned them over carefully. "Zancomi's, Stratford-upon-Avon; Zappelli's, Dudley; Zaruni's, Kidderminster; Zerusti's, Banbury; Zinkomi's, Bicester . . . yes, they appear to be in alphabetical order. All restaurants, or eating houses, I presume, from the tenor of your conversation with Trevor. It's a racket of some kind, of course. That goes without saying. And your job is to collect the doings in each instance. But what are these various café proprietors dubbing up for? That's the question that bothers me. Counterfeit notes that have been supplied to them by Trevor? From Middleton Hall, which he's using as H.Q.? Seems to me that's something like it." He looked extremely grave as he spoke. "I feel that I'm groping in the dark, Mr. Bathurst, and I don't cotton on to that position at all. Don't like it! It definitely disturbs my peace of mind when I'm in that condition. How do you feel about it yourself?"

"Much the same as you do, Andrew. Only more so. At the same time, I think my way is fairly clear, don't you?"

"You mean to go ahead as you've been directed and see what comes of it?"

"That's the idea. Don't you think it's a perfectly sound one?" Anthony waited for MacMorran's answer. It came.

"Don't suppose you can do better. As things stand. Keep your eyes open though, all the time, and let me know at once anything you think I should know. I'll leave that to your judgment. What will you do? Contact the various people in the order they are here?"

He tapped the file of papers with his forefinger. Anthony nodded.

"Yes, I don't think I can do better than that. I propose to work in the order they are there."

"O.K. And you'll be back here in a week's time. Is that the idea?"

"Either that, or before, some time. Depends on how I fare and on what I manage to find out. Agreed?"

"Yes. And I'll tell you this before we part company. I think I'm prepared for almost anything."

"Like that, is it, Andrew? Well—we shall see. And now you can do the disappearing trick and make yourself scarce."

When MacMorran had taken his departure, Anthony decided to walk to the railway station and look up the trains to Stratford-upon-Avon, As far as he could see, there was no reason to be advanced against his making an evening call at the establishment known as "Zancomi's." If there were a convenient train in the afternoon he was of the opinion that he should catch it. He hated delay in any shape or form and he was eager to tackle the problem which, indirectly, Trevor had handed to him. Examination of the time-table showed a train for Stratford-upon-Avon which left Wroxeter at 4.17. He would have time to return to the "Black Horse," settle his account and catch the train in comfort. On the point of straightening himself after bending to read the details on the time-table he was conscious of two figures passing close to him. One of the voices seemed particularly familiar to him and struck a chord of recent memory.

Turning quickly, he was able to recognize the two figures as those of Brodhurst and the man, Stanhope, whom he had met at 'Christopher's' a few evenings previously. His ear caught what Brodhurst was saying. Anthony heard him say, "You'll go from Liverpool St.

Margretham's a few miles from Chelmsford and the bundle will be placed in your arms. You and the girl will know what to do with it."

A second later and the two men were out of earshot. Anthony rubbed the ridge of his jaw. What was the association for which he was striving? Margretham! That was it! It had been mentioned in Regan's diary. No, it hadn't! What was the connection? Within the space of a couple of seconds, he had it. It was the address with which MacMorran had supplied him of the Sir Curtis Littlehales whose name it was that had been entered in the diary of Terence Regan. So Stanhope was on a journey there! And the bundle would be placed in his arms! Here, communed Anthony with himself, was food for thought. There are bundles and bundles!

As he walked slowly back to the "Black Horse," he thought matters carefully over. What was the link between Middleton Hall and Sir Curtis Littlehales at Margretham in the county of Essex? If I knew that, he agreed with himself, I should know a hell of a lot. He reached the inn and went upstairs to his room to pack his suitcase. In the action of tossing a pair of pyjamas into the case an idea came to him and he stood there, in the middle of the room, while the full realization of this idea flooded through his brain. Yes . . . that might well be the solution of the problem that had been troubling him for so long. The enormity of it almost made him gasp. And yet—! Anthony stood there, a little uncertain as to the best course for him to pursue. He himself was handicapped. For one thing he wasn't altogether free. He had work to do which was imminent. He had already decided to travel to Stratford-upon-Avon that same afternoon. And Inspector MacMorran had concurred with that arrangement. After a few moments' intensive thought, Anthony resolved to telephone to the inspector right away. He knew where to find him. He had heard MacMorran arrange to be with Inspector Foster at the police station that afternoon.

Having come to this resolve, therefore, he quickly made his way downstairs to the telephone. Events proved that his belief was right. MacMorran was at a conference with the local inspector. The "Yard" professional was, to put it mildly, surprised to hear Anthony's voice at the other end of the line. In addition, he said as much.

"Is that you, Mr. Bathurst? You're absolutely the last person I expected to hear from. In view of what you said to me at midday, You haven't forgotten, I'll be bound. What's that? . . . oh, I agree, as you say, circumstances certainly alter cases. What? . . . Ingot's Court, Margretham, Essex? What about it? That's right I sent you that information myself. After you asked for it. Yes . . . I remember it perfectly. The residence of Sir Curtis Littlehales. That's right. If you say so, I'll have inquiries made. It's not so easy as you might think. It's one of those things, you know, that's more easily talked about than actually done. So awkward to place the field. What? . . . all right then. I'll promise to see to it for you and I'll report any findings when we next meet. Will that suit you in the . . . yes . . . yes . . . don't worry about that . . . cheer-o, then, for the present."

Having delivered his message to MacMorran, Anthony hung up, went along to the receptionist and settled his bill. Ten minutes later he was on his way to the railway station.

4

PLOUGHING THE SANDS

THE journey from Wroxeter to Stratford-upon-Avon proved uneventful. Anthony was able to fix up for bed and breakfast at the "Singing Swan." After a quick and shortish meal, he sallied forth into the streets of the old Warwickshire town to find the establishment operated in its High St. by the gentleman known as Zancomi. It looked both good class and prosperous. Anthony pushed open the door and walked in. There were white-clothed tables, well patronized, and three or four waiters in conventional dress hovering between them. Anthony walked to the counter on the right-hand side at the entrance to the restaurant. A girl stood behind it.

"Yes?" she said interrogatively, as Anthony approached her. "I should like a word, if you don't mind, with Mr. Zancomi, the proprietor. Is he in?"

"Yes," replied the girl—"the governor's in all right. I'll go and fetch him for you. Wait a minute, please."

Anthony waited while the girl made contact with Zancomi. Eventually, she returned with a short, greasy-looking man well on in years who eyed Anthony by no means warmly.

"What do you want, if you please," he opened uncompromisingly.

"May I see you for a few minutes privately?" asked Anthony.

"Is it important . . . or can't it wait," said Signor Zancomi with something very much akin to a scowl.

Anthony smiled his best smile. "It is important. Extremely so—in fact. You will understand how important when you hear."

"All right. You will come please into my private room, then? This way, if you please."

Anthony followed Zancomi into a room at the back of the restaurant. It had deep red paper on the walls and was evidently used as a counting-house. "You take a seat—eh?" said the restaurant-proprietor.

"Thank you," said Anthony.

Zancomi wasted no time whatever. "You come on the business—eh?"

"Yes. I was asked to call on you, Signor Zancomi, by the gentleman whom you and I know as 'The Skipper'." Anthony stopped and waited for Zancomi's response. But of verbal rejoinder there was none. A strange look passed over the restaurant proprietor's face. Anthony was unable to assess it adequately. He was considerably puzzled. He wasn't sure whether the look was one of surprise or of stealthy cunning. He decided, therefore, to go ahead with the business of the evening. He lit a cigarette deliberately, waved out the match, placed the stub in an ash-tray that was on the small desk-table, leant back in his chair and said, "A great deal of profit can be made on caviare."

Zancomi regarded him critically for some seconds before he replied. "That depends," was his reply when it eventually did come.

"Oh," thought Anthony, "so you're not playing." He rose. "In that case, then, Signor Zancomi, I need detain you no longer. Good evening. There are many virtuous maidens in Nuremberg."

Zancomi also rose and stood staring at him. "I do not doubt it for a moment. And good evening to you. Pah!"

Anthony walked back into the restaurant proper and heard the connecting-door slammed to behind him. Back in the street he smiled to himself. He had certainly drawn a blank at his first port of call. Well—he wasn't to blame—he'd faithfully carried out the instructions which Trevor had given to him. Examination of his Z file had elicited the fact that there was another possible call in this same town. At "Zulani's"—the address of which was 8, Mop Parade. He would endeavour to kill two birds with one stone.

Anthony set out to find this second restaurant. Twenty minutes' tour of inquiry brought him to the appropriate locality. In appearance it was by no means so pretentious as the establishment presided over by Signor Zancomi. In fact, not to put too fine a point on it, its externals were far removed from a condition of cleanliness and certainly presented a most pressing invitation to Anthony (and probably many others) to keep away. But he entered. The door-bell heralded his arrival with a discordant clang. On the counter stood a tray of fly-blown cakes and a large urn with brass taps. Steam in clouds was issuing therefrom. A black-haired woman greeted him. Her arms were clasped avidly across her ample bosom.

All breasts and dirt, thought Anthony as he faced her. "Good evening," he said, and to himself in the same breath, "in for a penny in for a pound."

"Good evening to you, sir." He saw that her dark, heavy pouched eyes were not unkindly. In them were homeliness and sincerity.

"Can I see you privately for a few moments? On a matter of business."

She looked vacantly round the coffee-shop. "There is no one here."

"True! That is to say at the moment. But there may be customers in any second, may there not? Or is business so bad?"

The woman still looked as though she only half-comprehended what Anthony was saying. "Business is ver' bad," she said at length, "but perhaps not so bad as that would make out. I have a little r-room at the back 'ere. If you will come in, please, sir. Is it more of the forms to fill up? 'Ave I done them all wr-rong? Because if that is so, I am not too—"

Anthony shook his head in reassurance as he followed the dark woman into the little room. She motioned him to a chair.

"No, madam—you need have no fears with regard to the filling up of any more forms. That is to say, as far as I am concerned. On the contrary I am visiting you on strictly business terms." He bent forward and lowered his voice. "I have come from 'The Skipper'."

As in the case of his call on Zancomi, he waited and watched to see the effect of this announcement. But again, it elicited no obvious response, either by deed or word. The woman Zulani stared at him. She was either extremely cunning, he thought, or an excellent actress. Anthony went ahead. He crossed one leg over the other as he sat there.

"A great deal of profit can be made on caviare, Signora Zulani."

"Caviare," she said incredulously, "caviare would look str-range on my counter with the tea and the cheese-cakes. Surely a gentleman like you does not need telling that."

Anthony bit his lip. He felt many times the village idiot. He rose at once. "I will go then. There is no point in my staying. There are many virtuous maidens in Nuremberg."

The Zulani rose heavily from her chair. He could hear the disordered breathing as she got on her feet. "I 'ave never bin there. Milano, yes, and Messina, but never to the place you mention."

Anthony raised his hat. "Good night—I am sorry."

"Good night, sir," he heard come after him as he left the shop. Failure the second! Anthony felt more than a little mystified. He decided to sleep on the problem and tackle a similar proposition at Banbury on the following morning. He had never had a problem yet which wasn't the better for sleeping on whenever it assumed unpleasant proportions. But two lamentable failures in one day—!

5

NO CAKE AT BANBURY

ANTHONY entered the establishment, belonging as its front showed for the benefit of a curious world to P. Zerusti, at almost exactly half-past eleven on the following morning. A man of entirely different type from Zancomi came smilingly to meet and to greet him.

He was young, slim, graceful in his movements, fair-haired and smooth-skinned, and boasted a very trim fair moustache.

"Good morning," said Anthony. This looked more like the real McCoy, he thought to himself. "Have I the pleasure of talking to Signor Zerusti?"

The young man smiled and bowed. "Why, yes, of course. I am Paolo Zerusti. What can I do for you?"

Anthony met his smile with another of his own. "I want to talk with you for a few minutes if you can spare me the time. On a strict matter of business."

The young man smiled again, showing a row of beautifully white teeth. Then he looked round his restaurant. It was reasonably full. Some coffee "elevenses" were still remaining at their respective tables and a handful of early lunchers had already put in an appearance. Anthony realized what he was thinking.

"I'm afraid not in here. It won't exactly be convenient. For either of us. Shall we say—a little more private rendezvous?"

The young man made a treble of his smiles and nodded "Why yes, of course. In my own private little sitting-room. At the back here. What could be better?"

With a dramatic flourish of the arms he invited Anthony to enter a room at the end of the restaurant proper. Anthony followed him into it. It was comfortably furnished and gave eloquent signs, Anthony thought, that Paolo Zerusti was running a highly remunerative little business in this old Oxfordshire town. Anthony was gestured into a spacious arm-chair. He appropriately sank his long form into it.

"Now," said Paolo Zerusti, "we are comfortable, are we not? Which is as it should be. Is it not so? Now—we can talk the business! And plenty of it, if it is good and to our mutual liking. I am at your service, sir, and shall be pleased to listen to you. Proceed, if you please."

"This," said Anthony to himself once again, "is the real thing." He addressed himself to Paolo Zerusti. "You have probably guessed by now from whom I have come. For convenience shall I allude to him as 'The Skipper'."

At last, thought Anthony! But Paolo was either ultra-wary or definitely not swallowing any bait that there might be floating about.

"The Skipper," was all he said in reply and his tone conveyed little or nothing. Anthony decided to go ahead on his instructed lines.

"A great deal of profit can be made on caviare."

Paolo's face brightened perceptibly. "Oh, I see! I understand. You are what they call on the r-road? You travel in the sardines and the caviare? Ah—I see. It is now clear to me."

A sickening feeling invaded Anthony's throat. Here, facing him, was egregious failure No. 3! What the hell was wrong—anyway? This was the bundle as far as he was concerned. He'd get out of here forthwith. He proceeded to put his resolve into effect.

"No," he said, rising from the depths of the arm-chair, "you've got me all wrong. I am not trying to sell you anything. I think that I've probably been misdirected and come to the wrong shop. There are many virtuous maidens in Nuremberg."

The sun and the courtier-like smiles had vanished from Zerusti's face. "I do not understand you. Perhaps that will not be to my benefit. Who knows? Who cares?" He shrugged his slim shoulders.

Anthony waited in the shadowy hope that there would be an amplification of the reply. But none was forthcoming. He realized that he had performed his hat-trick of failures and that the only course he could adopt now, intelligently, would be to take his fare-well of Paolo Zerusti, as he had of Signor Zancomi and the lady named Zulani. Which he did. Zerusti bowed him out with punc-tilious ceremony and exaggerated courtesy.

"These misunderstandings do come," said Paolo, "to all of us from time to time. It is life! There is no blame attached. It is just one of those unfortunate happenings which can't be helped. Good morning to you, sir."

"Good morning," replied Anthony, "and many thanks for your forbearance."

He walked back deep in thought and resolved to return to Wroxe-ter immediately. His thoughts were the reverse of pleasant for he had considered that a little daylight had begun to reach him. The first thing, he decided, upon his return, was a conference with MacMorran. Anthony scratched his cheek. Trevor, evidently, was going to prove no mean adversary and was without a doubt more formidable than he had previously realized. Anthony walked to the station and caught the first train back to Wroxeter. On the journey he turned over many things in his mind.

6

MACMORRAN THINKS AGAIN

"I THOUGHT you said a week's time," said MacMorran, as he entered Anthony's room at the "Black Horse." "What's the idea of the speedy return? Am I to understand that the problem's solved and that success is seated on your shoulders?"

Anthony shook his head. "Far from it, Andrew! Let me explain. I've been back here in this town exactly forty minutes. I was able to come along here and book my room again. And as I wanted to see you very badly, Andrew, I phoned you at once. And on the contrary, in reply to your last question, I regret to say that the problem's a long way off being solved, and that we're almost back to where we started."

MacMorran shifted in his chair and began to fill his pipe. "I see. Tell me—what did you pick up?"

"Nothing."

"Nothing? Then why does our wanderer return so soon? And empty-handed at that? Why the sudden loss of form?"

Anthony grinned at MacMorran's pleasantries. "You wait till you hear, you old sinner."

"That's just what I am doing. Say your piece then."

"One thing emerges from my little activity, Andrew—and one thing only."

"What's that?"

"That I fell for it. I swallowed hook, line and sinker. Friends Trevor and Brodhurst, of Middleton Hall, played me for a 'sucker.' And as easy as kiss your hand! It must have been as simple for them as taking money from a blind man."

MacMorran wrinkled his brow when he heard this statement. "How do you mean, exactly?" he asked.

"Why—just this. The whole thing was 'baloney'."

"But how do you—"

Anthony intervened with scant ceremony. "My journeys relevant to the Z file."

MacMorran shook his head. "I don't—"

"Not one of the people on whom I called, knew the first thing about the 'Skipper'—Monsieur Trevor."

The inspector frowned. "You had better tell me the whole story. With regard to the various contacts, I mean."

"I suppose I had. Here goes then." Anthony described his calls at the establishments of Zancomi, Zulani, and Zerusti and the respective receptions thereat. MacMorran listened attentively, his fingers pulling thoughtfully at his upper lip all the time.

"Funny," he said at length. "Not funny ha-ha—funny peculiar, I mean. Looks to me as though you're about right. They drew a certain amount of waste liquid from your constitution."

"I can't see any other explanation, Andrew. That's frank. I wish I could believe otherwise."

"Let's have a look at the towns you visited. I've the shadow of an idea. Stratford-upon-Avon and Banbury. Counties of Warwickshire and Oxfordshire. Wonder if there could be anything in that. Where's your list again? The file."

Anthony produced the Z file for MacMorran's inspection. MacMorran glanced through it with some care. Anthony could see that he was working something out.

"I've an idea," he said eventually. "May be nothing in it. On the other hand it may be worth trying. Suppose you have a shot at another county."

"Why?" asked Anthony, "for what reason? I love to be logical."

MacMorran shook his head. "Couldn't tell you—so don't press me. Couldn't even pretend to tell you. Just a hunch—that's all."

"I'm not attracted by illogical hunches—never have been—and over that I'll be perfectly frank. Still—I'll hear you out. You've often been patient with me when I've fancied myself. Which county?"

MacMorran stared at the paper on the wall. "What other county is near here?"

"Worcestershire."

"Good! Try Worcester, then. Got any Worcester lines in the file?"

Anthony leant over and pulled the file towards him. He turned over the pages. "Yes. Three. Two at Kidderminster and the other in the town of Worcester itself."

"What names are they?"

"Zatuni and Zelli at Kidderminster and Zocali at Worcester."

"Well—to please me—try one of them, I don't care which. Pay your money and take your choice."

"All right," replied Anthony a little hesitantly. "I'll try the Worcester one. Zocali's. And woe betide you, Andrew, if you've put me on another 'stumer.' I warn you, you'll never hear the last of it."

"I'll chance that," said MacMorran, "it's always paid me to play my 'hunches'." He amended the statement. "Well—almost always."

"Very likely, I don't mind that. But there's a difference. This time you aren't playing them. You're getting me to."

"That's all right. You won't notice that difference. When will you go? First thing to-morrow morning?"

"If you think I should, I'm quite willing."

"You can go by bus. There's an hourly service from here. You want a 'Midland Red.' I'll go down to the bar and get a time-table. They'll be bound to have one there. Wait up here and I'll bring it."

MacMorran went and Anthony waited for him. The inspector was back within a few minutes. "Here you are," he said. "There's a bus leaves here at 11.5 which reaches Worcester a few minutes before two o'clock. How will that suit you?"

"All right," replied Anthony—"we'll have a drink on it. But, don't forget, Andrew—it's your hunch."

CHAPTER VI

I

MACMORRAN'S HUNCH

ANTHONY caught his "Midland Red" bus at five minutes past eleven on the following morning. It was crowded with passengers and he was compelled to join a queue some twenty minutes before the time of the scheduled start. Neither then, nor during the day previous, did he see any sign of Trevor, Brodhurst or Stanhope.

The bus ran through some remarkably pretty country and the orchards on each side of the route were heavy with fruit.

Worcester was reached at almost exactly two o'clock and the "Crown" provided him with an excellent cold lunch. He then considered the question of finding "Zocali's." The address given on the file Trevor had supplied to him was Burrows Hill. Inquiry of a uniformed constable in Broad St. elicited the information that "Zocali's" was located not far from the cathedral and near the river. Anthony made his way in the appropriate direction and was quickly rewarded with the discovery of a small street which led down to the Severn and which was inscribed with the name of "Burrows Hill." He saw that "Zocali's" was a small café on the right hand side. In external appearance it was most like the establishment of Zulani, of those upon which he had already called. As Anthony entered, the bell rang with a sharp, tinny sound. A little dark man, very obviously an Italian, stood behind the counter and smiled at the incoming customer.

"Good afternoon," Anthony announced himself.

"Good afternoon, sir."

Anthony walked straight to the counter. As he did so, an idea flamed into his brain. There was a glass on the counter, right to his hand. Good Lord—why hadn't he thought of it before? He put fingers round the glass and moved it in the circular fashion he had seen employed in "Christopher's" Bar at Wroxeter. The little Italian watched him curiously.

'Now,' said Anthony to himself, 'for the final test. I won't bother about getting him to take me into another room. I'll chance it here where I am.' He smiled at the little man. "I'm here from the 'Skipper'."

The little man nodded. Anthony crossed the Rubicon. "A great deal of profit can be made on caviare."

He waited for the fitting rejoinder. But alas—it was not to be. The little man smiled with his tiny currant-like eyes and emitted a sound which might have been "yes." On the other hand, with equal reason, it might not. Indeed, it might have been anything.

"There are many virtuous," begun Anthony—and then he broke off in ignominious surrender. "Give me a pot of tea, please, and a buttered scone, will you."

"Of course, sir—if you will please sit at one of the tables over there."

Anthony sat—and within a few moments was dealing with the tea and scone which the little Italian had brought him. His thoughts were bitter and his inclinations almost vindictive. So much for MacMorran and his hunch! He had made another entirely fruitless journey and was no nearer to any understanding of Trevor's business than he had been before. Anthony drank his tea, ate his scone, cursed Trevor and all his works, and shook the dust of Worcester from his feet. Giovanni Zocali watched him leave the café and then continued to watch him from behind a curtain in his window as he made his way down the street. "I do not understand," he muttered to himself.

Anthony was in touch with MacMorran again within an hour of arriving back in Wroxeter. The inspector came to Anthony's room at the "Black Horse" agog to hear the news.

"Well," he inquired jovially, "was I right?"

Anthony grinned at him. "So right, Andrew, that your score was exactly none in a hundred. Neither one more, nor one less. I extend my most hearty 'congratters.' Talk about a 'hunch,' and inspiration—well—words fail me."

MacMorran pursed his lips. "So you drew another blank—eh?"

"The great-grandfather of all blanks. Zocali was akin to all the others. He was the complete *Je ne sais pas.*"

"I'm surprised. I thought I was on to something. I really did. Funny!"

"That's what you said before. Sorry I can't agree with you."

The inspector sat silent for a few moments. "Don't know quite what to say," came from him eventually.

"I'm not amazed to hear you confess that. But I've got something to say, Andrew, and you can listen to me while I'm saying it. During my gaudy trip to Worcester and back—via your pestilent 'Midland Red'—I had a certain amount of time on my hands for contemplative meditation. Part of it I spent in a slap-up banquet at our friend Zocali's."

MacMorran raised his eyebrows. "I shouldn't have expected—"

"Pot of tea and buttered scone, Andrew. On the lavish scale! I was able to think certain things."

"Such as?"

Anthony spoke slowly. "I have come to the unhappy conclusion, Andrew, that not only has Trevor played me for a 'sucker,' but that he was aware of my real identity all the time. Have you got that, Andrew?"

The inspector surveyed him with a look of misgiving. "What grounds have you for saying that? Surely you don't—"

Anthony's eyes were eloquent. "I've endeavoured to cast my mind back to the entire conversation I had with Trevor on the occasion of our interviews. I've tried to recall, as far as I am able, the exact words which passed between us."

MacMorran nodded in approval. "Excellent idea. If you can do it with anything approaching reasonable accuracy. Can you?"

"I think that I have. As you say—reasonably!"

"With what result?"

"With the result that I'm distinctly worried. Because I've been forced to the conclusion, Andrew, that on one occasion, *Trevor was within an ace of addressing me as Bathurst*! Remember that I was known to him as Lotherington."

MacMorran opened his eyes. "What makes you think that?"

"Well—the devil of it is I can't remember the exact words. But on the occasion I'm thinking of he broke off rather precipitately and used a word beginning with a 'B' which somehow to my ear, at the time, didn't *seem* to be the word he had been intending to use when he commenced the sentence. I only wish I could recall it. But for the moment, it eludes me. It will come back, I don't doubt."

"It didn't convey anything at the time, then?"

"Merely what I told you a moment ago. I was off my guard and not paying proper attention, I suppose. Now that I've gone over the ground again, I can see a certain significance which escaped me at the time. *Peccavi*, Andrew!"

"Yes," said MacMorran, "and it's found you out, I'm afraid. The point is what are we going to do about it?"

"Agreed. What disturbs me is the unadulterated confidence the man must have in himself. He knows who I am which must indicate to him that he is suspected in some way—but does it worry him? Not on your life. He ignores all the unpleasant possibilities as far as he himself is concerned and calmly dispatches me on a fool's errand. Pretty cool, you know."

MacMorran grinned. "Pretty cool, as you say. I feel that I've got to hand it to him."

"It's evident that he considers that we've got nothing on him. So much so that he snaps his fingers at us."

MacMorran nodded. "In other words, although he may be guilty of having committed two murders, he's sure in his own mind that it will be impossible for us to pin them on to him. That's what it looks like to me."

"We'll see about that," remarked Anthony with grim determination, "he laughs best who laughs last—and I shall devote a lot of personal attention to that little matter of 'pinning'." He fell into a reverie. The only sound in the room was the ticking of the travelling clock on the mantelpiece. It was Anthony's own and he invariably took it with him on his travels. Suddenly Anthony came to action again.

"Andrew—I've thought of something. Something I asked for your co-operation over. Sir Curtis Littlehales's place in the heart of Essex. Ingot's Court—Margretham. Any news thereon or thereabouts?"

MacMorran shook his head. "None at all—up to the moment of my leaving to-day to come along here."

"Whom did you put on to it?"

"Evershed. Chatterton's otherwise engaged."

"He's pretty sound, isn't he?"

"Who? Evershed? Rather! Sound as a bell. No flies on Sammy Evershed—you can take it from me."

"And he's reported nothing?"

"Nothing at all. Not a 'squeak' of any kind whatsoever. But if there *is* anything fishy, you can bet your bottom dollar Evershed'll get on to it."

Anthony's eyes were far away. "Nuremberg, Andrew! In the conversation between Trevor and Brodhurst! What the hell's Nuremberg got to do with it? That's been worrying me for days now."

The inspector scratched his cheek. "Germany—eh? May be it all traces back to Herr Hun. It wouldn't be the first crime that has."

Anthony was silent. MacMorran was quick to observe this. "You don't think so? Judging by the lack of enthusiasm you show for my idea?"

Again Anthony was slow to answer the inspector. "You may be right, Andrew. And yet—" He paused.

"And yet—what?"

"Somehow I don't feel disposed to agree with you."

"I don't see why not! Nuremberg's in Germany, can one think?"

"Don't know! And that's a fact. Candidly, I don't get it."

"According to my memory of your account of the Trevor conversations, Nuremberg was mentioned in two connections. I think that's correct, isn't it?"

"Quite true, Andrew. There was talk of unsuccessful agents being transferred to Nuremberg and then there was the association of the 'virtuous maidens.' Those same maidens with whom nobody wants anything to do."

MacMorran grinned. "May be because of their virtue."

"I'm surprised at you, Andrew. You're a disgrace to a long line of Presbyterian forebears."

MacMorran laughed with him. "No," said Anthony, continuing the main line of the discussion, "I've got an idea firmly embedded in my brain that the Nuremberg association is not a direct one. There's something subtle about it. The meaning's hidden, enigmatic, cryptic. It's up to you and me to discover what that meaning is. I expect if we could tumble to it we should have gone a long way towards solving our entire problem. I shall have to make an investigation into the history of our German city. All I can remember at the moment is that it had a toymaker connected with it.

MacMorran shook his head. "I never heard tell of that, Mr. Bathurst. I thought it was famous for the manufacture of watches. They used to call 'em 'Nuremberg eggs'—to the best of my belief."

"Watches and eggs—eh? Neither of them gets us any forrader, I'm afraid. I can't connect the Trevor activities with either of those articles. Much too innocent. Wish I could. Might make things a shade easier."

Anthony had scarcely completed his sentence when there came a light tap on the door of his room. One of the chambermaids stood outside.

"Yes?" Anthony asked her. "Do you want me?"

"No, sir. But have you a gentleman with you by the name of MacMorran? That's the name I was to told to ask for, sir."

"Who wants him?" demanded Anthony with an element of suspicion in his voice.

"He's wanted on the telephone, sir, downstairs in the vestibule."

"O.K.," returned Anthony. "I'll send him down there at once."

"Thank you, sir. I'll tell them to wait till he comes." She turned and went downstairs.

"Andrew," said Anthony, "you're wanted on the phone downstairs. Don't know who it is that wants you."

"Must be Foster. At the station. He's the only person outside yourself who would know where to find me."

MacMorran left the room and hurried downstairs. Anthony stood at the door of his room and watched him go. The inspector was away for a matter of some minutes. When he came back to Anthony, waiting by the door, his face held a curiously strained expression. He passed by Anthony and entered the room.

"Come inside," he said quietly, "and shut the door."

"What is it, Andrew?"

"News from Evershed. Relayed to me by this local chap, Foster."

"I think," said Anthony quietly and deliberately, "that I may be in a position to anticipate you."

"How do you mean, man?"

"Just this," went on Anthony doggedly, "and I'll apologize in advance if I'm barking up the wrong tree. Your news, you say, is from Evershed. It concerns Sir Curtis Littlehales. More precisely it concerns that gentleman's daughter—the three-year-old Imogen."

MacMorran nodded slow acquiescence. "You're right! I'll hand it to you—"

"Never mind the explanations now, Andrew. Or the bouquets. They can wait for a more convenient time. What is it—the Lindbergh baby?"

"You've hit it, Mr. Bathurst. The little girl is missing. She was kidnapped from her bedroom some time during last night."

Anthony rubbed his hands and the gleam came into his eyes. "Right, Andrew! Now at long last we know exactly where we are. And I shall be able to measure swords with Capt. Lionel Trevor. Minus any complications concerning the letter 'Z'!"

2

THE NEWS FROM EVERSHED

MACMORRAN watched Anthony intently as he strode backwards and forwards across the room. There was no doubt that he meant business.

"If there's one wickedness, Andrew, that makes my blood boil this is that one. From now onwards Friend Trevor and Company have to contend with me! Till one of us goes under. I'll see him through with this to the bitter end. Give me the details, Andrew, please. Or as many as you were able to pick up from Foster."

"Evershed's story is roughly this. As you may expect, the child is normally in the care of a nurse. By name, Amy Otway. The child was put to bed yesterday evening at half-past six, which is her usual time, so Evershed says. The Otway woman sleeps in an adjoining room to the little girl's bedroom and there is a connecting door. This morning, as nothing was heard of either the nurse or her charge, Lady Littlehales went to their rooms. The nurse was found bound and gagged in her own room and under the influence of a powerful drug, and the child's cot was empty. A letter was found on the pillow. It was addressed to Sir Curtis Littlehales. These are the terms of the letter as far as I am able to remember them. Foster tells me that there was neither date nor address on it. 'Dear Sir Curtis, In these hard times one is compelled to take certain actions even though it may be against one's will and strongly at variance with one's inclination.'"

MacMorran broke off. "I'm giving you the gist of it. It went on like this. 'I wonder what the value is that you place upon the safety—or perhaps the actual existence—of your charming little daughter. The fact that she is your only child may even enhance that valuation. At least I may perhaps be pardoned for hoping so.'"

Anthony interrupted—almost savagely. "Sounds like Trevor. Sorry, Andrew. Go on, old man."

"The letter went on again to say this." MacMorran's words came slowly. "'For the moment, however, permit me to allay any fears that you may be entertaining on her account. The little girl is in safe hands and I can assure you that she will be well cared for. But as I said "for the moment." I am unable to make promises beyond that. Any attempt on your part to communicate with the police would inevitably mean that she would pass over—shall we say—to a happier existence. I am more than confident that this is positively the last thing that you would wish to happen. But let me get to business! If you will bring—or send—a parcel containing £10,000 (ten thousand pounds) in notes which must not be marked in any way, to the barrier outside No. 2 platform at Paddington station on Saturday morning next at 11 o'clock your daughter will be returned to you within 24 hours. You or your messenger that represents you must come alone and must wear a red rose in the coat and carry a brown attaché case, which will hold your parcel. *The* parcel! My agent will inquire concerning the right platform for Kidderminster and after handing over the parcel you must not move from the spot for at least a quarter of an hour. But don't forget—you must keep silent over this—but, alas, I must stop! I can hear Imogen crying a little distance away from me. I hate to hear a child crying. Yours always, "Capt. Kidd."' There you are—there you have it to the best of my recollection. What I've repeated I'm pretty sure is more or less right. But I *may* have left out one or two paragraphs."

"You've done darned well, Andrew. Pelman's a nit-wit by comparison. So our friend signs himself 'Capt. Kidd' does he? Double-edged. The combination perfect. Dual reference to the 'Skipper' again and the poor little girl he's put his foul hands on. Well, Andrew, this is where we get him."

"Don't see how! You may have plenty of suspicion, but there isn't an ounce of proof."

Anthony relapsed into silence, "Yes—and it may well cost that little kid her life. As I see things."

"Don't think that," replied the inspector. "They wouldn't dare in this country. We aren't in Chicago."

"Dare," retailed Anthony scornfully, "don't talk bilge! We may not be in Chicago. We're up against Chicago technique though—all the same. They'll kill without a scruple. You mark my words. Think of the two Regans and how they died if you're harbouring any doubt."

"That's all very well. But a lot of it is mere talk. How can these people know if Sir Curtis Littlehales has called in the police or not?"

"Trust them to find out, Andrew. They've probably half a dozen ways of discovering. People like this stick at nothing to gain their own diabolical ends. And I'm fearful for Imogen Littlehales."

"I've thought it over," continued MacMorran, "and I shall act. Sir Curtis's messenger will be there, as described, and the gentleman inquiring for Kidderminster will be promptly arrested on the spot. How does that strike you, Mr. Bathurst."

"It's all O.K. as far as it goes. Which isn't very far as I see things."

"How do you make that out?"

"I'm banking on one thing, Andrew. And that's this. People playing for high stakes, as this Trevor crowd are doing, are far too wily and cunning to commit elementary errors. You can go your limit on this, Andrew. If they suspect that Littlehales has communicated with you fellows in any way—the hunt will definitely *not* be up! And they'll circumvent your plans. Believe me, they won't walk into any trap with their eyes shut and their mouths open."

MacMorran made no reply for some seconds. When his reply did come he spoke a little grudgingly. "My idea's worth trying at any rate. I don't care what you say."

Anthony shrugged his shoulders. "I don't mind your trying it out. Because I think the mischief—from this child's point of view—has already been done. I don't like saying it, Andrew, but I'm sorely afraid that when Sir Curtis put the matter in the hands of the police he sealed his youngster's doom. This filthy technique is straight from the other side of the Atlantic and you well know what has happened over there more times than any decent person cares to remember. Once contact is made with the police it's all U.P. with the youngster."

MacMorran still sat silent with his arms folded and his lips pursed. At length he said, "I don't like to hear you say that. I'd give my right hand—"

"Giving your right hand won't help, Andrew. Or your left either. The gift would arrive too late. At any rate—that's my opinion."

The inspector got up quickly from his chair. "My mind's made up. As I said—it's at least worth trying. Will you come in on it?"

Anthony reflected. Then he shook his head. "I don't think I'd better. My best course, considering all the circumstances, is to keep well away from it. We aren't *certain* that they've got me taped. All the same—my future usefulness will be distinctly curtailed. No. I'll stay put here. You report progress to me as soon as you humanly can." He grinned. "Or the alternative condition, of course."

"Right-o. Suits me. On second thoughts, I think your idea's absolutely sound. There's no need for us to chuck all our advantages away. Even though one or two of them may be only problematically valuable. Where's a time-table? I'm getting back to town at once."

Anthony found him what he wanted. The inspector looked up a convenient train. Anthony shook hands with him.

"I'll await your report then, Andrew. With full details of the Paddington adventure. Yes?"

"That's the idea, Mr. Bathurst. And I have every hope that the report will be favourable—despite all your gloomy prognostications."

"Andrew," said Anthony, clapping him on the shoulder, "you're changing your spots. You're appearing as the incurable optimist."

3

PADDINGTON

THE following is a detailed account of what Anthony had chosen to describe as the Paddington adventure. As it was subsequently reported to him by Andrew MacMorran. The inspector himself went to the terminus together with Evershed and Supt. Hemingway. All were in plain clothes. In addition to these three officers a certain newly-attached assistant by the name of Arbuthnot (who has appeared in this history before), and who positively jumped at the opportunity to desert his long-endured passivity, also attended.

He, it may be said, carried an attaché case of the regulation colour and pattern, and (for the occasion and the occasion only) wore a red rose in his coat. If the information please the curious, this flower was a remarkably fine specimen of that particular species known to enthusiastic horticulturists as "General McArthur."

In obedience to arrangement, Arbuthnot approached the barrier outside the platform marked No. 2, at exactly three minutes to eleven. MacMorran, Hemingway, and Evershed were some distance away and in more or less suitable retirement. At any rate, nobody would have picked them out for what they were. Arbuthnot had been appropriately coached and instructed by the inspector as to his detailed duties and was loving every moment that passed. For some few moments he stood there apathetic—but intelligently apathetic. He looked the part that he was playing to a nicety. There was nothing whatever in his appearance to separate him from the hundreds of very similar young men who were strolling or hurrying to various parts and points of the busy station. But he wore a red rose and he carried a brown attaché case.

Arbuthnot continued to drift nonchalantly and naturally—a few steps in this direction—and then a few in that. The hands of the big clock showed the eleventh hour. MacMorran, Hemingway, and Evershed, adequately screened from the perils of observation, watched from their coign of vantage with feelings (it must be conceded) of ill-suppressed excitement. The minute hand of the big clock crept away from the position which indicated the hour. Arbuthnot still remained (from the point of view of the watchers) centre stage. Hundreds of men, women, girls and boys swirled and eddied round him until they found their respective personal objectives. Suddenly, as they watched, MacMorran caught Supt. Hemingway by the arm.

"Look," he said quietly, "that's our man over there—a thousand quid to a ha'penny cake on it—making his way slowly towards Arbuthnot. Do you see the fellow I mean? With the antiquated yellow straw hat on his napper."

Hemingway and Evershed each picked out the man MacMorran had described. He was a tall thin man with a long scrawny neck and a most pronounced Adam's apple. He wore, as has already been stated, an old-fashioned straw hat of the "boater" type, a linen stand-up collar open at the throat and a large white tie knotted at the base of the big white collar. On his left arm was crooked an unfolded umbrella. MacMorran classed him as either a teacher in an elementary school or an insurance agent and made a mental note that he was far from being of the type he had expected to see. His eyes were light blue in shade and protuberant.

"That's our man," the inspector repeated in a low-toned voice—"he's seen Arbuthnot and will be at his side in less than twenty seconds. Watch and see if I'm not right."

It did not take either Hemingway or Evershed very long to approve the accuracy of their chief's statement.

"Look out for developments," whispered MacMorran—"he's almost abreast of Arbuthnot."

The thin man sidled up to Arbuthnot and could be obviously seen speaking to him. Arbuthnot nodded in response to whatever it was that had been said to him. He then nodded again and placed his attaché-case in the thin man's hands. Both men stood where they were for the matter of some few seconds. MacMorran was surprised within himself that the thin chap made no attempt to open the attaché-case. Also, he thought, the fellow seemed extremely uncertain of himself. Arbuthnot walked a few paces away fro him. The tall man stared after him and then threw an anxious-looking backward glance over his shoulder. Then he began to shuffle away. MacMorran jerked himself from the role of spectator, to action.

"Get going, Evershed. Head him off as I arranged and don't take any chances."

Evershed slid off silently and relentlessly. The inspector, with Supt. Hemingway at his heels, moved off in the direction intended and entirely according to plan. Before they had traversed a hundred yards, they saw Evershed close with his man and tap him on the shoulder. The man turned round angrily. MacMorran and Hemingway were there with him at the psychological moment and with an entire absence of fuss the man was surrounded and in less than two minutes was being driven to Scotland Yard in a car which had appeared almost miraculously, it seemed, at the precise second when MacMorran had needed it.

The tall man made certain expostulations concerning the treatment he had received. To all intents and purposes he took an exceedingly poor view of the latest stage of the proceedings. But MacMorran cut him short in all his protestations.

"Don't talk! Wait! You'll hear all you want to hear in a few moments and probably a bit more thrown in."

They took him to MacMorran's room at the "Yard," overlooking the river.

"Sit down," said MacMorran, "and make a clean breast of things. That's my advice to you."

The man began to talk in a high, reedy, falsetto voice. MacMorran's gorge rose at him.

"This," said the tall man, "is an unwarranted outrage! And you shall pay for this or my name's not Richard Kent! I've never heard of such a thing! And in a free country at that."

"Cut it," ordered MacMorran, "and explain how you come to be in possession of that attaché-case. You're not charged with anything—yet—so let's have your story accounting for that case." The inspector paused and then continued again almost immediately. "And its contents," he added.

"Look here," said the tall man and his Adam's apple grew in proportion to the measure of his annoyance. "I'd have you know this. I'm a decent, honourable, self-respecting citizen and no man living—or dead come to that—can say to the contrary. My name's Kent. Richard Kent. I don't know who the devil you take me for, but if it's anybody other than Richard Kent, you're making a bloomer and a rotten bad bloomer at that. I'm a teacher in an elementary school, L.C.C.! And I was trained at Culham let me tell you. The name of the school is the 'Orchard House.' That's by the East India Dock. At the bottom of the Canning Town bridge. My headmaster is a Mr. Samuel Whiteman. I came to Paddington this morning to obtain certain information on behalf of my daughter *re* trains, platforms, connections, etc. She's going to Lyme Regis next Friday for her annual fortnight, and I promised I'd obtain the information she wanted. I always do every year. I believe in looking after my children—though thousands don't nowadays. I was just coming away with the necessary details when a lady stopped me."

His high voice, if anything, grew higher and more shrill. Evershed found it difficult to repress a smile and Hemingway looked extremely doubtful as to Kent's bona fides. The latter was quickly in his rhetorical stride again.

"'When I say 'a lady,' I mean 'a lady' and this one was a lady—a real lady—you can take it from me. She came up to me and asked me if I would do something for her. I think she described it as 'doing her a favour.' I said—naturally—what was it that I could do for her? Any man calling himself a gentleman would have done the same. She pointed a certain man out to me. He was standing near the barrier for No. 2 platform. Would I ask him if it were the right platform for Kidderminster? I said 'Why not ask a railway-official? A porter or something like that.' She said they weren't reliable—if you didn't tip them well they gave you wrong information—but this chap, she said, was on the special staff, 'he was always there and the details he gave you always absolutely to be relied upon and er—authentic.' So I promised I'd do it for her and I accordingly went up to this fellow she'd pointed out. I asked him exactly what she had requested me to. Then . . . to my surprise and I must admit, consternation, he pushed this attaché-case into my hands. I was dumbfounded. I didn't know what to do. I said to him 'What's this?' or words to that effect. He said 'In there's what you've come for' and moved a step or two away from me. Then it struck me that the case might be for the lady I was obliging and I turned away with the intention of taking it to her. The next thing I knew was your unwarrantable interference! Am I charged with stealing this attaché-case? I confess I'd like to know, Mr. . . . . er . . . I don't know who it is I'm supposed to be addressing."

"My name is MacMorran. I happen to be Chief-Inspector MacMorran if that information's of any value to you. Of the Criminal Investigation Dept.—New Scotland Yard."

If MacMorran's speech had been delivered with the intention of impressing Mr. Richard Kent it must be admitted that it singularly failed in its object.

"That's all very well," said Kent angrily, "but you haven't answered my question. As you yourself know full well. You're trying to get out of it. And you won't bamboozle me by tricks of evasion.

I'll tell you that. I repeat—am I charged with stealing that attaché-case? That's all I want to know."

For the moment MacMorran ignored the question. He turned quietly to Supt. Hemingway standing at his side.

"Open that case, Super."

Hemingway obeyed him. Inside was a square parcel. The superintendent took it out. MacMorran watched Kent's face carefully as it was disclosed. "Open the parcel, Super," continued the inspector. He continued to watch Kent. Hemingway bustled about and opened the parcel. He placed the string on the table with the utmost care and deliberation. All that the parcel contained were piles of used envelopes.

Kent's lip curled with derision when he saw what the parcel had held. "Don't you think you're wasting my time, Inspector MacMorran? And your own? But that's probably not as valuable as mine. Am I likely to endanger my reputation, my career and my professional pension for a few hundred used envelopes?"

MacMorran was nettled at Kent's attitude. "What was actually in the case may have been a very different proposition from what you may have thought would be in it. I wasn't born yesterday if you think I was."

"I'm glad to have the assurance," retorted Kent, "I was beginning to harbour certain doubts."

As MacMorran has admitted subsequently, in this particular respect Kent was by no means alone. Light was beginning to come to the inspector and it was up to him to find the best way out of an unpleasant position. In other words, what Anthony had predicted he was beginning to see had definitely come to pass. MacMorran turned to Evershed curtly.

"Ask him to get somebody to vouch for him. That's the best course for him to adopt. Perhaps that headmaster he mentioned just now would come along and give us the low-down on him. If he doesn't live too far away."

"Very good, sir," said Evershed, "I'll tackle him at once, sir."

Kent responded to Evershed's tactful approach. "Mr. Whiteman lives at Stepney. I daresay he would come along up here if you asked him. Though why it should be considered necessary I really don't know. I consider the whole thing's an outrage. Yes . . . he's on the telephone. STE 0606. You might find him in. I really can't say. On the other hand you might not. It depends. Very good, then—you try. And I wish you every success in your venture, I'm sure."

Evershed gave the inspector an almost imperceptible nod and used the telephone. Mr. Samuel Whiteman, to the good fortune of his assistant, Mr. Richard Kent, was in and when he understood the full terms of Evershed's message, he at once expressed his willingness to come to the Embankment to the aid of his colleague and do the necessary. The hour's interval which followed passed on leaden hands. But at long last, Samuel Whiteman arrived and was at once shown up to Inspector MacMorran's room.

"I'm Samuel Whiteman," he announced with gusto, "a head-master in the service of the L.C.C.—and there's my card. I believe that my services are required."

He produced a yellow-looking visiting-card, undoubtedly of many years' standing. MacMorran looked at it a little curiously. Before he could comment, Whiteman was talking again.

"And that gentleman sitting there is my esteemed colleague Dick Kent. Though why he's sitting there, I don't pretend to know." He chuckled almost boisterously. "Of Culham College and known to his friends and intimates as 'Cheesy' Kent . . . sometimes even referred to more irreverently as 'Old Cheesy.' I don't know what you gentlemen have got against him—if anything—but whatever it is, I'll give my word he's innocent."

His chuckle was transformed into a hearty rolling laugh. None of the police officials spoke. MacMorran was in a bad temper and the other two men waited for him. Whiteman looked from one to the other of them.

"Well—does that turn the scale in his favour? Or are you havin' him shot at dawn?"

MacMorran, more than ever mindful of Anthony Bathurst's anticipation, decided to make a clean sweep of the whole business as far as it affected Kent. He thanked Whiteman for his attendance and then turned to that gentleman's assistant.

"You may go," he said with a trace of sternness. "And next time don't be in such a damned hurry to oblige women that are unknown to you. If you go on doing things like you've done this morning you'll find yourself in a spot of bother before you know where you are; and next time you mightn't find a police-inspector as lenient as I am."

According to MacMorran, as he told the story to Anthony, Kent's eyes almost left his head and his Adam's apple moved spasmodically at the end of his larynx. He opened his mouth as though about to reply to the inspector in no uncertain terms. But he evidently thought better of the idea. His lips closed, his fingers grasped at his straw hat and he left MacMorran's room in the wake of his chief, Mr. Samuel Whiteman, and shepherded by Supt. Hemingway.

MacMorran turned quickly and made a sign to Evershed. The latter understood at once what was required of him and he therefore slipped out behind the others, completely unobtrusively, and started on his task a few paces outside the "Yard" building. This then was the history of the Paddington adventure as recited by MacMorran to Anthony on the afternoon of the same day.

Anthony had caught a fast train and gone straight from Paddington to the inspector's room at New Scotland Yard. MacMorran watched Anthony's face a little fearfully as he told him the details of the story. But all he saw featured there was cold gravity. There was no reaction of levity on Anthony's part either to his own accuracy of prognostication or to the inspector's personal discomfiture. Anthony's face was sad and remained grave.

"I don't like it, Andrew. I don't like it one little bit. As far as I can see, it means two things. And two things only. One—that they've called Sir Curtis's bluff as regards the police and secondly—" he paused abruptly.

"Well?" inquired MacMorran, a trifle testily, "what's the second thing?"

Anthony hesitated before replying. "Why, just this, Andrew. That I'm *afraid*—very much afraid, in fact—that they'll wreak their vengeance on the little girl. As I told you before. That, I think, must be the inevitable sequel, and I can see no hope whatever of it being avoided."

MacMorran's face whitened under its habitual tan. "You're looking on the worst side," he answered. "And as I see things, you're being hopelessly and most unduly pessimistic. Why on earth should they? I hate putting it in this callous way—but ask yourself, Mr. Bathurst, are they likely to kill the goose that's going to lay the golden eggs? Is it feasible—looking at it from the criminals' point of view. Where's the profit in it? Now—I ask you."

Anthony shook his head slowly. "But this particular goose hasn't laid any egg at all—let alone a golden one! And what's more—according to Sir Curtis Littlehales—it isn't even going to lay one! That's the position you have to realize. Which means that the unfortunate goose—presenting no profit while living—will surely die. And there's this, too, Andrew. The dead goose will be proof that the murderers mean business and will stick at nothing. Which will impress others. And *I* regret being callous, as you put it, every bit as much as you do."

The inspector looked glumly at Anthony and bit his lip. "You're convinced of what you say, I suppose?"

"Absolutely, Andrew. I wish that I weren't. But I can see no other reasonable possibility beyond the one that I have outlined to you."

The two men sat there silently for the matter of some seconds. MacMorran took out his pipe and began to fill it. Anthony Bathurst took the cue from him and lit a cigarette. They smoked for another brief period in silence. Until, as it happened, a knock sounded on MacMorran's door. The inspector looked up at the interruption.

"Come in," he cried curtly. Supt. Hemingway entered the room with a slip of paper in his hand. Anthony saw at once that the interruption was based on something more than the mere commonplace.

"What is it, Super?" asked MacMorran.

"News just come through, sir, from Chelmsford. Very important. They asked for Evershed, but, as you know, he's not back yet from that schoolteacher business you put him on. So I told Ashcroft to take it."

He put the slip of paper on the desk in front of the inspector. MacMorran bent over to read it. Anthony watching closely saw his face go the colour of cigar-ash and at that precise moment he knew without the vestige of a doubt what the news was that the inspector had been called upon to read. But he made no intervention of any kind. He waited patiently and let MacMorran read on in his own way and in his own time. When he had finished reading the inspector looked up and beckoned to Anthony. The normal colour had not yet come back to his face.

"I'm sorry," he said, "for doubting your judgment. Experience should have taught me better."

Without another word he handed over the slip of paper which Supt. Hemingway had brought him. Anthony took it and read it. It ran as follows. "The Margretham police have reported at noon to-day that the body of the child Imogen Littlehales was discovered early this morning in the grounds of her father's residence at Margretham, Essex, Ingot's Court. From the evidence it would appear that the child had been strangled."

Anthony handed the slip back to MacMorran. "Poor little golden goose," he said quietly.

MacMorran sat in his chair and nodded.

4

MURDER IN ESSEX

FURTHER information was soon to hand with regard to the murder of the little girl Imogen Littlehales. The doctor who was called by the police to examine the body gave it as his opinion that the child had been dead at least twenty-four hours when she was found in the grounds of her father's residence at Margretham known as Ingot's Court.

She had been killed, so he stated, by the pressure of a thumb on each side of the trachea. The marks of the severe pressure that had been exerted showed, so were his actual words after making his P.M., on the layer of ciliated epithelium which covers the mucous membrane lining the fibro-cartilaginous tube of the windpipe itself. Doctor Lamacraft, the doctor in question, also stated that the body was well-nourished and that there was every evidence to show that the child had been well fed and well cared for during the period of her absence from home. But there was absolutely no clue of any kind whatever in connection with the circumstances of the abduction.

The nurse who had had the care of the child at Ingot's Court was only able to make one statement. This was to the effect that whoever had attacked her had done so from behind. That she heard nothing before the attack had taken place and that she knew nothing. Beyond the fact that she had come to in the bedroom after her period of unconsciousness. The underclothes that were on the child's dead body were not Imogen's own. They were of but moderate quality and had doubtless been supplied to her by her murderers, either before or after her death had taken place. When she had been abducted from the house, Ingot's Court, she had been taken from the bed wrapped in a blanket.

Anthony discussed the various details of the case with MacMorran, Supt. Hemingway and Evershed, the detective who had been put on the case in the original instance by the inspector himself at Anthony Bathurst's general suggestion. Anthony had several questions to ask Evershed. But the man was able to give him little or no assistance. During the time he had spent in Margretham and its vicinity he had noticed nothing in any way suspicious and he projected it as his opinion that any menace which might have been directed towards Sir Curtis Littlehales or his daughter did not emanate from Margretham itself or any place in the immediate district.

"I've no doubt at all, sir," he remarked to Anthony, "that we have to look elsewhere for the home of the conspiracy against the little girl."

"I entirely agree with you. As a matter of fact I don't think there's any doubt about it. The district of Margretham came into the picture for the simple reason that Sir Curtis Littlehales lived there. Sir Curtis Littlehales who filled the bill in two directions. One, he's an unusually rich man and, two, he had a small daughter. You know what happened to Sir Curtis and you know also what has happened to the little girl."

There came an ominous silence. Evershed was so far affected by Anthony's statement that he clenched his fists.

"Beasts," he muttered, "bloody-minded beasts."

"Again I agree with you, Evershed," remarked Anthony quietly.

Hemingway watched MacMorran. MacMorran was his chief and whatever MacMorran needed or wanted it was up to him to do his best to supply. To do him full justice, he was actuated by both a sense of duty and by a flair for self-interest. Anthony began to speak again.

"I wonder if I shall be forgiven," he said, "if I enter once again the realm of prophecy." He paused. MacMorran knowing Anthony, knew, too, that the pause was deliberate.

"What do you want to say?" he asked.

"Merely this, Andrew." Anthony chose his words. "I was about to say this. And I don't claim or ask for any bouquets if events ultimately prove me right. That either Suzanne Polhill-Scott or Dudley Lee etcetera Spuyten will be the next little golden goose on the lists of those people whom Evershed here has just so appropriately described as 'bloody-minded beasts'."

The three professionals looked both scared and startled. MacMorran translated their doubts into words.

"You really think it's as bad as that?"

"I do." Anthony's reply was spoken simply and with little or no attempt at dramatic effect.

Hemingway spoke for the first time for some lengthy period. "May I ask, sir, why you are so sure of what you say?"

"You may, Super, and you shall have my answer. This is how I look at it. The little Littlehales girl was abducted for a reason. That reason was profit. I know you won't want to argue with me on that score. The desired profit was considerable. Consistent with the taking of the risk the murderers took. These people with whom we are called upon to deal don't play for small stakes. No profit was forthcoming. The little girl was thereupon promptly murdered. Reasons? To prove that only strict business is intended. To impress this horrible and brutal fact on the parents of poor little Imogen's successor or successors. Namely the small Dudley or the diminutive Suzanne."

Hemingway broke in impetuously. "But if you'll pardon me, Mr. Bathurst, what I don't understand is this. How is it you're able to name the families so certainly? It almost looks as though you're in the murderers' confidences." The superintendent shook his head. "That's the part I can't follow or understand."

Anthony smiled at Hemingway's difficulty. "Inside information, Super! Ask the chief here—he'll tell you all about it."

Hemingway looked towards MacMorran. The inspector nodded. "That's all O.K., Hemingway. Mr. Bathurst and I picked up some very vital information when we were at Wroxeter. We have reason to think that attempts may be made in the direction he has indicated. Although he's much more positive about that than I am. Than I *allow* myself to be."

Hemingway stared at him as he made the admission. "I see," he said, almost reluctantly.

"That's the explanation," continued the inspector, "but I'm hanged if I know what to—"

"There's one thing you must do immediately, Andrew," said Anthony. "And that's this. Both Polhill-Scott and Mrs. Spuyten must be warned to expect danger. That action should be taken at once."

"I suppose you're right," agreed MacMorran. He turned to the superintendent. "You go yourself, Super. To the houses of both of them. You'll find the addresses there in the—"

"I can give them to you, Super," broke in Anthony, "it will save you the time and trouble of looking for them. The Polhill-Scott address is number eleven Bryanston Square and Mrs. Spuyten lives in Mayfair, Little Clancy Street. I can't give you the number. It wasn't actually sent to me, but you'll have no difficulty in finding the house."

"Thank you, Mr. Bathurst. I'll jot them down." Hemingway suited the action to the word. As he did so, Anthony rose from where he had been sitting.

"Well I'm afraid that will have to be all for the present. I don't think there's any more that we can do."

"I agree," supplemented MacMorran.

"If you will let Superintendent Hemingway report to me what he finds at each of the houses he visits I shall be extremely obliged," rejoined Anthony.

"I'll see that that's done, Mr. Bathurst," said MacMorran. "Hemingway—you hear what Mr. Bathurst wants."

"O.K., Chief," returned Hemingway, "that'll go with me all right."

"Good," said Anthony, "and in the meantime we'll await developments."

CHAPTER VII

1

HEMINGWAY TOSSES A COIN

THE toss of a coin has decided many important happenings down the corridors of history. It has made all the difference between a hard wicket and a sticky dog, the gale dead into one goal as against the other, and the Middlesex as opposed to the Surrey side on that stretch of often popply water which lies between the respective points known as Putney and Mortlake on the championship course.

Hemingway, let it be recorded, tossed a bright new silver half-crown into the air as he left Andrew MacMorran's room and murmured as it descended into his outstretched hand, "Heads Dudley—tails Suzanne." The coin appropriately fell with Britannia uppermost, so Hemingway made his way towards the residence of the Polhill-Scotts.

The father of the little Suzanne and the third son of Lord Clamness was at his London address. A week previously he and several friends had been at his country house at the back of St. Margaret's Bay. It may be observed, therefore, that Supt. Hemingway's luck was well in. Polhill-Scott was standing with his back to the mantelpiece of his morning-room when the tall figure of Supt. Hemingway was shown into the room. Polhill-Scott's eyebrows went up a little as his eyes took in the superintendent's presence.

"Good morning," said the latter. "I insisted on seeing you, so you mustn't blame any of your servants. As a matter of fact, sir, my business is . . . er . . . highly important and extremely urgent. That must be my excuse, sir."

Polhill-Scott's tone was supercilious when he answered. "Who are you?" was all he permitted himself to say.

"There's my card, sir," replied Supt. Hemingway.

Polhill-Scott took the proffered card and read it. "The police— eh? May I ask to what I owe the pleasure of this visit?"

Hemingway embarked on his already prepared explanation. "You've nothing to fear, sir. I mean—to be apprehensive about."

"Thanks for the information," cut in the chilling voice of Polhill-Scott. "I'm much obliged to you for the information, I'm sure." Hemingway realized that he had begun to flounder. So he made an attempt to pull himself together. "What I meant, sir, was from your own personal point of view. Actually, this visit of mine is to do with your daughter."

"My daughter? What on earth are you talking about, man? Do you happen to be aware of my daughter's age—amongst other things? She's not one of the Bright Young Things—yet."

"Yes, sir. I am aware of her age, sir. Fully. But this is the point—is she with you . . . at this moment?" Hemingway propounded his question almost fearfully, as though he himself dreaded what he knew would be the inevitable answer.

"She is not," came the incisive answer. "But is the fact of terrific importance?"

"She's not, sir?" returned Hemingway weakly.

"She is not. I said she wasn't. What's wrong with that?"

By this time Hemingway's initial nervousness had gone and he had become master of himself. "Then do you know where she is, sir?"

Polhill-Scott stared at him incredulously. "Of course, I know where my daughter is. I make a habit of so doing. One would think she was on the road to Gretna Green with Caliban himself the way you're talking. My little girl is at my house at St. Margaret's Bay—near Deal—in the county of Kent. Now does that satisfy you . . . Superintendent"—he looked at the card he still held—"Hemingway."

The superintendent breathed freely again. His worst fears had been allayed. "Is your wife with her, sir?"

Polhill-Scott put his hands rigidly behind his back. "Look here, Superintendent. Where's all this leading up to? Because I candidly confess that I credit you with enough intelligence not to ask me this catechism of questions unless you had an excellent reason. Now what is that reason? Out with it, man, for the love of heaven." Hemingway looked round. He was perfectly calm and collected now. "May I sit down, sir?"

"You may. My apologies for not having offered you a seat before this." The tone of invitation was still curt.

Hemingway found a chair. Without knowing it he was sitting on the most valuable chair that he had ever sat on. Perhaps it was as well that he didn't know it, because the fact might have disturbed him and militated against his efficiency.

"Well, sir," he began, "it's like this. Information has reached us that your little girl is in great danger."

Polhill-Scott paled a little. "How do you mean exactly?" he queried quietly.

Hemingway began to do his best work. "I take it, sir, that you have heard of the murder of the little girl—the little girl who was stolen and taken away . . . the daughter of Sir Curtis Littlehales . . . in Essex?"

The face that watched him was ashen now. "I have. But please tell me how that in any way affects Suzanne."

"Well, sir, it's like this. We have every reason to believe that a similar attempt is to be made on your little girl."

The Hon. Michael Polhill-Scott was a different man now. His face worked anxiously and his hands trembled. "Every reason? What do you mean by every reason? I don't know that I properly understand you."

"Well, sir," began Hemingway again, "let me put it like this— good reason! I take it that you know that the little girl's all right up to now?"

There were fear and horror in Polhill-Scott's eyes. Shorn of his social decoration and racial tradition he had reverted to primitive man. "No news must be regarded as good news, Superintendent Hemingway. That's true, isn't it?" he asked hoarsely.

"Yes, sir," replied Hemingway eagerly. "And is your wife with her, sir?"

Polhill-Scott nodded. "She is. They've been at St. Margaret's Bay for over a month now. It is my intention to join them there some time next week. Or rather rejoin them. But I'm bewildered? How is it you know all the things you assert that you know? All these things you're warning me against? If you know so much, why don't you—?" He paused, as though uncertain how to finish the sentence he had begun.

"These are the facts, sir. There's a gang at work in this country. Who they are and where they operate from we *don't* know. But they're probably from America. This sort of thing, as you know, is very prevalent out there. One of their most profitable rackets. If they take your child you'll be presented with an ultimatum. Same as Sir Curtis Littlehales was. Pay up—or—! And the 'or' can be very ugly, sir. Very ugly indeed! I'm sure that you don't need any reminding of that. Bearing in mind the Littlehales business."

The man he spoke to sat crumpled up in his chair. The picture which Hemingway had drawn for him had played havoc with his imagination and hit him hard. He looked up, his eyes still haunted by the dragon of his fears.

"I must find out. Suzanne must be all right. Otherwise I should have heard." He started up from his seat. As he did so there came a light tap on the door.

"Come in," cried the Hon. Michael Polhill-Scott. A servant entered.

"You are wanted on the telephone, sir. In the library, if you please."

Polhill-Scott, a strange hunted look on his face, nodded and followed the man out, excusing himself to Hemingway as he went.

It was with unsteady fingers that he picked up the receiver. His voice, when it came, sounded unfamiliar to him.

"Polhill-Scott speaking. Who is that?"

The voice that answered him was soft and cultured. It would have been absurd to deny even that it was an unusually attractive voice.

"Is that the Hon. Michael Polhill-Scott?" it inquired.

"That's what I said," replied Polhill-Scott with a trace of acerbity. "Who are you?"

"If you were with me now you would probably call me an attractive woman. Most men do. And your reputation leads me to believe that you would be no exception. But that's neither here nor there. I want to speak to you about something else. Suzanne! Your only child, I believe. You'll get a letter with regard to her. Some time to-day. Please treat this letter seriously. Any other course on your part will be fatal."

It was here that Polhill-Scott found words to interrupt. Previously words had simply refused to come to his aid. "Who are you?" he cried emotionally into the telephone. But all that he heard now was, "Well, good-bye for the present and please don't forget what I've said, will you?"

Polhill-Scott was left standing with the telephone-receiver in his hand. All the colour had drained from his face. He replaced the receiver and steadied himself by putting his hand to his head. His whole body trembled violently. He made his way slowly back to his room and Supt. Hemingway. He seemed to have aged ten years in less than ten minutes. As soon as he entered the room, Hemingway sensed trouble. Polhill-Scott nodded at him vacantly . . . weakly.

"It's come," he said in a broken voice. "What you warned me against. I've had a message on the 'phone about Suzanne. That was it."

Hemingway came to full alertness. "Tell me," he said with sharp insistence, "tell me all about it."

In broken, disjointed sentences, Polhill-Scott recounted to Hemingway the purport of the message he had just received. The superintendent's face grew graver as he listened. "I don't like it, sir. I don't like it at all. They must be very confident to act in this manner. Looks to me as though they've already gone a long way."

"What do you mean by that?" Polhill-Scott almost glared at the Scotland Yard man. His eyes held entreaty and desperate fear.

"Well, sir, I don't want to sound pessimistic, but I shouldn't be surprised if they've already struck. But about this letter, sir. That will tell us more about matters when it comes. Perhaps the worst." Hemingway wished he hadn't used the last word so he quickly changed his tack. "How about seeing if a letter's been delivered? It's just on the cards that it may have been."

Suzanne's father made an effort to pull himself together. "That's an idea," he said. "I'll ask Grice."

He rang the bell and the man appeared who had come in before. Polhill-Scott asked him the necessary question. The man answered. "I will inquire for you, sir."

The two men waited in silence for the return of Grice. They were not compelled to wait for long. The man returned within a couple of minutes.

"There is a letter, sir. It was in the box. It appears, sir, if I may say so, to have been delivered by hand. Within the last hour, I suggest."

"Let me have it, Grice. At once, please."

Grice handed over the letter. Polhill-Scott took it. "That will be all for now, Grice—thank you." He made as though to open the envelope. "It's addressed to me," he said in a flat, toneless voice, "typewritten address." But his fingers refused to act so he handed the envelope to Supt. Hemingway. "Open it for me, Superintendent—do you mind?"

"Not at all, sir. I was, in fact, going to suggest that I should."

Polhill-Scott gave the letter to Hemingway. Hemingway opened it. "I'll read it to you, sir," he said at length, "and you must prepare yourself for a shock."

"Tell me the worst," replied Polhill-Scott.

"This is what it says," went on Hemingway. "There's no address and it isn't dated. But knowing what I do know—I'm not surprised at that. 'To the Hon. Michael Polhill-Scott, 11 Bryanston Square, W.1. In the early hours of this morning and from purely altruistic motives, your daughter Suzanne came into our care. On certain conditions we shall look after her and care for her to the full extent of our power. Those conditions are as follows, (1) Enclosed is a stall ticket, Row D, No. 22, for to-morrow evening's performance of *Love in Idleness* at the Flamboyant Theatre. Please occupy that seat and bring with you to the theatre the sum of £20,000 (twenty thousand pounds) in one pound currency notes. These notes must not be in any way marked. When the lights go up in the auditorium for the first entr'acte the occupant of D.21 seat will say to you, "This play might have been written by Pinero." You will then hand over the price of your daughter Suzanne's safety. "Safety" in this relationship is synonymous with life. (2) You must in no way communicate with the police authorities. If you do I can assure you that you will never see your little girl again—*alive*. If you should be foolish enough to doubt the accuracy of these statements may I in this connection draw your attention to the sad and recent instance of Imogen Littlehales. Sir Curtis, you see, acted so very foolishly! And the bill eventually was heavy.'"

Polhill-Scott sat with ashen face. "I'm frightened," he said, "because in a way I *have* communicated with the police! That means that Suzanne will be—" He stopped abruptly.

"They need not know that, sir," countered Hemingway. "After all, you didn't send for me. It was just sheer coincidence. I came of my own accord and just happened to be here when the letter was received. There's no call for the devils that sent this letter to be aware of that."

"But what do I do?" said Polhill-Scott. "I'm in a cleft stick as far as I can see. And again, what about my wife? I've heard nothing from her yet. Why haven't I heard from her? She must know that something has happened to Suzanne."

Hemingway thought it out. "You will hear, sir. You're bound to. And soon at that. These scoundrels have moved at once, you see. Quicker than your wife could. Probably had the letter all ready beforehand to slip in to you directly the little girl was in their clutches. Now I'll tell you what I propose to do. I'll report back to the 'Yard.' You can keep out of the affair altogether. And I'll promise you this, sir. We'll take no action in any way that will endanger your little girl."

Polhill-Scott looked doubtful. "Yes—but how can I be sure of that? The mere fact of your knowing—"

"Leave that to me, sir. I'll see to that. I'll give you my word on it. Also—I'll let you know what course to adopt *re* to-morrow evening's do. The child's safety must come first."

The man nodded. "Yes. The child's safety must not only come first. It's to be the *only* consideration. If it means the sacrifice of every penny I possess. You understand that."

"Yes, sir. And if I may say so the sentiments do you credit, sir. Now I'll get straight back and then we'll get into touch with you. But you understand it will be all on the Q.T. and you need have no fear of any official action. Goodbye, sir; it seems to me that I turned up here at what one of my colleagues calls the 'psychological moment'."

Polhill-Scott nodded without speaking and Hemingway took his departure. He walked back to the "Yard" at a brisk pace and within ten minutes of reaching there was closeted with Chief-Inspector

Andrew MacMorran. Five minutes after the interview started, MacMorran 'phoned for Anthony Bathurst.

2
AT CLOSE QUARTERS

ANTHONY Bathurst and MacMorran heard Hemingway's story without comment and minus interference. When the superintendent had finished, MacMorran looked at Anthony and presented a question.

"Well—and what's the plan? How do we act? I'd like to hear your ideas first of all, Mr. Bathurst."

"Well," replied Anthony, "there's one thing that sticks out a mile isn't there?"

"You mean?"

"That our first consideration must be the life of the little girl. No move, or semblance of a move, must be made by us to endanger that. All the same—our luck's in. The fact that Polhill-Scott was able to give Hemingway all this information without obviously contacting him was very definitely a slice of cake for us. And Dundee at that. We know—and they don't know that we know! And if Polhill-Scott remains quiescent and stays 'put' they'll set on the assumption that we don't know!"

"They're quick on the draw," commented MacMorran. "I've been on to St. Margaret's Bay. But the reply hasn't come through yet."

Hemingway nodded and then turned to Anthony again. "Well, sir—as the chief said—what do we do?"

Anthony shook his head.

"I don't want to make plans too quickly. So much is going to depend on them. Let me think things out. There's always the little girl, you see." Anthony rose and paced the room. "It's like this. Any interference we may make to cause their scheme to go awry or even to disrupt the smooth working of their schedule might mean the child's life. That's where these beasts always hold the whip hand. Which brings us to Plank No. 1—that Polhill-Scott must occupy stall D.22 at the 'Flamboyant' to-morrow evening as he has been instructed. With the cash—which he must hand over under the prescribed conditions. Now, he has to be told what he has to do.

First problem—by what means or route shall we tell him? This gang, whoever they are, must not entertain the veriest suspicion that the police are on the job for the sake of the little girl. The Polhill-Scott household will be watched—you can bet your life on that."

"Tell him by ordinary letter," said MacMorran.

"He may not receive it. Delays in the postal services are not unknown. You see—we can't afford to take the slightest risk. That's the situation as I see it. Plus—this communication must be made to Polhill-Scott himself by word of mouth. One of us must go there. Neither you, Hemingway, nor MacMorran. And I should keep out likewise. Think it had better be Evershed. Can you get him all right? Is he conveniently available?"

"He will be," said the inspector, "if I say so."

"Good. Rig him up as a Water Board employee or something of that sort. Nice suitable uniform. You know the kind. Peaked cap, etc. Nothing ornate. Just the suggestion of the man come to look at the water supply. Fix him up with appropriate impediments. You know. Evershed turned into a respectable imitation of a turncock. Anyhow—so that he'll pass commonplace muster. He must get in, contrive to see Polhill-Scott and pass the message to him re the 'Flamboyant.' You'd better vouch for his identity, Andrew, in such a way that Polhill-Scott can't possibly doubt it. Is that all O.K.?"

MacMorran nodded his agreement. "Yes. I think so."

"That brings us to to-morrow evening itself." Anthony paused. MacMorran's telephone bell had rung. Anthony waited for the inspector to answer it.

MacMorran listened. They heard him say, "Yes—I've been expecting to hear for some little time now. Last night, you say? As I thought. Very good. That's satisfactory as far as I'm concerned . . . if I do . . . and anything should come along this end . . . I'll ring you and pass it on. Many thanks."

MacMorran hung up and looked at the others. "The news is through from the Kent coast. The little girl was taken last night. In circumstances very similar to those of the Littlehales youngster. Well—we know exactly where we are now. There's that about it."

"We did before," intervened Anthony grimly. He started to pace the room again. "What worries me so intensely," he said, "is that virtually we have to let these people go—because of the child. We can't move. If we lift a finger—" he paused again. "Is Helen Repton available for to-morrow evening?"

MacMorran nodded. "Yes. If we want her."

"I'm certain you can't beat her for the particular job I'm suggesting for her. Arrange with the 'Flamboyant' people that she sells the programmes for D row of the stalls. Let her in, of course, Andrew, on what we're after. Tell her to get going directly our man arrives and not to give herself away. He'll never suspect her if she's as good as I know she can be. Let her report all he does but not to trail him if there's the slightest danger of her being spotted. There now remain we three. You and I, Andrew, and Supt. Hemingway. I'm not quite sure yet as to our best policy. You see," he concluded almost whimsically, "there's always Master Dudley Van, etc., Spuyten."

"What do you mean exactly?" asked MacMorran.

"That we always have him in reserve. I don't intend to be callous. I'm simply trying to deal with the case as a problem requiring solution. See what I mean?"

MacMorran stared at him. "I'm not altogether sure that I do. Do you mean that we sit tight on the Polhill-Scott job, let these people levy their ransom and return the child, and then wait for them to move again?"

"Almost, Andrew. Not quite. But you've cottoned on, perhaps, to my general idea. Do you find it commendable?"

The inspector shook his head. "No. Too uncertain by far and I'll tell you why, Mr. Bathurst. They may never go for the Spuyten job."

"Why not?"

"If they bring the present one off, they may be satisfied with what they collect out of it and lay off the other. That's entirely feasible, isn't it?"

Anthony took some little time in consideration of the inspector's argument. When he eventually replied, he said, "I'll grant you this. They may 'lay off,' as you describe it, for a time. I'm perfectly certain, however, they won't stay their hand altogether. But—again, as you say—the delay—or the interval—may be a long one. Too long. It would mean having our plans in pickle, as it were, over too protracted a period. It would not be too easy for us in those circumstances." As he finished, Anthony nodded. "Yes, Andrew, I agree with you. The little Dudley must be ignored as a practical proposition. Which means that we are brought back to the consideration again of our present problem."

Hemingway spoke. He had been silent for a long time. "Shall I see Evershed—or would you rather I waited for a little while?"

"Leave it, Super," replied MacMorran, "till we've got the whole thing cut and dried. I don't want to put part of our problem into being until I've seen and decided on the pattern of the whole lot. Then there's Miss Repton as well. I must see her, too. So leave it till I give you the O.K. generally. Now let's look at to-morrow evening. Re the arrangements. Had I better go to the theatre? I'd like to and arrest the brute on the spot. Nothing would give me greater pleasure, I assure you."

Anthony nodded. "I know. But that procedure would spell disaster for Mlle Suzanne. Therefore it doesn't arise as an attractive adventure. As to whether you should go—my reply is 'no.' You're too well known—and any chance incident might serve to give you away. How do you react to that opinion yourself, Andrew?"

MacMorran seemed a little disappointed but he answered readily enough. "Candidly I think you're right. I don't want to agree with you, but I feel that I must. That brings us to Hemingway here. Should he go or should he keep out?"

Anthony hesitated before answering this question. He could see advantages and disadvantages in each possibility. "In my opinion," he said eventually, "the super should keep out. Mainly on account of the presence of Polhill-Scott. He knows him, you see. They're acquainted. And the circumstances of the acquaintance are so inseparably connected with the affair that will take him to the theatre to-morrow night that it would be unwise, in my judgment, for Hemingway to be present anywhere in Polhill-Scott's personal circle."

MacMorran smiled what Anthony has always called his "dourest" smile, "That leaves you only—of the three of us. Do you want to go? They may know you—if what you're thinking and what I'm thinking are on correct lines. How about the risk there?"

"I regard it as a thousand to one against my being recognized as I shall appear to-morrow evening. I know the danger from A to Z and I shall, therefore, be most thoroughly on my guard against it. Yes, Andrew, I think that finally casts the die. I shall be present at to-morrow evening's performance of that modern comedy entitled *Love in Idleness*."

MacMorran sat and drummed with his fingers on the blotting-pad in front of him. "All right, I'll accept the situation as you have put it to me. I'd leave you to the devices and desires of your own heart. Meanwhile there are Evershed and Miss Repton for me to interview with regard to their instructions. When shall I see you?"

"Unless anything extraordinary occurs, I'll come round after the show. For one thing I shall want to hear Helen Repton's report."

"If it's here by then, yon mean."

"If it isn't, Andrew, I'll be pleased to wait for it. I've a high regard for that young woman—from every point of view."

"What about your ticket?" said Hemingway.

"Ticket?" queried Anthony.

"Yes—your seat for to-morrow evening. At the 'Flamboyant'— you'll want a stall for yourself, won't you?"

"Oh—I see what you're getting at, Super. For the moment you had me on one leg. I'll see to that myself. You needn't worry. Leave all those personal arrangements to me. I don't think, though, that I shall need a stall. I'm rather inclined to the opinion that another part of the auditorium is definitely indicated." He grinned. "I might even betake myself to the Olympian heights—you never know. Still—it can wait. I'll work all that out sometime to-morrow." He leant forward and touched MacMorran on the kneecap. "Something I want you to do for me, Andrew. As soon as possible. In your official capacity and in *re* telephones. Analyse the incoming calls to Middleton Hall near Wroxeter, Warwickshire, say for the last two days. House in the occupation of a certain Capt. Lionel Trevor. Cover the full forty-eight hours. And check up also to-morrow evening on all calls put through, say from a two miles' radius from the 'Flamboyant' Theatre, after a certain time. That time will be, I venture to predict with some degree of certainty, very soon after the end of the first act."

MacMorran nodded. "Good idea. I follow your reasoning. You're reckoning on him 'phoning."

"I think he's pretty certain to, whoever he may be. With the news that the machinery, so far, has run, and is running, quite smoothly. His confederates, at the other end, will be requiring and waiting for that precise piece of information."

MacMorran nodded again, "Yes. I think that's perfectly sound, I'll have that idea of yours seen to. And I'll expect you here, then, after the performance."

"That's the idea, Andrew. We shall meet at Philippi."

3

THE REPTON SLASH

HELEN Repton had been attached to the women's side at the "Yard" for nearly three years now and, as far as the respective judgments of Anthony Bathurst and MacMorran went, stood in a class by herself from the point of view of intelligence, initiative and general ability. Her father was a Fellow of History at Oxford, and Helen, before insisting on a career for herself, had taken an Economics degree at London. She was tall, thin and darkish and a bundle of dynamic energy which functioned all the time she was engaged for any special duty, and did not relax until that particular duty had been well and truly performed.

She moved in and about the stalls at the "Flamboyant," black-habited and white-aproned, with her programmes in her hand and two eyes unobtrusively focused on seats D.21 and D.22. The curtain was timed for eight o'clock. At ten minutes to the hour, the stalls were comparatively empty, there being not more than thirty people in the entire rows. The rush, she knew, would come just before the curtain. The minutes passed slowly for her but the stall-holders now were beginning to put in an appearance and the demand upon her stock of programmes grew at a steady rate. The orchestra began to tune up and at 7.55 sharp swept into the overture. At three minutes to the hour she saw Polhill-Scott come in and take his seat. She knew him from the description she had been given of him by Supt. Hemingway. His seat, she observed, was the end seat of the centre block on the left-hand side as you faced the "foots." She worked her way slowly towards him without the slightest show of undue hurry and sold him a programme. She noticed that he carried a square parcel under his arm and that his fingers, when she handed him his change, were trembling and unsteady.

He took his seat, wiped his forehead with his handkerchief, glanced apprehensively towards the seat on his right-hand side, saw that it was as yet unoccupied and then plucked nervously at the edges of the programme that Helen Repton had just sold to him. That lady passed along the front row of the stalls neatly and quickly, as business for her by this time had become definitely brisk and was demanding by far the greater part of her attention. The time now wanted but a handful of seconds to eight o'clock. Just as the "foots" went on full, a tall man came from the cloak-room and made his way slowly towards Polhill-Scott and stall No. D.21.

He was a man not without a certain personal distinction. Helen Repton, at the moment that mattered, was fortunately placed. She happened to be walking towards the man who entered from the cloak-room. He sank into D.21 coincidentally with the orchestra finishing the overture. Careful as always, she sold two more programmes before arriving near him. She fluttered a programme in his direction without speaking and, as she did so, her heart gave a leap, for she was able to see, pocketed in the palm of his right hand, the cloak-room ticket which had obviously only just been handed to him. Her quick eyes told her that it was Number 113. The man put half-a-crown in her hand for his programme and she mechanically counted out his change. At the same time she commenced on her mental picture of his description. Meanwhile Polhill-Scott stared straight ahead at the stage and at the curtain which was just going up.

4

FROM REPTON TO UPPINGHAM

ANTHONY Lotherington Bathurst at that same moment was in the centre of the third row of the dress circle. He had chosen this seat deliberately and after a certain amount of careful planning. Not only was he able to see the occupants of the stalls perfectly and under the cover of his opera-glasses, but he was also well screened from observation by two rows of human bodies seated in front of him. His glasses, trained on the appropriate seats, showed him the arrival of Polhill-Scott and he watched with acute interest the slim, trim figure of Helen Repton as she adroitly moved along the various rows of stalls and sold her stock of programmes to many customers and as to the manner born.

Anthony waited with infinite patience for the appearance of the man to whom he himself had given, for his own understanding, the appellation of the "Antagonist." This was how Anthony was thinking of him as he kept his glasses focused on the seat that he knew the man was destined to occupy within the space of the next few minutes. Then he saw the man come in just as Helen Repton saw him. Anthony watched him walk to D.21 and sit in it, simultaneously with the strains of the overture dying away. And, as he looked, Anthony knew that he had seen the man before. He had half expected to see Trevor. But this man was not Trevor. But figure and face were familiar and Anthony confronted the problem as to remembering where and in what circumstances he had seen the man before. And while Anthony was debating thus, the orchestra faded out and the curtain went slowly up.

5

AND BACK TO REPTON

WHEN the first act of *Love in Idleness* had played for ten minutes, Helen Repton slid silently and efficiently into the cloak-room. She showed the surprised-looking and startled attendant certain significances and credentials.

"No. 113," she said curtly. "The clothes left here. I want to look at them, please. And as quickly, please, as you can possibly manage it."

The attendant nodded and looked round at the assembled collection of coats, hats and scarves. She turned over and examined several heaps before saying, "Here you are, Miss. Here's the lot with the 113 ticket."

Helen Repton moved swiftly to the pile of clothes which the attendant had indicated. They were entirely normal and conventional, opera-hat, overcoat, gloves and white evening scarf. She looked inside the hat. It was innocent of initials but the hatter was "Duke, Aston St., Birmingham." She noted the size and deftly pushed the hat to one side. The coat was innocent, like the hat. There was nothing whatever to be found in any of the pockets. But the tailor's name-band by the collar showed "Elmslie, Molineux Terrace, Wolverhampton." Helen Repton made a rapid assessment of the size. The gloves were of dark *suède*. The scarf was just a white evening wrap and yielded nothing.

Helen Repton pushed the clothes along the counter and back to the attendant and slipped into the darkened auditorium again. Her wrist-watch showed the time to be seventeen minutes past eight. She had already instituted inquiries and knew, thereby, that the first act played thirty-three minutes if faithful adherence were paid to the script and accurate timing. Which meant that she had approximately a quarter of an hour to wait for the entr'acte. She stood near the "foots" and stole a furtive glance at Polhill-Scott and his seated neighbour. Polhill-Scott was still staring almost blankly at the stage and the members of the cast who happened to be on. He was sitting bolt upright now in his seat, tense and rigid. To Helen Repton, who had been informed of the reason why she was in attendance that evening, he conveyed the impression that his body was present but that his soul had temporarily discarded it and was a great distance away.

The man next to him, or (as Helen thought of him to herself) "that vile beast," sat coolly and easily in his seat. The "Flamboyant" management allowed "smoking" during the performance, and this man was taking full advantage of the concession. A cigar was held idly and nonchalantly between the first fingers of his right hand. Every now and then he would lean forward gracefully and knock the ash off into the little tray in front of him that had been provided for that express purpose.

6

TO RETURN TO UPPINGHAM

ANTHONY had seen the temporary disappearance of Helen Repton and he had fallen to wondering as to the cause thereof. He puzzled as to whether anything had already passed between Polhill-Scott and the "Antagonist" which her eyes had been quick enough to observe and which had eluded his own, bearing in mind the relative distances which she and he were away from Row D of the stalls.

While he was cogitating thus, the reminiscence for which he had been groping stabbed into his brain as to when and where he had seen the "Antagonist" before. It had occurred on the occasion of his first visit to "Christopher's Bar." The realization of this was warm and comforting. Any doubt which he might have been harbouring as to whether he was casting his line in the right reaches was now thoroughly and effectively dispelled. As he looked down to the stalls he could see that Miss Repton had not returned to her more immediate post of duty. What the heck had bitten the girl to send her scramming like that? Must have been something, he concluded, that she considered pretty important. He trained his glasses on the two men of his acute interest. Nothing had happened so far. Polhill-Scott was obviously taking no risks of any kind. Well, Anthony couldn't find it in his heart to blame him. A kid like that—

Then he saw the figure of Helen Repton again. But he did not notice from where she came. As he had seen it, one moment she was not and the next moment she was. But he was satisfied to know that she was in her place again and he certainly wasn't in the mood for meticulous analysis. Just as Helen Repton had done, down there near the stalls, Anthony checked up on the time. It was just on twenty minutes past eight. Or from his most important and persistent angle, another thirteen minutes to go before the "Antagonist" declared himself.

Then Anthony's thoughts sped back to his recently-born remembrance concerning the man's identity. In his anxiety with regard to Helen Repton his mind had relinquished this and the idea been temporarily forgotten. He saw himself again on the point of entering "Christopher's Bar" on the evening he had first visited Wroxeter.

As he had come to the revolving door a man had been standing there in the company of two ladies. Or had it been three? Anthony attempted to resurrect the entire scene as it had actually taken place. Yes—there had been three ladies. Very smartly dressed at that. And the "Antagonist" had been their escort. They, as a party, had come out of the bar as Anthony had gone in. So Trevor was not the big fish after all. Or might he be? Was the man in seat D.21 of the stalls the Triton himself, or merely one of the bigger minnows? Anthony's thoughts rioted as he considered the question. The answer to it might be some considerable time in coming but that it would eventually come he held no doubt, and he would be content to wait until then for the solution of that particular problem.

Under the influence of his impatience he looked at his watch again. It was now twenty-eight minutes past eight. Five minutes yet to go. Anthony leant forward in his seat and trained his glasses again on the two vital seats in Row D of the stalls. He could detect a slight change in the attitude of Polhill-Scott. Instead of looking straight ahead at the stage he was now, Anthony noticed, stealing occa-sional, but regular, sidelong glances at the man seated beside him. The "Antagonist," however, remained, as far as could be seen from where Anthony was, completely oblivious of these looks of Polhill-Scott, moved not a muscle, and turned not a hair. Anthony could tell from the incidence of the dialogue and the general stage-group-ing for action that the moment for the first curtain was very near now. He held on steadily with his glasses to the main objects of his scrutiny and he then saw the trim figure of Helen Repton come a little nearer to the two men.

7

THE HUNT IS UP

THE finale of the first act of *Love in Idleness* demanded a slow curtain. As it began to roll downwards, Anthony leant forward, his glasses pressed to his eyes, so that he should miss nothing. Leaning forward as he was, the thought struck him that it had been a far cry from Arbuthnot, the bank clerk, to the present critical phase of the drama. As far as he could see, for the curtain was by now down, the two heads of the occupants of seats D.21 and 22 had gone closer together. Beyond this indication Anthony could detect nothing to excite his interest. People were moving and chattering all round him, heads were turning in all directions and programmes being used as face-fans with all the restless activity which seems to be inseparable from this exercise.

Then Anthony, by dint of craning his neck, spotted something much more significant! The "Antagonist" rose from his seat, to his full height, and carelessly stretched his arms to their full length above his head, as though he were ridding himself of the effect of cramped muscles. Anthony, watching every movement like a hawk, saw him take a cigarette from the pocket of his dress-coat and light it. Every gesture the man made was accompanied by a studied nonchalance. Then, as though he had suddenly made up his mind with regard to something, he turned and made his way out of D row of seats, courteously passing by Polhill-Scott as he did so with every indication of consideration and personal care. Anthony saw him make as though to enter the cloak-room, but pause on the threshold. Then he turned away and Anthony watched him walking up the right-hand aisle towards the back of the stalls. "Clever," said Mr. Bathurst to himself, "going to the bar for a quick one. When his genuine exit does eventually come it will be quiet and entirely unobserved." It was at this precise moment that Anthony noticed the second disappearance of Helen Repton.

8

HELEN PICKS UP THE SCENT

HELEN Repton, keeping herself all the time in the comparative background, had seen the transfer effected between Polhill-Scott and his neighbour. She saw the latter make for the cloak-room just as Anthony had, and noticed him, too, make his way towards the bar at the rear of the stalls. She had been prepared for something of this kind to happen and she made a rapid mental calculation that she had at least a matter of five minutes to spare. She therefore ran quickly to a place concerning the convenience of which she had already made arrangements, divested herself of her programme-seller's costume and revealed to anybody who might have been there to see that she was wearing below that a telegraph messenger's uniform minus the trousers. These, however, were to hand (also by arrangement) and it was the work of but a moment to pull them on. The appropriate cap was also there and she crammed it on her head and made it comfortable. This was the work of another second. With cigarette hanging loosely from her lips she made her exit from the front of the theatre, walked a few paces and took a bicycle from the man standing with it all ready for her on the edge of the pavement.

Helen's plans were always well thought out prior to execution. This was one of the main reasons why she was always so successful. With one leg over the saddle and the other on the kerb she waited there, commanding the exit from the theatre. She was certain that the man in whom she was interested had not yet had time for his drink and to leave the building. Also, she reasoned, he had no intention whatever of hurrying. Everything he was about to do he would do quietly. With an entire absence of flurry or fuss. In all probability, she continued to reason, he would remain in the shadow of the bar until the curtain went up on the second act. As the bar *habitués* swarmed back to their respective seats, their minds intent on that one object, he would slide gently out, pick up his wearing apparel from the cloak-room, and say goodbye to the "Flamboyant" Theatre for that one evening at least. Thus Helen's thoughts as she straddled her bicycle and watched and waited for her man. Subsequent events proved to the hilt the soundness of her reasoning.

Five or six minutes later she saw her man emerge. He stood on the pavement outside the theatre for a few seconds looking in each direction. Helen Repton cupped her hands round her cigarette, as though in the act of lighting it from a match. She had contrived to be on the right side of the road from the point of view of travelling on it. The man she watched held up his hand and signalled to a passing taxi. She saw the parcel under his arm as he got into the taxi. She made a pretence of tossing away the match she had pretended to be using. She knew that it would be a comparatively easy matter for her to follow the taxi on her bicycle through the streets of theatre-London with so many traffic lights on the way.

Also, the traffic at the time was congested, which suited her book from all angles. As the taxi moved off, Helen Repton pressed down the right-hand pedal of the cycle and moved off in its wake. By now there were several vehicles between her and her quarry, but she could see it easily and had no difficulty whatever in keeping it in sight. It was travelling in a westerly direction. The time was now thirteen minutes to nine.

CHAPTER VIII

1

GATHERING THE FRAGMENTS

Anthony Bathurst, MacMorran, Hemingway and Evershed sat in MacMorran's room on that same evening. Anthony looked at the clock. The time now was twelve minutes to ten—just over one hour since Helen Repton set out behind the taxi which contained the man who had occupied seat D.21 in the "Flamboyant" stalls. MacMorran interpreted Anthony's glance and nodded in acquiescence.

"I agree, Mr. Bathurst," he said meaningly. "I know what you're thinking—we ought to be hearing from Miss Repton before very long. Unless—"

"Unless what, Chief?" interjected Hemingway.

"Unless something unexpected has turned up and she's gone after it. She's not one to miss a chance, you know. Especially if that chance looks like being productive."

Anthony cut in. "That's the one contingency I'm a little afraid of. That she's chasing our friend of the stalls and that the chase has proved to be a long one and a stern one. It may be some hours before we see her. I don't know that I altogether wanted that to happen."

"What will you do?" asked the inspector. "Will you wait?"

"I most certainly shall, Andrew. For another hour or so at least. Or even longer than that. As you already know, I have abundant faith in Helen Repton."

A knock sounded on the door. "Come in," cried MacMorran.

The door was pushed open, rather unceremoniously, and a voice called, "Policewoman Repton to see Chief-Inspector MacMorran."

"Send her in," rapped MacMorran, and within a few seconds Helen Repton entered the room. Anthony grinned at her unusual attire and the girl smiled back at him.

"Good evening," said MacMorran. "Glad you're here—we were getting a wee bit anxious about you. Now what have you got for us?"

Before she could reply, Anthony grinned at her again for encouragement. "I've come to report, sir," she opened to MacMorran, "in accordance with the instructions conveyed to me from you. As was instructed, I attended at the 'Flamboyant' Theatre for the performance this evening and carried out duties as a programme-seller attached to the first six rows of the orchestra stalls, to be precise from Row A to Row F. I observed that when the curtain rose promptly on time seats 21 and 22 in Row D were occupied as you had intimated they would be. I have no doubt that seat 22 was occupied by the gentleman whose name you gave me and just before eight o'clock seat 21 was taken by a man exactly as I had been led to anticipate. His description is as follows. Height just under six feet—say, 5 feet 11 inches—iron-grey hair, frosty-blue eyes with very prominent nose, clean shaven, takes size 7 in hats and size 8½ in gloves, age probably between 55 and 60. Well-preserved man for his age. Has or has had connection with the Midland districts."

Helen Repton spoke with the utmost confidence, but Anthony smilingly interrupted her.

"I'm sure you will pardon my asking you the question, Miss Repton, but may I inquire, in all humility, how you are able to make those precise statements *re* gloves, hats and locality?"

Helen returned smile for smile. "I expected to be asked that, sir." She proceeded to explain how she had been able to obtain the information. The others nodded and expressed their approbation.

Anthony rubbed his hands appreciatively. "Excellent, Miss Repton. My congratulations. A touch after my own heart."

Helen Repton flushed with pleasure. Anthony was by way of being a firm favourite of hers and from her point of view this was "praise from Sir Hubert."

"Go on," instructed MacMorran. "Let's hear the rest."

"Very good, Chief. When the first act finished the man I have just described spoke in an undertone to Mr. Polhill-Scott and a parcel was handed over to him. I was close by—and watching all the time. Rut I took good care that neither of them should notice me—notice me—er—that is to say—unduly. The tall man then rose and made his way towards the cloak-room, but on the threshold stopped and evidently changed his mind about something, because he turned and made tracks for the bar behind the orchestra-stalls. I thought out and made my plans. I had this on underneath my frock—or best part of it"—she indicated the uniform with just the soupçon of a blush—"and I had arranged for a cycle to be ready for me in the event of my requiring one. The result was that when the man left the theatre I was in position, as it were, and all ready to follow him in whatever direction he decided to go."

She paused and looked round at the four faces of her companions. On these she read no criticism but marked approval. She continued her account.

"When he came out he hailed a passing taxi. I followed it at a respectable distance. Thanks to the 'hold-up' at the various traffic lights I was able to trail it without the slightest difficulty. In fact, I never actually lost sight of it. His destination turned out to be Paddington station. I cycled up behind him at a time interval of a few seconds. He didn't see me arrive. I'm perfectly certain of that. I mingled with the crowd—wheeling the 'bike'—and gradually worked my way towards him. Then I had a stroke of unexpected luck. As unexpected as it was fortunate. In the crowd I spotted two messengers in similar uniform to that which I was wearing." She smiled. "And am still wearing! I placed myself as near them as I conveniently could so that I shouldn't be too conspicuous. After a longish wait about I was able to watch the gentleman I was following right on to his platform. The train he caught—I checked up on it afterwards—was scheduled for Oxford, Evesham, etc. Which proves again, I think—or perhaps 'indicates' is the better word—that he has a Midland contact somewhere."

Helen Repton sat back in her chair and concluded her recital of events. "I thought when that happened that I had better report back, Chief. My instructions from you didn't carry me any further. I hope that I have done the right thing."

MacMorran nodded. "That's all right. You need have no regrets. You've done a good job of work. Our hands are tied, you see. By reason of the little Polhill-Scott girl, I dare not show them too clearly. It's imperative that we should protect her. But you've given us an excellent lead which, with reasonable luck, is bound to get us somewhere."

Helen Renton flushed with gratification at the inspector's tribute. Hemingway winked at Evershed and said, "Very pleasin' to work for someone who appreciates you. May be my turn one day. You never know." He grimaced at Anthony Bathurst. The last-named spoke to the girl again.

"You're quite sure, I take it, Miss Repton, that our friend of D.21 stall didn't phone to anybody after he took the parcel from Polhill-Scott? That is to say, between taking the parcel in the theatre and entering the train at Paddington?"

"Almost, sir. As reasonably certain as I can be. He was only out of my sight for about five minutes. I know that's a long time from many points of view. But he went to the bar at the theatre. I actually saw him enter. There's no 'phone near there. And if he had gone from there to a 'phone in another part of the theatre I feel positive that he couldn't have left the theatre at the time he did. That's how I'm judging it."

Anthony nodded. "I agree. Seems pretty sound to me."

MacMorran doodled on his blotting-pad. He began, "If we—" and then checked himself. The others waited for him to elaborate. MacMorran produced the elaboration. "I'm worried about the next step. The next safe step. We can't afford to tread anywhere and put a foot wrong. If we do—" he checked himself again. Anthony came in.

"There's this to it as I see things. These people *must* establish communication before long. It's absolutely vital for them. Between this end as we've seen it this evening and the end where they're holding Mlle. Suzanne."

Hemingway leant forward. "May I butt in?"

"Of course. We can do with all the heads we can get on this job."

"Well—I agree with what you've just said, Mr. Bathurst. But it seems to me there's another possibility. One that's been so far overlooked. With regard to this communication, I mean."

"And what is that, Super?" inquired Anthony.

"Why, this, Mr. Bathurst. That the man in the stall D.21 may have had a confederate in the theatre. I mean in the theatre itself at the time when the parcel was passed over. You see, sir, it would have been dead easy. Money for old rope! The man could have been sitting just behind them. In the stalls. Or it may even have been a woman. Waiting for a sign of some kind. Which could have been conveyed to him—or her—in a very simple manner. D.21 chap might, I suggest, have stood up, or waved his hands, or moved his arms. And the other person would have understood what the gesture meant—whatever it was. I don't think we ought to disregard the possibility, Chief."

Hemingway sat back—a little flushed with the mental and verbal exertions of his argument. Anthony smiled at him. "As a matter of fact, Super, Monsieur D.21 did stand up! And, which is perhaps more to the point still, he stretched his arms. High above his head. You can corroborate that, Miss Repton!"

The girl nodded her agreement. "I can, Mr. Bathurst. That is quite true. A few seconds after the curtain had come down. I think certain words passed between him and Mr. Polhill-Scott. Their heads seemed to be very close together for the space of a few seconds."

"I am of the opinion," added Anthony, "that the Super's suggestion is well worth bearing in mind. That the communication *must* be made seems to me an absolute certainty. If they haven't employed the medium of the telephone we shall be forced to explore these other possibilities. Are all the arrangements in order with regard to the telephone calls?"

"They are," said MacMorran. "I've seen to all that personally. We shall have tabs on all the calls both to and from Middleton Hall for the next week."

Anthony shook his head. "In all deference, Chief, I'm afraid that won't be adequate. It's not going deep enough. Let's look at it from the personal standpoint of Comrade D.21. We'll *assume* that he's in the train now *en route* for Wroxeter. He may 'phone from a public call-box directly he leaves the train. Look at the field that opens up! Bit staggering, isn't it? I confess I'm unhappy when I think of it."

"It's not so bad as it looks on the surface," said MacMorran. "I'll brighten you up a bit. If he does 'phone he'll have to do so between Wroxeter Station and Middleton Hall. Ten to one on that. The time, you see, in that way becomes fairly well indicated."

Anthony nodded. "That's excellent, Chief. We want to check up on all outgoing calls from public call-boxes between Wroxeter Station and Middleton Hall during the period between the time the train runs into Wroxeter and our friend's arriving at his destination. Two hours should cover it. Send for an *A.B.C.*, will you? We'll start calculations now."

MacMorran spoke on the telephone. Anthony swung round to Helen Repton. "What train was it he caught, Miss Repton?"

"It was scheduled to leave at 9.49, Mr. Bathurst."

MacMorran opened the *A.B.C.* which had been brought in to him.

"You hear that, Chief," said Anthony—"9.49 p.m. out of Paddington."

MacMorran fingered the pages. "9.49 ex Paddington. Gets to Stratford-upon-Avon at 12.9 a.m. That's an hour and twenty minutes. No. I'm wrong. I can't count. Two hours and twenty minutes. How far's Stratford-upon-Avon from Wroxeter?"

"With stops at all stations," replied Anthony, "about half an hour. On this train—say 20 minutes. Turn up Wroxeter and clinch it."

MacMorran took the tip. "Yes. You're about right. Reaches Wroxeter at 12.31 a.m. Now if I phone Foster at Wroxeter—"

"Don't," said Anthony curtly. "Remember the super's promise to Polhill-Scott. No action till the youngster's sent back safe and well. Still—you've got your time pretty well fixed. Say from 12.30 a.m. onwards. There's an advantage in that. There shouldn't be many calls at that time in the morning—and what there are—the few, I mean—will be all the easier to trace."

"Yes. There's that in it. Evershed—see to that, will you? With regard to those telephone calls. I'll leave that matter in your hands entirely. Don't sit on it. Get to work at once."

"Very good, Chief," said Evershed, and took his departure.

MacMorran looked at Helen Repton. "Well, young lady, I don't think we can be expected to do any more this evening. No good rushing matters. Let me say again that you've done well. Extraordinarily well. Many thanks." He nodded to her and Helen Repton withdrew. "Good girl that," he said to Anthony.

"I told you that, Andrew," said Anthony. "Many moons ago. So don't pretend to come it now, as though you've been a bright lad and just made a discovery. I knew she was 'class' the first time I clapped eyes on her. She was in mufti and I liked the way she swung her skirt. It hung on her, not round her. There's a difference."

Anthony dropped an eyelid in Hemingway's direction, which the superintendent suitably acknowledged. The latter rose to go. Anthony went and sat on the corner of MacMorran's table. "I take it you'll communicate with me directly you pick up anything? Yes?"

"I shall, Mr. Bathurst. You may rely on that. But I'm a wee bit despondent over this case. I'm by no means too confident that we shall get anything. Don't know why exactly—I'm just explaining to you how I feel about things."

Anthony dangled his feet. "That's strange. Because I don't feel at all pessimistic. We know such a lot. Compared with other cases that you and I have come our way in the past. Sometimes we've known so little. If we allow this gang to slip through our fingers after all this we deserve to be boiled in oil." He leant over and patted MacMorran on the shoulder. "Which I've always understood, Andrew, is a singularly unpleasant business."

MacMorran stood up from his chair and shook hands. "I won't argue with you about that. Good night, Mr. Bathurst—and you'll be hearing from me. I hope before very long."

2

STALEMATE

Two mornings after the evening when Helen Repton played programme-seller at the "Flamboyant," Anthony walked back into MacMorran's room at the "Yard." MacMorran was sitting at his desk. He looked up as Anthony entered.

"Well?" remarked the latter as he came to MacMorran's side. "What's the game?"

The inspector affected failure to understand him. He looked down at his papers and then up again. "How do you mean?" he asked.

"How do I mean?" echoed Anthony mordantly. "You know very well what I mean, you old reprobate! Wasn't I expecting to hear from you? Concerning such matters as telephone calls and Middleton Halls? To say nothing of ships and shoes and sealing-wax! Anyhow—why the appalling silence, Andrew? What's gone wrong? Tell me the worst."

MacMorran's face and voice were grave when he replied. "I'm worried, Mr. Bathurst. Dead worried! And that's a fact! Nothing has come through to us whatever. Not a 'phone call from Middleton Hall! Not a 'phone call *to* Middleton Hall! They mightn't have the ruddy 'phone on there for all the use that's made of it."

Anthony sat quiet in the seat he had taken. "Nothing—eh, Andrew? Nothing at all. H'm! Wants thinking out, that does.' He sat there quiet again for ten seconds or so. Then he spoke. "Half a minute, Andrew. What about the time he left the train? Just after midnight. Nothing picked up there?"

"Not a sausage, Mr. Bathurst. There wasn't a call-box used round about that time anywhere in the vicinity. In the reasonable vicinity."

"What time was Miss Suzanne returned?"

"Half-past eleven yesterday morning. To her father. To his place in Bryanston Square."

"I thought so. From what Hemingway told me on my way up. I understood him to say something like that. Darned funny, isn't it?"

MacMorran looked a trifle sour. "Depends on how you regard fun."

"Don't be sore. You know what I mean perfectly well. The necessary communication must have been established in some way. That stands to reason. How did the little lady come home?"

"An older child brought her. A girl of about 12 years of age. Gave her name as Irene Deacon. Had a story, of course. A lady stopped her and asked her to convey Suzanne to the home of the Polhill-Scotts. Her description of the lady, naturally, was beautifully vague. We could get nothing of value from it."

"Where was she stopped for this encounter to take place?"

"A few streets away from the Polhill-Scott home. She wasn't sure of the name. But from what she told us I should imagine it must have been in Whittaker Street. All Suzanne says is that she stayed with a lady."

Anthony relapsed into silence again. MacMorran sat drumming his fingers. Suddenly Anthony came to life again.

"Remember the night Helen Repton was here?"

"I should say I do."

"Remember the suggestion that Hemingway chucked at us?"

"About there being a confederate in the theatre, do you mean?"

"Yes. That's exactly what I do mean, Andrew. And I'd go even a bit further. I'm inclined to think that there may have been something in the suggestion. In view of what you've told me this morning."

The inspector made a wry face. "I don't like the sound of that. It's very helpful, isn't it? The needle and the haystack won't be in it. What chance have we of tracing him? A complete impossibility." MacMorran shrugged his shoulders at the mere thought of the task.

Anthony made no immediate reply. He sat there thinking matters over. "If our friend of D.21 did have a pal in the theatre, he communicated with him either by a pre-arranged sign or by word of mouth. Agree on that, Andrew?"

"No. Not altogether. He might have written a message and passed it on by a third party present in the theatre. You can't ignore that possibility."

Again some seconds passed before Anthony replied. "We have no evidence from Helen Repton that he wrote any note."

"He was out of her sight for a time. She can't account for all his movements. She thinks he went to the bar."

Anthony nodded. "You're quite right, Andrew. That's perfectly true. For the moment I overlooked it." He paused and then continued. "If it were done by pre-arranged sign, I agree our chances of tracing anybody are pretty hopeless. And, like you, I take a pretty dim view of it. Your needle and haystack conditions are well in the picture. Not so good, Andrew! Definitely not so good!" He fell to musing again but then suddenly slapped his hand on his knee-cap. "Andrew, you old image, I've thought of something! Have I been slow? Or have I?"

"What is it?"

"The bar, Andrew! The bar we've heard so much about! In this instance, the bar becomes decidedly sinister. Monsieur D.21, according to Helen Repton, went to the bar at the back of the stalls. I've never sat in the stalls at the 'Flamboyant,' so that I'm not dead sure of its exact location. If he had a message to pass on, he could have easily passed it on in there. Remember this. It was the very first contact he made after Polhill-Scott had handed over the money."

"You may be right," said MacMorran lugubriously, "but it doesn't help us overmuch as far as I can see. We're still faced with the same predicament."

"Which one?"

"Why, the needle and the haystack one, of course. Anybody could have met him in the bar."

Anthony smiled and there was a tinge of boyish mischief in the smile. "That may not be the case, Andrew."

"How's that?"

"Think it over."

MacMorran furrowed his brows. "You mean that he might have conveyed the information to somebody employed in the bar? That is to say, one of the theatre staff?"

"That, Andrew, is precisely my contention. How does it strike you? Feasible or the reverse?"

The inspector made the concession. "I suppose the possibility's there."

"I consider it something more than a possibility, Andrew. Much more like a probability. Bearing in mind all that we know. At any rate there's a chance."

"I think, perhaps, that we ought to follow it up."

"I'll go further than that. To my mind we must follow it up. Any other treatment of it would be sheer negligence."

"O.K. When?"

Anthony looked at his wrist-watch. "The box-office should be open by this time. What do you say to running along to the 'Flamboyant' now? We should find somebody there who could tell us things."

"Very good, Mr. Bathurst," replied Inspector MacMorran, "that suits me. I'll come along with you right now."

3

MR. BATHURST DRAWS BLOOD

AT THE box-office of the "Flamboyant" Theatre, MacMorran produced his credentials and asked to see "anybody with authority." The girl to whom he addressed the request was obviously impressed by the association with Scotland Yard.

"Mr. Noyce is in the theatre, sir," she said eagerly, "you can see him. I'm sure he'd be pleased to give you any information you happen to want. I'll 'phone through to him, now, sir, on the internal line."

She spoke on the 'phone to the authority-possessing Noyce. Then she hung up the receiver and came out to tell MacMorran and Anthony what she had been able to effect. "Mr. Noyce says he will see you, sir, with pleasure. Will you please wait just inside the theatre for a minute or two? He won't keep you waiting."

The inspector thanked her and he and Anthony awaited the arrival of Mr. Noyce. The last-named came within five minutes. He was a tall, fresh-faced, eager-looking young man with thinning hair but a spring in his tread.

"Good morning, Inspector ... er ... MacMorran. Good morning to you, sir" (this to Anthony). "I understand from Miss Kelso that you wish to see me. Well, here I am—at your service."

MacMorran thanked him. Could Mr. Noyce take them to the refreshment-bar which served the orchestra stalls?

Mr. Noyce both could and did. "We are endeavouring to check up something, Mr. Noyce," explained the inspector. "Nothing particularly serious—but nevertheless important."

Noyce nodded. "That's all right. I understand. What is it you want to know exactly?"

"What staff do you employ here?"

"Two girls. Women if you like. They work the bar between them. Practically all the custom that comes in here is between the acts."

"Always the same two?"

Noyce hesitated. "Well—that's a—"

MacMorran broke in. "Suppose I put it like this. Who were the two on duty the night before last?"

"A Miss Bainbridge and a Mrs. Landry."

"Old servants?"

"The former—yes. Been with us about nine years. The latter's a recent addition to the staff. By the way—that reminds me of something. I rather fancy she's resigned. I've an idea Miss Kelso mentioned it to me yesterday. I can easily find out for you. Just a minute."

Noyce disappeared and Anthony looked at MacMorran with uplifted eyebrows.

"Hear that, Andrew? A little significant, don't you think? Feeling as we feel? Still—we shall hear more about it, no doubt, in a moment or so."

When Noyce returned to him he nodded his head affirmatively. "Yes. I was right. Miss Kelso has just confirmed it. Mrs. Landry left last night."

"In the middle of the week," remarked MacMorran. "Rather unusual that, isn't it?"

Noyce pursed his lips. "Yes. I suppose it is. But we get it that way sometimes. It's casual sort of labour, you know."

"Why did she leave?" asked Anthony. "Did she give any reason? Or wouldn't you ask her?"

Noyce shook his head. "No. I don't suppose we would question her. They come and go—these people. Drift from one job to another. Miss Bainbridge of ours is an exception. As I said—been with us years. Very steady, reliable girl. But during the time she's been with us, I should say another dozen at least have come and gone. It's like that, I can tell you. You never can tell with that class of employee."

Anthony persisted in his inquiry. "Any chance of your Miss Kelso knowing?"

"Why Mrs. Landry left, do you mean?"

"Yes."

"I'll ask her with pleasure. Won't take half a sec."

Noyce dashed off again—to return even more quickly than on the previous occasion. "Mrs. Landry told Miss Bainbridge that she and her husband were moving away from London. Down to some place in the country. Miss Bainbridge did tell Miss Kelso where it was but Miss K. can't remember the name of it. They're leaving very shortly, I believe, from what she told Miss Bainbridge."

MacMorran by now was as much alive to the portents as Anthony himself had been. "Thank you for your information, Mr. Noyce," he said affably, "you may rest assured that as far as you are concerned, it will be treated as entirely confidential. Now there's one more point I'd like to cover before we part company. Can you give me this Mrs. Landry's address as you knew it when she was employed here."

"Easy. I can get that for you, Inspector, from the staff register. Come into my office, do you mind?"

Anthony and Inspector MacMorran followed Noyce into his office. "Seen the show?" he said over his shoulder, as they entered.

"I have," said Anthony .

"What do you think of it?"

"Good show—on the whole. Should have a good run."

"You think so. Well—it's funny how one's judgment can fail. I'd have banked on it being a 'flop' on the first night. I was wrong—*premières* are bad to judge by—and I've been in the 'show' game for years."

He sat down and pulled a book towards him, "Here we are. Theatre establishment staff. Mrs. Landry we want. I'll soon turn it up for you. Landrv—L. Here we are, Number 7, Hudson Road, Nunhead."

Anthony made a note of the address. MacMorran expressed his thanks again, they shook hands all round and the interview terminated. Outside the theatre Anthony was articulate.

"We progress. Andrew! We very definitely progress! *N'est-ce pas?*"

MacMorran nodded in acquiescence but whether he understood Mr. Bathurst's question must be regarded as no more than an even-money proposition.

4

THE LANDRY CONTACT

As THEY moved into Hudson Road, Nunhead, Anthony became critical.

"I've always found this, Andrew, a most depressing district. It's dull and drab and deadening."

MacMorran surveyed the prospect. He grunted. They had walked up an incline by the side of an unattractive cinder-path and the houses, all around them, seemed to speak of sadness and sorrow much more than of merriment and mirth. Hudson Road was entirely typical of the general scheme.

"Apart from any other considerations, Andrew," said Anthony, "I entirely sympathize with the desire of the Landrys to migrate to the country somewhere."

Again the inspector grunted. It seemed that he was in no mood for conversation. Anthony continued.

"It may be, of course, that our birds have already flown. And the words 'too late' be found inscribed upon your heart. But we will be optimistic and hope otherwise."

"Here's No. 7," remarked MacMorran, "so we shall soon know."

They passed through the gateway of a house which, if possible, looked a trifle more squalid than most of its immediate neighbours. MacMorran used the knocker effectively and the clamour it made offended the ear as much as the house itself offended the eye.

"The birds have not flown," observed MacMorran dryly, "I can hear—"

"The flutter of their wings? Don't be too sure! They may belong to the wrong birds."

But Anthony's doubts were ill-founded for it was Mrs. Landry herself who had come to the door. MacMorran's first question to her established this, if, of course, the lady's admission were founded upon truth. Mrs. Landry listened to MacMorran's opening remarks and then looked vaguely round. Her look was accompanied by a statement.

"My husband works late every Friday evening."

This *non sequitur*, for such it was, was ignored by the inspector. He went on to explain who he was and suggested to Mrs. Landry that the interview might proceed better if it were conducted within the house.

"You can come in," she said somewhat grudgingly, "and it'll be a pleasure to ask you—but I've done nothing wrong. There's nothing on my conscience. I'm an honest hard-working woman and you and your kind have got nothing on me. I don't know what you want of me, I'm sure."

Anthony and MacMorran followed her into her parlour. They sat down on black, uninviting, horsehair chairs.

"Now look here, Mrs. Landry," said MacMorran, "understand that nobody's accusing you of anything. All we've come for's a little information. First of all cast your mind back to two evenings ago. You were on duty then in the bar of the 'Flamboyant,' which caters for the stalls. Is that so?"

"Quite true. And it caters for the pit as well. In case you don't know that. We may as well have everything ship-shape and correct to begin with otherwise there's no knowing where we'll get to. I wasn't born yesterday, you know." Mrs. Landry sat back in her chair, her arms folded and her lips set in lines of prim and proper determination.

"Quite so," replied MacMorran tactfully. "I agree with you. Now what I want to know, Mrs. Landry, is this. You aren't bound to answer me. I can't make you. I'm simply asking for information as I told you before and I hope you'll help me."

"It depends," said Mrs. Landry guardedly, "before I make any rash promises, let's hear what it is you want."

"Go back to the evening before last, Mrs. Landry. You were on duty in the bar."

"You've said that once and I admitted that it was so. Now what about it?"

The inspector remain unruffled. "Can you recall any of the people who came into the bar at the close of the first act."

Anthony saw the woman change colour. The change was but slight, perhaps, but when he saw it he knew that he and MacMorran were not wasting their time.

"You're askin' me something, aren't you?" The tone of her voice was not devoid of defiance.

"I am. I've come here for that express purpose."

"There's a rare crowd comes in, you know, and you've got to serve 'em all in double-quick time—else there's trouble. The intervals aren't so long that you can take it easy. They don't pay you for nothing at the 'Flamboyant'."

"I am aware of all that, Mrs. Landry. Even then, I think that you may be able to assist me. The man I'm inquiring about—we *know* he came in your bar—was tall, slim and clean-shaven. A distinguished-looking man with an extremely prominent nose. In age, say between fifty-five and sixty. Or thereabouts. Do you remember him?"

Anthony was watching her intently. She had gone tight-lipped again and a wary look had entered her eyes. She appeared to be debating within herself as to whether she would or would not tell the truth. Eventually she seemed to make up her mind.

"Look here," she said defensively. "I've done nothing wrong. I told you that when you started this third degree business with me."

"If that's the case, Mrs. Landry, there's absolutely no reason why you should hide anything from us. You must see the sense of that statement."

She swayed slightly from side to side as though, within her mind, there were a pendulum swinging between the points of acceptance and refusal.

"All right," she exclaimed, almost suddenly, "I'll come clean with it. I've done nothing that I'm ashamed of. I do remember the gentleman you describe. I served him with a 'double Scotch and Polly'." She stopped abruptly.

"Yes," said MacMorran gently and persuasively, "and did anything else happen while he was there in the bar?"

"Yes," she answered sullenly, "he asked me if I'd oblige him and do something for him."

"And what was that something?"

Mrs. Landry's sullenness remained with her as she replied to the second question. "He asked me if I would send a 'phone message for him." Again she stopped. The inspector kept his patience.

"Please give me the full facts, Mrs. Landry. I have no wish to keep on pestering you with questions."

"Well—I *am* telling you. What else am I doing, I'd like to know? You don't give me a fair chance."

"What was this telephone message you sent for this man?"

"It was quite innocent—and quite harmless. Couldn't have hurt anybody. All it said was that he was catching a certain train that evening from Paddington. I forget the exact time of the train but it was something to ten."

"Thank you. Now what was the name of the person you 'phoned?"

"Smith. Mrs. Smith. And Mrs. Smith answered the 'phone and took the message. The whole thing didn't take me more than a few seconds."

Her tone was still aggressive and resentful. Anthony caught MacMorran's eye.

"Smith." Always "Smith."

The inspector returned to his interrogation of Mrs. Landry. "What was the 'phone number?"

There was no answer. MacMorran repeated the question. Mrs. Landry bridled. "Look here," she said fiercely. "What's all this leading to? Can't a woman oblige a gentleman over a little thing like that without having to undergo a proper Spanish Inquisition?"

"Be reasonable, Mrs. Landry. Tell the truth and no harm will come to you."

She reverted to her previous condition of sulkiness. "Oh—all right then, have it your way. You're a 'rozzer'—I suppose you'll get what you want in the end. It's no good the likes of me trying to put up a fight against you. The number I 'phoned was Hengist 222. Easy to remember, you see. I couldn't very well forget it if I tried."

"What happened after you had conveyed the message?"

"Oh—nothing at all. Mrs. Smith—I asked for Mrs. Smith as I had been told to—came to the 'phone. I repeated the message I had been given about the train, she said, 'Thank you very much' and rang off. And that's all there was to it."

Anthony came in here with his first query. "Are you sure, Mrs. Landry, that that was all she said?"

"Why—yes—" Mrs. Landry broke off. She appeared to be thinking about the question. Anthony saw this, but purposely made no attempt to prompt her. Both he and MacMorran kept silent.

"No," said Mrs. Landry at length. "She said, 'Thank you very much. I understand.' I remember now. She said, 'I understand.'"

"Thank you, Mrs. Landry." MacMorran leant forward towards her. "And what was the inducement you had offered to you to deliver this message?"

The woman flushed a little. "The gentleman gave me a pound note. And pound notes aren't so plentiful with me that I could afford to refuse it. We're not like some people—me and my hubby—we have a pretty hard struggle, I can tell you."

"I don't doubt that," replied MacMorran gravely, "and as far as I can tell at the moment I have no quarrel to find with your action." He rose on the words. "I don't think we need trouble you any more for the time being. And many thanks for the information you have passed on to us." He turned to Anthony. "Do you want to ask Mrs. Landry any other questions, Mr. Bathurst? Because if not—"

Anthony shook his head. "I don't think so, Chief. I think you've covered the ground pretty thoroughly."

"In that case, then, we'll say good-bye to Mrs. Landry and proceed on our business."

The lady in question looked somewhat surprised. She had been fearful as to how the interview would terminate and now that the finale had been reached in terms by no means unpleasant the unexpectedness had caused her something of a shock. As she watched her two visitors depart, the colour came slowly back to her cheeks and she heaved a prodigious sigh of relief.

"Ah—well," she said to herself, as she regarded their retreating figures from behind a window-curtain of the front room, "they weren't so dusty, considering what they signify."

CHAPTER IX

1

HENGIST 222

THE village of Hengist, as everyone knows, is in the county of Kent. About eleven miles south of Blackheath. As their car travelled the miles towards it, MacMorran remarked to Anthony that the sun was too hot and the road too dusty. The trees wore all their green beauty and the hedges were a riot of full-leafed green.

"Kent, Andrew," said Anthony, "the garden of England! I might remark that St. Margaret's Bay also owes allegiance to the 'White Horse.' Please observe the coincidence."

"I've thought of that besides you." The inspector was curt. Anthony put out his hand and waved a fast-travelling motor-coach past the car. Across the road to the south a ridge fell away steeply and to the right, for a long sweep, ran the grey lines of the South Downs and there could be seen beyond them the line of cloud and sea.

"A delectable county, Andrew," said Anthony, harking back to his previous statement, "a county, indeed, after my own heart." MacMorran yielded nothing to this last expression. "The name," continued Mr. Bathurst, "of the gentleman presumably responsible to the Postmaster-General for the rental of the telephone identified as Hengist 222 strikes me as definitely unusual."

"Ay," returned MacMorran. "I'm with you all the way with regard to that. Not altogether English, to my way of thinking."

"Chester Moran," quoted Anthony with some relish. "To be precise, Colonel Chester Moran. I must confess that the name has both flavour and savour, Andrew. A cousin of yours—do you think?"

MacMorran ignored the question and grunted. "American—to my way of thinking. American—every syllable of it."

"I think you're right. And I don't mind if you are. It suits me. It fits in with the unholy pattern of things. This child-stealing racket is un-English. America has been its *'fons et origo'* for a long time now. Oh—by the way, Andrew, do you expect to find the dashing colonel in residence when we present ourselves. Do you anticipate that the flag will be flying high on the ancestral castle?"

"Don't you run on so fast. I didn't say that I intended we should present ourselves. Seems to me that might well be a technical error on our part. For one thing, it means disclosing ourselves to a certain extent which mightn't do us or our cause any good, and, for another, we can't produce a shred of complaint against the said colonel that we can support by proof."

"Unless we bring Polhill-Scott."

"Who is most disinclined to move in the matter. Let me tell you! We shall have to hold the kidnappers of Suzanne under lock and key, I'm afraid, before Polhill-Scott will move an inch against them on his own account. He's dead scared of what they may do to the little girl. Others of the gang who mightn't be rounded up. I suppose in a way it's understandable."

Anthony thought it over. After a time he translated his thoughts into words. "What steps do you propose to take, then?"

"Have a dekko at the house and then repair to the best inn in Hengist for a nice lunch and the best information we can glean in the saloon bar in respect of Colonel Chester Moran. Any fault to find with that?"

"No-o. That's sound enough and I see your point. And the prospect you've painted is by no means unattractive. But you've got to realize one thing, Andrew, and that the sooner the better."

"What's that?"

As he spoke Anthony swung the car into a side road whose signpost read "Hengist 4 miles." "Why, this! You've got to make a decisive move at some time or another. You can't keep on delaying the evil day. In other words, it comes to this. You've got to get the bracelets on the members of this racket. To do this you need certain proof. If that proof isn't forthcoming in the ordinary way—you've got to go in at close quarters and get it. And candidly, Andrew, I see nothing else for it."

MacMorran's reply to this was somewhat slow in coming. "Easier said than done," he remarked somewhat brusquely.

"Maybe—but very necessary all the same, I'm afraid."

MacMorran gestured towards the road ahead. "Running into Hengist. Not a bad little place from the early look of it."

The car began to climb a hill and the square tower of a church showed behind a belt of trees. There were red roofs, too, just visible here and there, dotted about the adjoining country. The car came to a junction of three roads. The main road ran into Hengist, and it could be seen that the other two would speedily degenerate into mere lanes. A long brick wall lay on their left as the car entered the village proper. A few yards beyond it stood a house of undoubted Tudor origin and a hundred yards or so past the house was the inn. Anthony fell in love with it at first sight. It rejoiced in the sign of the "Three Cups" and Anthony at once called MacMorran's attention to it.

"Here we are, Andrew. We encounter the promise, as publicly proclaimed, of liberality, of prodigality and profusion. Not one cup, mark you, but three. I commend it to you."

He ran the car into a wide parking-space and with the entered the house of rest and refreshment. The bar was comfortably full and most of the company belonged to the rustic type. Anthony and MacMorran went to the counter and Anthony ordered two pints. For a time they stood there and listened to the conversation. As he had expected, Anthony found the chief topic to be agriculture. Figuring prominently in that topic was the vicar's marrow of 1937. Several references were made to it and many glowing tributes paid to its weight and size. Summed up, "it wurr a fair monster."

MacMorran ordered a second round and at a sign from Anthony they took their blue china pint pots to a table that already afforded accommodation to five people. But there was ample room round it, so Anthony and the inspector made a bee-line for it. One or two of the locals moved up to make seating more comfortable. Gradually and by the exercise of infinite care, Anthony was able to insert himself into the give-and-take of the conversation. For some time he held the compass of the conversation to the agricultural, but then by a few carefully seeded remarks he brought it to matters affecting Hengist itself and the adjoining vicinity. Eventually he felt that the psychological moment had arrived for him to strike.

"By the way," he remarked almost casually, "isn't there a well-known military gentleman residing in this neighbourhood? A man who writes in the reviews on Army tactics generally?"

There was no response to his remark. The locals looked at each other blankly. A man who had been consistently addressed as "Mr. Abbs" took upon himself the responsibility of reply.

"Don't know the gentleman you're referring to, sir. There ain't no writer fellows living in this district as fur as I know. And I've lived nigh here, man and boy, for over sixty year now."

Anthony affected an endeavour of memory. "Really? I must be wrong then. Barking up the wrong tree probably. But I had the man's name on the tip of my tongue a moment ago. Funny! Perhaps if I try I shall be able to recall it."

They waited for him—grave-faced and round-eyed. Suddenly Anthony raised a finger with a gesture which betokened triumph. "I've got it. I thought the name would come back to me if I persevered long enough. The name was Moran! Was it Major—no—I know what it was—it was Colonel Moran. Colonel Chester Moran! Funny how a name will elude you and then come back to your mind all of a sudden. Memory plays sharp tricks on all of us."

The venerable Mr. Abbs immediately registered both interest and knowledge. "Oh—him! A gentleman of that name certainly lives here—but I never heard tell that he was one of them writin' chaps. That be a new 'un on me."

There came a chorus of agreement with the Abbs statement. "No more have I." "Me naythur." "Noa—nor me."

Anthony affected surprise. "Is that so? Well, perhaps I'm muddling two different people and have got the names all wrong. You who live in the district should certainly know better than I."

Mr. Abbs nodded with benevolent understanding. "That be quite all right, sir. But if the colonel what lives here does a bit of pen-pushin' in his spare time, it be unknown to us here in Hengist. That's all there be to it and all. As a matter of fact, sir, the colonel do come in here upon occasion. That's his house way back down the road there. Not a quarter of a mile from here." Mr. Abbs indicated with the stem of his pipe the direction from which Anthony and MacMorran had just come.

Anthony nodded understanding.

"I remember seeing it as we came by in the car. Tudor, I should say, from the design."

Abbs nodded with an extraordinary suggestion of profound sapience. "1500 or thereabouts, if it be a day, sir. Round about the time of Good Queen Bess, so I've allus been led to believe."

Another of the locals broke into the conversation. Anthony had heard him addressed as "George." His surname appeared to be Pilcher. He drained his tankard, set it down on the table with an air of irrevocable decision, licked his lips and remarked oracularly, "That colonel feller you're talkin' about is an American. What some people call a 'Yank'."

"How do you come to know that?" asked his crony Abbs.

"I don't know it. Leastways—for certain I don't. I'm just usin' the judgment I've had given me. Got ears and eyes, haven't I?"

"How do you mean," said Abbs with a wink in the direction of the others.

"I can hear him talk, can't I? And see the clothes he wears, can't I? He's a Yank and I'd lay my next week's wages on it."

"Good for you, George," said Abbs encouragingly. "Any takers?"

There was no reply from those who looked as though they might represent the sporting fraternity of the company. Anthony was by no means displeased to hear Pilcher's opinion. He looked straight at "George" and, seemingly addressing him directly, remarked, "Well—whether he comes from the other side of the water or not— he's got a nice place down the road there. Took my eye directly I saw it. Want a good price for it, I expect, if he ever came to sell."

He then turned in the direction of the bar-counter and ordered "pints" all round. At the glad news George Pilcher warmed to the fray.

"Doan't doubt that, sir, for a moment. Tidy big place that. 'The Gables'—the name of that is. That's the funny part about it. Folks around 'ere think as 'ow it's far too big for the colonel's wants. Outside the servants there's only 'im and 'is daughter livin' there. Must 'ave a rare bit of room to spare."

"No wife—eh?" said Anthony.

"Never seen one, sir. Folks do say as 'ow the lady died many years ago."

It has been often said that Fate itself yields second place to no other agency as far as the power goes of the arrangement of the dramatic. It was at that moment that Fate chose to assert itself and certain it is that no theatrical producer ever staged a more dramatic or a more timely entrance. A woman walked into the bar of the "Three Cups." Anthony looked up almost idly. Only to avert his face immediately. For the woman at whom he looked was the woman who had companioned Trevor in "Christopher's Bar" at Wroxeter and to whom the waiter had given the name of Iris Underwood. A second or so after he had first glanced at her Anthony saw that she was not alone. A young man in the twenties had entered the bar just behind her. He was dressed in a well-cut suit of plus fours and had an eager, intelligent-looking face.

Anthony bent over and whispered a word of warning in the inspector's ear. The inspector acknowledged it by stroking his nose with his finger. Anthony whispered to him again.

"I don't imagine that she'll recognize me. I've only been near her once to my certain knowledge. But, of course, she may, you never know. So I'll play for safety. I'll keep my face averted from her."

Anthony executed a half-turn so that Miss or Mrs. Underwood received the benefit of his back. MacMorran, on the other hand, took the opportunity of facing front and taking a good look at her. She was engaged in a quick, low-toned conversation with her companion. Strive though he might, however, he was unable to catch a single word of what was being said. Ten minutes passed without bringing any alteration in the situation. Anthony continued his varied discussions with Messrs. Abbs, Pilcher and Co., and then MacMorran gave him the signal for their departure.

"Drink up, Mr. Bathurst," he said quietly. "I don't think we've anything to gain by staying on in here. To say nothing of the fact that you may be recognized. Unless you wish to—"

Anthony closured him with a shake of the head. "No, Andrew— I'm with you as regards to that. We'll clear!"

On the return journey, past the Tudor residence now inhabited by Colonel Chester Moran and presumably his daughter, they compared notes. Anthony was, unusually for him, inclined to despondency.

"The job in front of us, Andrew, is to pin it on them. That's our task. The two houses are both in it, there's not a doubt of that—this place here in Hengist and Middleton Hall at Wroxeter. Trevor is in all probability Moran's chief of staff. Brodhurst and Stanhope serve Trevor at Wroxeter and the barman at 'Christopher's' acts as one of their 'intelligences.' But how the hell are we going to bring the crimes home to them? That's what's biting me. For I'm blessed if I can see a way."

MacMorran's fingers explored his cheek. "I quite agree. Look at the confident way in which Trevor dealt with you. It was downright contemptuous."

"You needn't remind me, Andrew. I haven't forgotten it I assure you."

Anthony drove on for some distance in silence. MacMorran considered the problem that Anthony had just enunciated. And, like Anthony, for the time being he could find no solution.

2

ANTHONY BATHURST DECIDES

WHEN they reached the "Yard," Anthony parked the car and accompanied MacMorran back into the latter's room. Anthony took his favourite seat on the corner of the inspector's table. MacMorran lit his pipe and Anthony began to smoke a chain of cigarettes.

"Well, Andrew?" he asked at length, "found the issue to the problem?"

MacMorran shook his head. "No. I don't know that I'm even inches nearer. All we have to work on is suspicion. Mere suspicion. Not an ounce of proof."

"There's an accumulation of suspicion, though, even though there's no accumulation of evidence." Anthony blew smoke away from him as he spoke. He continued. "There are the Regan murders. And there are these child abductions with one child dead. As I see it, there's only one thing in front of us. From the angle, that is, of definite action. One thing stands out a mile."

MacMorran looked at him steadily. "And what's that?"

"I shall have to get to grips with them. At close quarters, Andrew. If you like—the Nelson touch. Get right alongside."

The inspector grimaced. Anthony noticed it and rallied him. "Well—what's the matter with that? I mean it. I'm not shooting a line."

MacMorran shrugged his shoulders. He repeated Anthony's question. "What's the matter with it? Just that I don't like it."

"Why not?"

"The stake's too high for a profit that's only problematical."

"That may be true. But my dear old Andrew, look at it for yourself—we've simply *got* to do something! We can't let this collection of blackguards put their fingers to their noses and grin at us with unconcealed derision. And if we take no action—that's simply what is going to happen. You need have no illusions about that."

MacMorran grew moody again. "I know."

Anthony followed up the advantage he had gained from the admission. "Well then, it comes to what I said. I've got to take the war into the enemy's camp. There's nothing else for it. I shall pick up something if I do—don't you fret."

"Ay. That's exactly what I'm afraid of. You'll pick up something all right. A bullet between the eyebrows or a knife in your back. That's what you'll pick up."

Anthony imitated MacMorran and shrugged his shoulders. "Don't fancy the prospect—I admit. But I must take the risk."

"It's not a risk, Mr. Bathurst, it's more like a ruddy certainty. I'm thinking of your own words. They're men that will stick at nothing."

Anthony gave vent to impatience. "All right, Andrew. Let's suppose for the sake of argument that I give in to you and abandon the idea. It's up to you, then, to suggest something in place of it. What's your alternative?"

MacMorran was silent under the thrust. Anthony struck again.

"Come on! No begging the question! What's your alternative?"

There was no answer. Anthony came a third time. "Have you got one?"

"I don't know that I can rightly say that I have."

"Right. You admit it. Then I'm going back to Trevor and Co. at Middleton Hall. Ten to one, too, I shall find Colonel Chester Moran there. But if I don't, I guarantee I'll find *something* that will help us put the rope round their dirty necks."

"How?"

Anthony hesitated a second before he replied. "Don't quite know at the moment. Shall have to wait for the inspiration to come. There's a tide in the affairs of men—you know the rest, Andrew."

MacMorran's face grew graver. "I still don't like it. You'll be placing yourself absolutely within their power."

"I've been in tight places before. I can take care of myself."

"No man can protect himself properly when the odds are against him. In this instance they'll be overwhelmingly against you."

"Not altogether. You can cover me to a degree. When I bearded the lion before you covered me. And I got out that time all right."

"That, Mr. Bathurst, was a preliminary skirmish—this is the final round. There's an almighty difference."

Anthony forsook his mood of persistence for one of cold gravity. "My mind's made up. I've figured as an amateur burglar before this—when the cause warranted it—and I'm prepared to play the part again. But I'll promise you this. You shall have full details of all my intentions before I start the ball rolling. Because I shall want all the help you can give me, Andrew—I'm fully aware of that."

MacMorran looked up and shook him by the hand. "And you shall have that help, Mr. Bathurst."

CHAPTER X

1

ANTHONY STRIKES AT CLOSE QUARTERS

ANTHONY Bathurst left MacMorran at Wroxeter station. They had travelled down by the only fast train of the evening. They had made their plans and had established a complete understanding with each other. Anthony had told MacMorran exactly what he proposed to do and MacMorran had agreed as to his own plan of campaign granted that certain circumstances arose.

The weather was dullish when Anthony said good-bye to the inspector and started off on his long enough walk to Middleton Hall. One of Anthony's troubles was that it was summer time and, therefore, there was far more light than he desired in order to bring off the first step of his venture with success. His wrist-watch showed the time to be ten minutes to eleven when he arrived outside the gates of Middleton Hall. His plan was to obtain cover from the bushes near the side of the road—the same clump that he had used on a previous occasion—and wait for a car to come to the Hall. He always regarded himself as a good judge of character and he felt pretty certain in his own mind that at least one of the Middleton Hall *ménage* would come home somewhere about midnight. Anthony intended, when that happened, to use his ingenuity and effect an entrance.

With this purpose in view, therefore, he squatted down in the clump of bushes, made himself as comfortable as he could in the circumstances and hoped for the best. As he did this, he patted his pocket to assure himself that the revolver he had brought with him was safe. He commanded the road and while he could see that there was no approaching vehicle he allowed himself the luxury of smoking. Fortunately for him and his enterprise, the moon was in its first quarter and by now conditions of relative darkness were setting in. Anthony crouched there waiting for over an hour. To him, the waiting period seemed interminable and much more like three hours than one. It reminded him more than once of the time when he and MacMorran had waited near the tents of the fairground when they had investigated the problem of the "Ladder of Death."

Just after his watch had showed him the time to be between ten minutes and a quarter past midnight, he heard the sound of an approaching car. He quickly stubbed out the glowing end of a cigarette in the grass at his side and awaited developments. A few seconds later he could distinguish a car coming up the straight road to the gates of Middleton Hall. Now that the time for action was so close to him, the car seemed, to his eager and expectant sight, to be arriving at a snail's pace, although he knew full well that the idea was an absurdity.

The car came up nearer to the gates and stopped. By now, and from this position, Anthony was behind it. It was fairly dark and before he moved Anthony waited to see if an occupant of the car got out in order to rouse the lodge-keeper. His caution turned out to be thoroughly justified because all the driver did in this direction was to sound his horn repeatedly. Anthony, therefore, held to his ambush to the very last vital second. He lay in the bushes perfectly still until the lodge-keeper sauntered down to the gates, opened them, and the car began to move slowly between them. Anthony then crawled from his hiding-place, ran swiftly and noiselessly across the road and was just behind the car, on the lodge-keeper's blind side, as it moved through the entrance. The lodge-keeper, with his back to Anthony, walked to fasten the gates again and the car quickened in speed on its journey to the house. As the car darted away, Anthony, hoping against hope that the driver would look straight ahead and avoid his driving-mirror, crouched down by the offside back wheel and then slithered off at a tangent into the darkness. His luck held.

The car vanished from sight and by the time the sleepy-eyed lodge-keeper had closed the gates again, Anthony had found some sort of cover away from the main approach to the house. This, as he knew from his previous experiences, was situated nearly half a mile away.

He decided to wait where he was for a few minutes and then make for the pergola of the crimson ramblers in case other inhabitants of Middleton Hall had yet to arrive home that evening—or rather morning as it now was. No sooner was the decision made than he translated it into action. In addition, too, it proved to be soundly foundationed, because in less than a quarter of an hour's time, the car-entrance performance was repeated and Anthony, unobserved, was able to see a second car, with Brodhurst driving it, come up the path leading to the house. His own judgment told him that this should be the last and eventually his judgment was proved to be accurate. Or, at least, accurate enough for some time to come.

The night, although dullish and dark, was warm in the extreme and Anthony settled down again to a waiting game. His resolution was to wait in the grounds until somewhere around two o'clock and then attempt to enter the house in some way which his ingenuity should discover, improvise, or devise. For one thing, he was considerably more comfortable where he was than in the clump of bushes outside and after all, he argued to himself, audacity is usually a profitable suit. He hoped to enter the house and by a bold stroke, acting in concerted arrangement with MacMorran, turn the tables on Trevor and company. Away in the distance he could hear the Town Hall clock of Wroxeter chiming the hours. A long time seemed to elapse before one o'clock struck and the following hour-period between one and two seemed interminable. The strokes came at last, however, quivering over the summer morning air, and Anthony moved swiftly and silently towards the house of Trevor and his associates.

When he reached the front door of Middleton Hall, he decided to make a tour of the outside of the house. He prospected accordingly. Up to the moment, he had no clear idea of the lie of the land, beyond that part of the house he had already actually entered. As he walked to the back of the building an idea came to him. He remembered that in many houses of this type and standard, there was often a conservatory attached which frequently led into one of the main rooms. If he could find something of this nature it might lighten his task considerably. He began to creep noiselessly round the outside of the house. At the back, to his infinite joy and satisfaction, he found what he was looking for. A magnificent glass-house that might have been erected and placed there for his own especial benefit. To remove a pane of glass near the door was the work of but a few moments. Anthony then inserted his hand through the aperture and felt for the key. But, to his keen disappointment, no key discovery rewarded him. He realized then that the door must be fastened by a bolt. And that this bolt must be found and manipulated. The play of his electric torch showed him where the bolt was. It may here be remarked that it was invariably Anthony Bathurst's habit to travel when on strict business bent with fountain-pen, pocket-knife, electric torch, revolver, rope round waist, and a length of string. He had learnt more than once down the avenue of experience the consistent usefulness of the last-named article. When he saw where the bolt of the conservatory door was, he felt that judicious use of the string *might* enable him to move it! He cut, therefore, a convenient length of string, looped the length, and then, with the help the torch afforded him, put his hand through the aperture again and angled for the head of the bolt.

The task proved by no means easy. He had but scant room to manipulate the string-length and to handle the torch in addition imposed on him a severe handicap. For some minutes the string dangled over the bolt-head and provocatively persisted in just missing attainment. But Anthony set his teeth and persisted. Eventually, and probably more as a result of good fortune than by the exercise of skill or judgment, this persistence and perseverance succeeded and he was able to secure a string-hold on the bolt-head, pull it up gently towards him, and then by a steady movement of the wrist turn it sufficiently for his purpose. He then tried the handle of the door and, to his triumph, it yielded and he had effected entrance.

He closed the door quietly, listened intently for any sound or sign of life-proximity, assured himself that he could neither hear nor see either, and then brought his electric torch into play again. What he saw in front of him pleased him. A spacious living-room opened into the conservatory where he was standing, and although the doors *appeared* to be closed, he fervently hoped that they *weren't* fastened against him! With noiseless strides, he made his way to them and tried them. His luck still held. The doors were not locked and within another second he was standing on the threshold of the room. Here, he repeated his performance in the conservatory. And again he could hear or see nothing. Also, his nose could detect no smell of tobacco-smoke, which caused him to think that the room hadn't been occupied for some little time. Certainly not within the last hour or two. His problem now was where to advance next. His intention, if possible, was to find either Trevor's private apartment, where he probably conducted his business, such as it was, or alternatively to gain access to the curious museum-room where he had been taken when Trevor and Brodhurst had interviewed him in relation to the farcical Z file.

He stood there and attempted to think in what direction this room lay. As far as he could remember, the house had been built to run north to south and he estimated that the "museum" room as he called it to himself, lay to the south from where he was now standing. It was on the ground-floor—he felt certain of that—so he crept silently out of the living-room which opened on to the conservatory and made his way in what he judged to be the proper and correct direction. He passed down a long and thickly-carpeted corridor, with several closed doors and then, to his complete and utter relief, he recognized where he was and knew that he was standing in that part of the house where he had been before. The door he could see just in front of him was the arched door of the room where he had sat with Trevor and Brodhurst.

He tried the handle. The door gave to his pressure and Anthony went in. He flashed his torch in order to get his bearings. The room was empty. So far so good—if his ideas were sound, all the occupants of Middleton Hall at this hour were safely packed away in bed. If he played his cards skilfully, he would bring his venture to a successful conclusion. He walked over to the table-desk at which Brodhurst had been sitting when he and Trevor had initiated the Z file mare's nest. The coats of armour, the animal specimens and the ancient implements of warfare were still there in the same places that they had previously occupied. The huge box-like arrangement next to the desk was also in its accustomed position. On the table part of the desk was a tray full of papers and documents. Most of them appeared to be letters. On another corner of the desk lay a number of green cardboard files. Anthony let the light of his torch play on them. Some of the docket-titles carried no interest for him but eventually one caught his eye and arrested it. The subject-matter was shown on a typed slip as "Cases or Clearance." He quickly opened the file and found, as he had expected to find, certain correspondence neatly arranged in chronological order. So far as he was able to see from a cursory glance they were reports by agents with regard to people and he turned over three or four when the sight of the name "Spuyten" caused him to hold his breath. He flicked these documents over as rapidly as he could and discovered a most concise report on the personnel, etc., of the Spuyten household in Mayfair and a full description of the child, Dudley Lee Spuyten. Anthony extracted this report from the file and carefully placed it in his wallet. He had by now reached the determination to search for a second docket. At the bottom of the pile, his efforts were rewarded and he found it. The typed slip-title pleased him immensely. It was "Cases Cleared." On the top were several documents—some marked "Polhill-Scott Dossier" and others "Littlehales Dossier." Anthony grabbed them, folded the whole lot into two and crammed them into his breast-pocket.

He thought intensively for a few racing, throbbing seconds and decided that he had obtained enough for his purpose and that his immediate concern should be to put as big a distance as possible between himself and Middleton Hall. He crept cautiously out of the "museum" room and began to retrace his steps the way he had come. At length he reached the conservatory, padded softly through it, closed the door behind him and stood outside.

'They'll see the missing square of glass,' he thought to himself, 'but what the hell will that matter? Too late, too late,' he chuckled. 'My problem now is to get past the lodge-keeper and his everlasting bars.'

He began to walk quickly towards the gates and was just abreast of the pergola when to his consternation and horror he saw the headlights of a car approaching him. The turn in the drive had prevented him seeing the car before. Would he have time to dash into the arbour before he was seen? The query was answered for him without delay and Anthony knew with a sickening feeling round his heart that the game was up. Two men sprang from the car and advanced towards him. He saw that the one in the van carried a gun pointed at him. Anthony, thinking quickly, decided that discretion would most certainly be the better part of valour. Discretion allied to the ever-valuable quality of audacity. As the men came up to him, Anthony was able to identify them. They were Trevor and the man he took to be Colonel Chester Moran, who had sat in the stalls. Trevor brandished the gun.

"What the hell are you doing here?" he exclaimed. "Put your hands up or I'll let daylight into you."

"My dear Trevor," said Anthony coolly, "I find your welcome just a little boisterous and, if I may say so, a trifle unfriendly! And I have always regarded you as the perfect host."

"Who is it," barked Moran, "who is it, Trevor? And when you've told me that, tell me what he's doing here at this hour of the morning?"

Anthony hoped they wouldn't observe the bulge in his breast-pocket. Before Trevor could reply to Moran, Anthony cut in again.

"I may have arrived at an unusual hour, I admit! Put the matter down to, shall we say, inadequate transport. But I have an excellent reason for coming. Surely I don't have to remind you, Capt. Trevor, that I am here by appointment?"

"What's he mean?" exclaimed Moran, turning to his companion.

Anthony was in again before Trevor could find words. "I repeat. By appointment! In the matter of the Z file." Anthony realized that Trevor, for the time being, at least, was nonplussed. "As I couldn't make anybody hear, I concluded that you were all in bed and that I'd better return in the morning. So I came away. An entirely sensible idea—don't you think?"

Trevor muttered something under his breath to Moran which Anthony couldn't catch. Nor could he catch the gist of Moran's reply. But suddenly Trevor came back to normality.

"Come on," he said, "quick march! Back to the house, my very clever young gentleman, and we'll investigate matters. I fancy there's a great deal that needs looking into."

Anthony felt the gun poked unpleasantly into his ribs and was forced to accept the inevitable. The procession wended its way towards the house.

"What about your car," said Anthony, "won't it be rather in the way where it is? Accidents, you know—"

Trevor interrupted him brusquely. "You needn't do the worrying over that. Worrying—like charity—should begin at home. You'll have plenty of time for that—believe me."

"I'm delighted to hear it," replied Anthony.

2

INSIDE MIDDLETON HALL

ANTHONY was escorted, if the word may be used, through the front door entrance, and to the "museum" room.

"Sit down," said Trevor curtly.

Anthony obeyed. He sat in the same chair that he had favoured on the occasion of his first visit.

"Would you mind, Colonel?" said Trevor again, with a significant nod. "I don't think we need take any chances."

Moran slid his hands round Anthony's body and appropriated his revolver. "As you say, Trevor," he said quietly, "we may as well be on the safe side."

His voice was not unattractive, but there was a cold glint of cruelty recognizable in his eyes which had the effect of making Anthony feel far from comfortable. When Moran had passed his predatory hands over his pockets he had been mortally afraid that he would investigate the wad of papers in his breast-pocket, but the "colonel's" mind had evidently been so centred on revolvers and their like that the feel of papers aroused no suspicion in his mind. But Anthony's thoughts instantly reverted to two other contingencies—one—the green docket-files on the table in the corner where Brodhurst had sat, and two—the missing square of glass in the conservatory. He knew that the moment that was discovered he would be in a pretty hopeless position. Not that his present one was any too rosy!

"Question him, Trevor," said Chester Moran sharply. "What puzzles me is the fact that you and he seem acquainted."

Trevor reddened a little at the remark. "We are, sir. I'll explain how a little later on." He addressed himself to Anthony. "Why are you here?"

Anthony affected surprise. "Why am I here? That's a good one, I must say. You know as well as I do that I'm here at your invitation. In the matter of that little commission I undertook for you a few days ago."

He had chosen the word "commission" deliberately and he saw Moran look steadily and searchingly at Trevor. Trevor's flush deepened. Things weren't going the way he would have liked. He essayed explanation.

"This man was here about a week ago, Colonel," he said and the annoyance in his voice was easy to detect. "I don't know why he came exactly, although I entertain very shrewd suspicions. Ostensibly he wanted to muscle in on one of the rackets, but I suspected he wasn't all he pretended to be—so I sent him on a fool's errand. Gave him the Z file to canvass. You can guess the rest."

"Oh, no, he can't," intervened Anthony. "You can't get out of things as simply as all that. You took me in as a partner. And it's no use your denying it. Brodhurst and Stanhope knew all about it. And if that isn't true, why did your lodge-keeper let me in to-night when I first came along?"

Moran looked from one to the other of them. "I see," he remarked eventually, "that's what you mean by 'commission.' I see! Now I'd like to hear something else from you, Trevor. You say you have your suspicions as to what his real game is. I'd like to hear them now. Kindly oblige, will you?"

This gave Trevor his chance. Anthony could see the relief reflected on his face. "I believe this man, Colonel, to be connected with the police authorities. His name, in my opinion, is Bathurst. What he imagines he's here for I haven't the slightest idea. Perhaps just nosing round aimlessly. Who sent him I don't know. Whom he represents I don't know. But that he's proved and is still proving himself a confounded nuisance I *do* know. And I suggest, Colonel, with your approval, of course, that we demonstrate to him that we have a certain simple but effective way with nuisances."

Moran remained icy cool. Anthony endeavoured to emulate him. "I see," said Moran again. "So that's your opinion, is it, Trevor? Well—there'll be no harm in us trying to find out whether you're right or wrong. It will be a comparatively simple matter for me to question him."

He turned to Anthony and Anthony could see the snake in his eyes. "You heard what Capt. Trevor said. You understand the implications. What have you to say in reply?"

Anthony now knew that the tide had gone against him and that it would take him all his time to extricate himself. He decided to make a clean breast of things—up to a point and up to a point only.

"That's all right, Colonel," he said as easily as he was able. "There's a certain amount of truth in what Capt. Trevor says. I have had associations with the police, I admit, and I also, upon occasion, undertake private investigations."

Moran's eyes narrowed. "You treacherous hound," he said softly. There was a silky menace in his voice which Anthony couldn't fail to recognize and understand. "You treacherous hound," he repeated, "you have the brazen effrontery to admit that to my face! I sincerely trust that you are not reckoning on getting away with it. Because if you are, my dear Mr. Bathurst, your optimism will prove to be singularly misplaced. Singularly!" His voice changed from silkiness to vibrant mordancy. "Tell me," he snapped, "what investigation are you running now that you're found on my property at this time of night and in these circumstances."

Anthony regarded him steadily. "Your discourtesy amazes me, Colonel. I should never have believed you capable of such a gross breach of manners and good taste. Crime is certainly these days becoming the pastime of the essentially vulgar. However, you asked for certain information and I'll give it to you. I represent a family by the name of Regan. Does the name convey anything to you?"

Moran and Trevor, as though actuated by one thought, turned and looked at each other. The look on the face of each was significant.

"So," said Moran, "the Regans—eh? H'm—very interesting! I do happen to recall the name, as it happens. I remember reading something about them. Now—what was it? Can you assist me, Trevor? I'm afraid my memory's not what it was."

"They died, Colonel. There was a strange coincidence about their deaths. Each was a road fatality. Probably crossed the road without exercising sufficient care. Very—very sad! Ah, well—there's nothing like Safety First."

Moran's lip curled. "Ah—yes. I remember. And you, my dear inquisitive Mr. Bathurst, will be able to find out all about them that you desire to know. For you shall have the exquisite privilege of taking the same journey."

"Via Nuremberg," put in Trevor, giving full articulation and enunciation to every syllable.

The word raised echoes of remembrance in Anthony's mind. What was the horrible and sinister meaning behind it? "The journey that the Regans had travelled." He was destined to be not long in doubt. For the reason that Moran was repeating what Trevor had said.

"Yes. Via Nuremberg! I think the route will be most appropriate. We will endeavour to make the punishment fit the crime."

Anthony was conscious of a shiver running down his spine. There were cruelty and cold-bloodedness in Moran's voice. "Show him his transport, Trevor—let him taste the joys and pleasures of anticipation."

He chuckled and all the venom and malice known in hell were present in that chuckle. Trevor rose and strolled nonchalantly over to the corner which held the desk which Brodhurst had used. Anthony watched him. Fascination was impossible to evade. Anthony saw Trevor pause before the large box-like apparatus which had aroused his interest on previous occasions. Trevor bent down, seized the box by its corners and stood it on end. It was as much as he could do to effect this. To his surprise Anthony saw that it had folding doors similarly placed as in the case of a man's clothes-closet or wardrobe. Its height, he judged, to be between six and seven feet. Moran's voice broke in unceremoniously on his thoughts.

"That, my dear Bathurst, is a highly-interesting contrivance. One that, I am sure, will make an instant appeal to you. You will be able to describe it to your companions on the Styx, in a few hours' time. I regret excessively that I shall be denied the opportunity of listening to that recital. I am convinced that it will be well worth listening to. Ha ha, I've thought of a good one. Listen here, Trevor! On Hell's radio to-morrow. 'The postscript to-night will be by Mister Bathurst, *late* of the world. He will describe the details of his journey to Hades.' Ha ha—damned good that—though I say it that shouldn't."

Anthony made no reply. Though this was the most ticklish situation perhaps that he had ever been in, he wasn't giving any sign of that to Colonel Chester Moran. The latter continued in his previous vein.

"But I digress. This apparatus, Bathurst, on which your eyes are fixed with such fatal fascination, which fact, of course, is quite understandable in the circumstances, is a modern edition of the famous 'Iron Maiden.' The Grim Maiden of Nuremberg."

Anthony winced a little at the words and Moran was quick to perceive this shaft had gone home. "The Iron Maiden of Nuremberg," he continued maliciously, "was the name given to a medieval instrument of torture used in that home of culture, Germany, for heretics, traitors and parricides, etc. You will observe the type of people indicated, and judge how appropriate it will be to deal with your own case. Briefly, it was a box. But a box large enough to admit a fully-grown man. It had folding-doors. They were studded, I think that's the right word to use, with sharp, iron spikes. When the doors were pressed to, these spikes were forced into the body of the victim, who eventually died after undergoing a rather horrible form of torture. Our modern version of the 'Grim Maiden' works on rather different lines. Would you care for me to describe them to you? I assure you I shall be most happy to oblige."

Anthony made no reply. He was too busy calculating the chances of escape.

"Ah," said Moran, "you are silent. I shall assume that in this instance silence betokens consent. Inside the doors of our 'Grim Maiden' there are fixed a number of iron bars. The doors themselves are manipulated by a device similar to that which is used for lengthening or shortening a dining-room table. In other words, my dear Bathurst, when the handle is slowly turned the doors close in equally slowly on the occupant of the 'Maiden'—that will be you before very long—and he is crushed—well I leave the remainder to your vivid imagination! It's an intensely convenient method, because so many people killed by fast-moving vehicles do sustain broken ribs and spinal injuries."

Anthony still remained silent. Moran turned to Trevor.

"I don't think," he said, "that we need be too precipitate in this matter, Trevor." He ostentatiously made play with his watch. "I think it would be an excellent idea from all points of view if our friend Bathurst were left with a few hours' contemplation of the delights of the journey he is so soon to take and, after all, 'dawn' is traditionally the appropriate moment for executions and firing-squads."

Anthony's nerves tingled. This was good news. The delay would give him a slender chance to cheat these devils after all. It depended to a large extent on what interpretation they would put on the word "dawn." He determined, therefore, on a policy of no resistance for the time being and resolved to submit without a struggle.

"Tie him up, Trevor," he heard Moran order. "Tying up dirty dogs is something that you have a distinct flair for—I can say that from experience."

Trevor disappeared for a few moments to return with a length of rope. "You will be found, my dear Bathurst, or rather your body will be found, early to-morrow evening on a road in the near neighbourhood. Would you care to nominate the place where you will lie? I've an open mind on the matter—personally. You don't answer! Well, then, somewhere between Wroxeter and Bridge Ferry! A little whisky poured round your mouth and lips will indicate to your friends the police that a few hours earlier you may have been a little indiscreet, shall we say, at 'Christopher's Bar'."

Moran chuckled again and lounged out. He paused on the threshold.

"Truss the dog, Trevor. Let him lie awake and contemplate the caresses of the last maiden he'll ever know in this world."

Trevor advanced towards Anthony with the coil of rope.

3

ANTHONY CHOOSES HIS BREAKFAST

LEFT alone in the "museum-room," trussed and helpless as any fowl, Anthony soon knew why Trevor had laughed when he had gone to rejoin Moran. He had turned off all the electric lights except the one directly over the "Maiden." This sole illumination left to the room became as a refinement of cruelty. The "Maiden" was the only object in the room which Anthony's eyes could properly comprehend. A chiming-clock right away in another part of the house was his one means of measuring the passing of time. At last he heard it strike four, and again he fell to wondering as to when would be "dawn" according to the reckoning of Colonel Chester Moran. The passage of the succeeding hour seemed interminable, but at long last Anthony heard five strokes come from the distant clock. Soon after that he heard footsteps and he realized with a queasy feeling in the pit of his stomach that his position now had become almost desperate. The footsteps came nearer and the door of the "museum-room" opened to admit Trevor.

"Good morning, Bathurst," was his greeting, "and a really glorious morning it is, I can assure you. You're a lucky man. You couldn't have chosen a better day for your—er—excursion!"

Anthony's mind groped to grasp a shred of dignity. He hoped that he found it by forcing a smile to his lips. "Good! I'm delighted to hear your news. I have never taken kindly to rain in the summer."

"Excellent," returned Trevor. "I've news for you. It concerns a whim of the colonel's. He's a real sportsman—you can't get away from it! He has a fancy, he tells me, to do the thing in style. He argues that we owe it to you. He says that a journalistic phrase which has always appealed to him is 'the condemned man ate a hearty breakfast.' He's sent me to inquire whether you would care for 'a gammon and two'? That was his rather crude way of putting it."

Anthony summoned a second smile to grace the occasion as well as he was able. "Your friend the colonel has a turn of humour. I'll fall in with it. I'd like a few cherries—Napoleon's, if possible—a cereal, eggs and bacon, toast and marmalade."

"That's excellent," replied Trevor. "I'm sure that the gesture will appeal to Colonel Moran immensely. He'll account you as a man after his own heart. I think I can manage the cherries. But there's one thing you haven't instructed me on. Tea or coffee?"

"Oh—coffee," said Anthony, "coffee—most certainly."

"I'll arrange that breakfast is served at six o'clock for you. You should finish by, say, half-past. We'll book the other little ceremony for seven o'clock sharp."

"That's only allowing me half an hour after breakfast. Cutting things rather fine, don't you think?"

Trevor smiled amiably. "My dear Bathurst—you will find half an hour ample—believe me. In fact I'm rather inclined to imagine that you may even find it a trifle too long. I'm sure that I should in similar circumstances."

"That," replied Anthony, "may yet remain to be proved."

"I'll order your breakfast." Trevor strolled to the door of the "museum-room."

"You missed my point," said Anthony. "I was alluding to your execution."

"Shucks," returned Trevor, "there are times when you annoy me."

"Even then I can go one better, Trevor. You always annoy me—and, by the way, I like the yolk of my eggs set. Please remember to tell the cook."

Trevor's answer was to slam the door.

4

ANTHONY COMMITS AN INDISCRETION

AT SIX o'clock precisely Anthony was released from the ropes of his bondage and served with his breakfast. It was a strange thought to him that within little more than half an hour he stood an excellent chance of solving his last mystery. The breakfast courses were exactly as he had chosen. He started to eat at three minutes past six. At 6.22 he had finished. At half-past six Trevor returned, this time accompanied by both Moran and Brodhurst. The latter looked more sinister than ever.

"I had to come," he said malevolently, "if only to wish you good-bye and a pleasant journey, Bathurst. Remember me to the two Regans, will you? They should be pleasantly acclimatized by now, I should imagine."

"I will," said Anthony, "with pleasure. And also to the little Imogen Littlehales."

There followed an icy silence. It was Moran who broke it. "I see," he muttered. "So that's how the land lies, is it? Most illumin-ating! Trevor—this man has certainly lived too long. Any doubts I might have harboured are removed. Clear these breakfast things away and give him the works at seven o'clock sharp." He turned to Anthony. "That last remark of yours, my dear Bathurst, was a blazing indiscretion. So unlike you!"

"I don't know. I may as well be hanged for a sheep as a lamb."

"Hanged," retorted Moran. "You flatter yourself—hanging would be ecstasy compared with what you're going to enjoy. Your sense of values needs drastic readjustment."

Meanwhile Trevor and Brodhurst were removing the breakfast things and Anthony was glancing at the time by his wrist-watch. He had barely twenty minutes remaining to him.

5

ANDREW MACMORRAN RISES EARLY

The time was now ten minutes to seven. Anthony found that he was straining his ears for any sound from the outside world. But he could hear nothing. He would wait for another five minutes and after that he was resolved to sell his life as dearly as possible. After all, a bullet would be a kindly end compared with the agonies of that hellish box.

Trevor and Brodhurst were busy placing it in position. Brodhurst had opened the folding-doors and Trevor was at work inserting a handle in an aperture at the back of the contrivance. At that second a gleam of hope came to Anthony. He fancied that his straining ears had caught the sound of a shout some appreciable distance away. He scanned the faces of the others to see if any of them had heard it. But no face gave any sign of this. Anthony concluded that he must have been mistaken and as a last desperate chance he decided to play hard for a delaying action.

"Get him ready," cried Moran curtly. He swung round on to Anthony again. "I've given you your choice of breakfast, but I can't supply you with a 'sky-pilot.' Devil-dodgers aren't in our line at Middleton Hall. So you'll have to rely on your own efforts. In other words, you hound, say your prayers."

Anthony faced him. "And I have something to say to you, Colonel Moran. And what goes for you goes also for the remaining members of your blackguardly gang. I'll make you a promise. You will be arrested, every man jack of you, within the next twenty-four hours. The warrants are out and the Crown's case against you is a degree better than cast iron."

If Anthony had expected to shake them he was disappointed. "Baloney," said Moran. "The Crown couldn't prove a thing. It's no use you putting up that bluff. Hoist him into the 'Maiden,' Trevor."

Anthony backed to the wall. But he realized that the odds were three to one against. These, however, he had diminished to a certain extent by choosing the strategic position. As Brodhurst came at him, Anthony landed him a clipping left, straight to the mouth, and Brodhurst staggered back. But before Anthony could recover Moran and Trevor closed in on him. Moran ran in under his guard and Trevor closed with a fierce upper-cut to the chin. As his head rocketed back, Moran struck him hard below the belt and Anthony went down like a felled ox. Moran and Trevor flung themselves on him like hounds on a fox and Brodhurst came at him from the side. After a few seconds' ineffective struggling he was overpowered and Trevor lashed his arms to his sides while the two others held him prisoner.

"Shove him in the 'Maiden' and have done with him," cried Moran, and the three of them lifted him from the floor and carried him to the death-box. "The pressure is but slight for a time," said Moran bitingly, "but it gradually increases as the sides of the box come together and the iron bars are just a little, shall we say, relent-less! You cannot argue with them and in the end they get their own way. You'll hear your own ribs crack like egg-shells—rather a unique experience, I suggest."

Anthony was now within a couple of paces of the "Maiden" and his last thought was, as the folding-doors opened in front of him, as to what the exact time was. If it were well past seven—but Moran's mordant voice interrupted his train of thought.

"And it's not even *au 'voir*, Bathurst—it's most definitely *adios*! You are now about to keep your last assignation with a lady."

Anthony felt his body lifted higher into the air and then, quite close at hand, and eminently business-like, came a familiar voice: "Put up your hands, every one of you! I can assure you that you're covered from every direction."

Moran, Trevor and Brodhurst faced round to three levelled revolvers as though actuated by some hidden piece of mechanism and Anthony crumpled through their arms to the floor.

"Better late than never," said MacMorran, as he advanced, gun in hand, to the centre of the room, "and my apologies, Mr. Bathurst, for cutting it a trifle fine. Evershed, Sergeant Foster, arrest these men, will you please?"

"What the hell are we charged with anyway?" demanded Moran truculently.

"The attempted murder of Anthony Lotherington Bathurst," replied MacMorran cheerfully, "which will do nicely to be going on with. But if you're really interested, even more serious charges will be communicated later."

As Evershed and Foster went swiftly to their work, MacMorran stooped down and untied Anthony's arms. He looked up, on one knee, to the three handcuffed men he had netted.

"There are ten more of my men in the grounds at various points," he said, "so go quietly. It will be much more comfortable for everybody."

Anthony got up. "Thank you, Andrew," he said simply. "I had begun to think that your watch must be a second or so slow."

6

NEARING THE END

MacMorran walked over to the Grim Maiden. "H'm," he observed dryly, "interesting affair—very. What's it all about?"

Anthony explained the niceties of the procedure as Moran had described it to him.

"Nuremberg—eh?" said the inspector, "good old Jerry! Trust him to think up something gentle and refreshing. And it goes back to the dark ages, you say?"

"Not quite that, Andrew. It's patterned on a medieval prototype. There was much more blood about the original. It possessed sharp spikes as compared with iron bars. You can see, though, how the Regans died—poor devils! My body was to have been discovered on the road this evening."

"Actually," replied MacMorran, "we were here a minute or two before I played my ace. I waited until their backs were turned to us. It was a super proposition. I knew that when they tried to force you inside that box, that must almost certainly happen. I was right. It did." He looked at Anthony searchingly. "Don't tell me you were afraid I'd let you down."

Anthony grinned. "No-o. But it was a trifle too close to be pleasant. How did you get on at the lodge-gate?"

MacMorran grinned back. "Put the fear of God up the lodge-keeper. Our strength was a dozen. Bar Evershed, Foster produced the others. Take it from me, the bloke on the gate didn't argue the toss when he clapped eyes on us." He paused. "Now you haven't told me yet. How did you fare last night?"

Anthony supplied the necessary details. As he concluded, he handed to the inspector the various papers and documents he had extracted from the files. "And there, Andrew," he said, "you have, I think, ample evidence to drive your case home. But for running into that blessed car, I should have got out of the place all right and brought the bacon home with me."

MacMorran nodded. "That was tough luck, I agree. What was wrong with you was your sense of timing." He grinned at Anthony as he delivered the shaft.

"There are still a few more birds for the fowler's net," said the latter, "there are Stanhope, Joe, the bar-tender at 'Christopher's,' and the lady we saw in the village inn at Hengist whom I know as Iris Underwood."

MacMorran nodded. "I know. Joe will be brought in this morning. Foster will see to that. And I shall make immediate arrangements with regard to the lady we encountered in the 'Three Cups' at Hengist. Stanhope, though, may present certain difficulties. But difficulties, Mr. Bathurst, are created to be surmounted. I know that you would be the last person to deny that."

Anthony smiled. "How well you know me, Andrew! Better, perhaps, than I know myself. By the way—there's a certain tour I've been promising myself for some little time now. And that's a tour of Middleton Hall, inside which you and I now stand. I'm interested, for instance, in the production of 'dud' notes. What do you say to coming round with me now? Some time may elapse before such a good opportunity comes our way."

"My idea exactly, Mr. Bathurst. I was on the point of making the suggestion a moment ago. We'll take the bull by the horns and do the job now."

Anthony and the inspector walked from room to room. Everywhere they went the appointments were ornate. The expenditure which had been necessary to set up the establishment had been lavish in the extreme. Eventually they came to an upper room. The equipment, furniture, and general layout were certainly different from those in the other rooms of the house. The press, chemicals, the engraving-blocks, the various bowls and apparatus all bore evidence and clear testimony as to the prior purpose to which the ordinary uses of the room had been put.

Anthony turned to MacMorran and smiled. "No doubt about this place, Andrew. This is where young Regan and his clever-fingered confrères turned out the 'dud' notes on behalf of Moran and company. I wonder how many strings Colonel Moran *did* have to his bow."

7

THE END OF THE CHASE

Anthony Lotherington Bathurst, Chief-Inspector Andrew MacMorran and Supt. Hemingway sat in the smoking-room of the "Black

Horse" Inn, Wroxeter. Anthony put a glass down on the table and looked at his watch.

"What are we waiting for," asked MacMorran. "Am I to take it that there's an additional guest who has not yet arrived?"

Anthony smiled and nodded. "Andrew, you've holed in one. As a matter of fact there are three additional guests. So that our full party will number half a dozen. The three to come are due to arrive by the train known as the 7.3. Dinner will then be served at 7.30. I hope that it will be a good one. As I'm in the chair on this occasion, the hope is fervent and intense. I selected the courses with discrimination."

Hemingway beamed. The statement was as music to his ears.

"Three more guests?" queried MacMorran. "Is one permitted to inquire who they are?"

Anthony smiled again. "Certainly, Andrew. I shall be delighted to tell you. Their names are the Hon. Michael Polhill-Scott, Richard M. Arbuthnot Esq. and—I hardly care to mention the third name, Andrew."

"Why—don't I know him?"

"Oh—yes. You've met him on innumerable occasions."

"Who is it?"

"Sir Austin Mostyn Kemble, Commissioner of Police."

MacMorran almost choked over his drink. "You would do that," he remarked dolefully.

"I regarded the party as incomplete without him," returned Anthony. He looked at his watch again. "They should be here any minute now," he continued. "I've given an order for dinner to be served directly they put in an appearance."

The joy which Hemingway had experienced at the mention of the dinner had diminished somewhat at the thought of the presence of Sir Austin. He was sorely afraid that the proximity of the head of Scotland Yard must inevitably cramp his own style. Previous encounters had been not altogether unconnected with certain matters of discipline. He sat quiet therefore, and hoped for the best.

At a quarter-past seven the door opened and the three men whom Anthony had awaited came in. After another round of drinks, Anthony took his five companions in to dinner. Sir Austin began to talk. The others listened. Very soon the conversation became general and both Hemingway and Arbuthnot began to feel at ease. When the "sweet" had been served, the Hon. Michael Polhill-Scott pushed back his chair and stood up. He had caught Anthony's eye and the latter had nodded back. Anthony felt that he knew how Polhill-Scott was feeling and could imagine something, at least, of what he wanted to say.

"Sir Austin," he said, with just a trace of emotion in his voice, "Chief-Inspector MacMorran, Supt. Hemingway, and you two also, Bathurst and Arbuthnot, I want to say to you all—thank you! I am not a speaker—but if I were I doubt whether I could do myself justice here this evening. But I, my wife and my little girl can never repay what you fellows have done for us. That's all! You understand. Thank you!"

The Commissioner, by now feeling amicably disposed to the remainder of the human race, including even those who happened to be the guests of His Majesty, turned to Anthony.

"Now—Bathurst, my boy, it's time we heard from you."

Anthony shook his head. "For once in a way, sir, I have but little to explain."

MacMorran leant across the table. "If I may be allowed to interrupt for a second, I've an item of news for you. A man, by the name of Joseph Burton, was arrested this morning at Kingsley. He was an old travelling-companion of Mr. Arbuthnot here."

Arbuthnot's eyes reflected excitement. "Oh—good! That's excellent news. I've been wondering about that for some days."

"I'm also glad to hear it," said Anthony, "because it gives me a starting-point. Just as it gave one to Arbuthnot. In fact I think he's the man whom Mr. Polhill-Scott should thank most of all. Him and his sharp eyes. But let me start with the *'Seamark' Omnibus*—the book of which friend Burton was so inordinately fond. If it ever comes into your hands, MacMorran, I'll guarantee that you'll find that there's a thin 'compartment' between each page which will hold the flimsy body of a currency note. This book was used as the container when the 'dud' notes were distributed in the Kingsley area. And, I fancy, in other areas as well. Other copies are probably in circulation. The binding, that of an ordinary public libraries' book, was, of course, used in order to distract attention. Anybody seeing it would naturally take it to be exactly what it was represented to be. Regan's skill with his hands was the cause in the first place of the offer that was made to him. In other words, he joined the staff at Wroxeter. When he discovered what he was being used for he kicked a bit, I imagine, and thereby signed his own death warrant, for the Moran collection took immediate action. While he was being kept in confinement, or even perhaps after he had been first warned, he communicated with his sister without the gang being aware of what he was doing. He couldn't put his suspicions into actual words because, no doubt, his correspondence was censored, but he managed to convey what he wanted by subterfuge. And at the same time provided evidence to be used against the people who were threatening him. I was fortunate enough to be able to understand his messages."

"There's a point there, Mr. Bathurst," said MacMorran, "that I'd like cleared up. He wrote that letter to his sister from his own house. Yet you speak of his being a sort of prisoner. How do you explain that?"

"I think in this way, Andrew. They 'moved in' on him. Took possession of his rooms. If only for a short time. Eventually he was removed to Middleton Hall and 'dealt with' there. But he managed to get his message through. From acute reminiscence I can assure you the poor fellow has my sincere sympathy." Anthony's face was grave and there came a brief period of silence.

"How did they get on to his sister?" The question came from Arbuthnot.

"That's a good question," answered Anthony, "and I've given a certain amount of attention to it myself. My conjecture is this. When they had murdered young Regan they watched his sister, night and day, in case she took any action concerning his disappearance. He had, no doubt, mentioned to somebody in Wroxeter that she was his only relation. Their Kingsley end took on the job. When she communicated with me they knew she was apprehensive. I was traced to Wroxeter. That opened their eyes. So they inveigled her down there in my name and finished her. I don't care to think about that part of it." Anthony paused abruptly.

"So that, in your opinion, Bathurst, they knew you were in on the case?" put in Sir Austin Kemble.

"Yes, sir. I think they knew that all the time. But they were contemptuous of the idea that we could bring anything home to them, so they treated the opposition in cavalier fashion."

"There's another point there," said MacMorran. "*Moran* didn't know. According to what you've told me. Trevor hadn't informed him. How do you explain that?"

"I ascribe that," said Anthony, "to Trevor's belief in himself and in his own powers. In effect, he said, 'Leave this fellow to me. I'll deal with him. No need to worry the colonel with it.' I think Trevor did most of the work of the organization. Moran may have put up the necessary capital in the first place, but Trevor was the chief executive officer."

"Well," said the Commissioner, "it's another feather in your cap, Bathurst. I must admit that."

"I don't know about that," was Anthony's rejoinder. "I rather incline to the opinion that I've run no more than a moderate third."

"Whom to?" queried Sir Austin.

"To Arbuthnot and Hemingway," replied Anthony. "If it hadn't been for Arbuthnot's original alertness we shouldn't have had a dog's chance, and if it hadn't been for Hemingway we might never have got to grips with Moran."

He turned and raised his glass to the two men he had named.

"I suppose," returned Arbuthnot, "the swine have no chance of getting away with it?"

"Not an earthly," said MacMorran, "there's enough evidence in the house at Hengist to hang the principals twice over."

"What a pity we can't," said Anthony Bathurst.

THE END